THE *Great* MISFORTUNE OF *Stella* Sedgwick

ALSO BY S. ISABELLE

The Witchery

Shadow Coven

THE *Great* MISFORTUNE *of* Stella Sedgwick

S. ISABELLE

STORYTIDE
An Imprint of HarperCollinsPublishers

HarperCollins Children's Books, a division of HarperCollins Publishers,
195 Broadway, New York, NY 10007

HarperCollins Publishers, Macken House,
39/40 Mayor Street Upper, Dublin 1, D01 C9W8, Ireland

Storytide is an imprint of HarperCollins Publishers.

The Great Misfortune of Stella Sedgwick
Copyright © 2025 by S. Isabelle
All rights reserved. Manufactured in Harrisonburg, VA,
United States of America. No part of this book may be used or reproduced
in any manner whatsoever without written permission except in the case
of brief quotations embodied in critical articles and reviews.
harpercollins.com
ISBN 978-1-335-00696-7
Typography by Andrea Vandergrift
First Edition

25 26 27 28 29   LBC   5 4 3 2 1

For Odessa, the brightest star in my life

PART ONE

A proper lady has a soft demeanor, but mustn't be too shy to defend her values.

—"Letters to Fiona Flippant"
August 1860

I

Addyshire, England
March 1868

Contrary to appearances, I do not usually begin my mornings by shoving delivery boys to the ground.

I know it's horribly unladylike of me, but if I may defend myself, the scoundrel deserved it.

"Oh!" I shriek, though *I'm* not the one hunched over in pain. "Heavens! Are you all right?"

"*Am I all right?*" the boy shouts furiously, laying in the gravel path leading up to the house.

A warm breeze passes, and I straighten the feather in my hat. Well, I don't really care if he's all right or not—I only asked to regain some sense of politeness. I can't ignore the fact that, violence or no violence, a boy my age and so low in society would never have raised his voice at a lady with a fairer complexion.

Then again, a proper lady would never have shoved him.

Then again, "proper ladies" were never described the way he described me.

He hadn't said it to me directly, and judging by Mr. Wilson's face when he saw me stop dead behind the cart, I wasn't meant to hear it. I'd been minding my own business, having just managed to slip away from Mrs. Smith's cross-stitching lessons to pick some flowers from her garden for my aunt's table. I'd wanted the quiet time to work out the kinks in my latest short story—one that currently exists only in my mind but will make a lovely piece if I ever get around to putting pen to paper. Anyway, as I rounded the corner of the house and came upon the fruit delivery wagon, I heard it.

Such a lovely country estate. And how nice of dear Mrs. Smith to take in some Blacks for house-training.

House-training. As if cousin Olivia and I are overexcited dogs with bladder issues. See, I couldn't very well ignore that, even as Mr. Wilson awkwardly cleared his throat to end the conversation.

The younger Wilson had spun, and with just one look at his face, I found myself overcome with anger. You may imagine me as a fierce heroine if you wish, but it was actually rather clumsy, more so me jabbing my finger at him than a real shove. The boy was even clumsier than I—quite an accomplishment—and he stumbled backward over a sack of apples and hit the ground.

Honestly, it was as much the apples' fault as it was mine.

"Stella Sedgwick!"

Mrs. Smith screeches behind me, and I reflexively duck as if the sound were a physical object thrown at my head. She scurries out of the house red-faced, her straw-colored hair braided down

* 4 *

her back, the skirts of her high-collared day dress bunched up in fists at her sides. I rub my temples. I'd already felt a headache coming on from the tight plaits Aunt Eleanor had done my hair in, and now this.

Mrs. Smith gives me a cold look before turning to Mr. Wilson with the warmest of smiles. "Good afternoon. What's happened here?"

Mr. Wilson waves a wrinkled hand gently. "Nothing at all, ma'am. We'll be on our way."

I furrow my brow. I'm not sure what's compelled Mr. Wilson to defend me. Likely it's nothing to do with me at all and more that he simply can't be bothered with all this, or maybe he finds Mrs. Smith as intimidating as the rest of the village. Perhaps he's an old friend of my uncle's—the good pastor, may he rest in peace—and simply pities the orphan girl standing before him.

But Wilson's son scrambles to his feet. "Not true! She pushed me to the ground!"

Mrs. Smith whips to me, her lips in a tight line.

"I—well. He fell. I might've pushed him. A little." I don't bother explaining what he said. It wouldn't matter to Mrs. Smith anyway.

Blood rises in her cheeks. "You and your temper! Well, I suppose I'm not surprised, considering—" She pauses to look me over before turning back to Mr. Wilson and his son. "Her behavior is impossible for me to control, please, accept her apology—"

"She *hasn't* apologized," the boy sneers, rubbing his right thigh dramatically.

I nearly sneer in return, but Mrs. Smith snaps back to me before I can. "Go on, then!"

"I do apologize." I offer a bowed head, only half an inch lowered, more than he deserves. "In the future, I'll have to throw you onto your left side as well, so at least the pain would be even—"

Mrs. Smith lets out a sound between a gasp and a wail. "*You ungrateful child!* Get in the house now!"

As she apologizes on my behalf, I spin on my heels. I've half a mind to run all the way home, but Stella Sedgwick is no runner. That was something my mother used to say. I was a headstrong child, and never fled from punishment after misbehaving. If she's looking down on me from the heavens, I hope she's proud. I also hope she can't see the mud on the hem of my dress. Sorry, Mum.

My cousin, Olivia Witherson, watches from up the steps. She's wearing a soft day dress of creamy blue muslin with yellow ribbons, and her loose curls are pushed back behind a daisy-patterned scarf. My cousin is a sweet, mild-mannered beauty. When she makes her foray into society, I can only imagine how the suitors will be tripping over their own feet to, well, *suit her.*

She's here to learn things for ladies who will come out into society and be married off to good men. She spends her days practicing the piano, singing, painting, and keeping her opinions to herself. She'll make a lovely wife one day. Poor thing.

There is no such fate in store for me, thank the heavens. Not that I enjoy my lessons any more than Olivia does. While Aunt Eleanor aims to make a smart match for her daughter, she thinks that becoming a servant in a wealthy household is the best future that a girl of my situation can make for herself. Mrs. Smith is meant to show me the way, but I can't stand it, because she's horrible and mean, and I don't want to be a servant—how am I supposed to care for some family and their brats when I can barely remember to feed myself when enamored by a good book?

Mrs. Smith says reading will rot my brain. Yes, reader. Mrs. Smith is an utter fool.

"What have you done now?" Livvie asks, her voice more worried than angry. "Could you not have let it be, Stella?"

I shake my head. "If you had heard him, Livvie."

She sighs, leading me into the drawing room. "Oh, you're in for it."

Sure enough, Mrs. Smith comes in, raving mad, nearly colliding with the hideous paisley armchair. "Well? What do you have to say for yourself?"

"I'm sure there's nothing I could say to set your opinion of me to rights," I answer.

She gives Livvie an exhausted look, as if to say, *Can you believe her?* I think it's a plea for help, which Livvie answers by fiddling absently with her shawl.

Mrs. Smith turns to me. "Miss Sedgwick, I've given you more chances than you deserve as a favor to your uncle and at great potential cost to myself and my reputation. What will people say of me when you've hopped from house to house, let go from jobs for your poor talents and poorer behavior?"

"Well, they'll say you did a poor job," I offer plainly.

She sucks in a breath, and it pinches her face like she's taken a great bite of lemon. "*I* did what I could with a girl so fond of savagery and unpleasantness!"

"Mrs. Smith, you've done nothing but insult my intelligence

since I arrived here." And strike me with a ruler when my needlepoint didn't please her, but I keep that to myself.

This response seems to anger her more than finding that little fiend wailing in the dirt. "I beg your pardon? I've taught you the ways of a proper lady for nearly a year now, and that's all you have to say?"

My brow twitches upward. "I would thank you, Mrs. Smith— only, I've found this entire experience to be unpleasant, if not utterly useless, and so I'm not sure what I'd be thanking you for." I pause. "Though you do make a fine scone, I suppose."

Livvie fidgets behind me, and I know she's just dropped her head into her hands. I can almost hear her tinny internal scream.

Mrs. Smith's face grows pale. Between the ghost-white face and the furious eyes, I think she looks rather like an undertaker of hell.

She wrenches her mouth into a scowl. "Get out!"

I nod. "With pleasure."

I turn to Livvie, and for a moment, I wonder if she's staying. But she's by my side so quickly that I feel a little guilty for thinking she'd do otherwise. Though we hold differing opinions in many things, she truly is my best friend.

"Good day, Mrs. Smith," Olivia says sweetly, every bit the result of her training in this awful house.

Mrs. Smith continues her huffing and puffing as we set out on the path back toward home. Normally, Aunt Eleanor sends Mr. Chapman with the rickety gig at the end of our lessons, but that won't arrive for another two hours, and I have no desire to wait on the steps of this hellish house. It's an hour's walk to the parsonage, but the weather is quite nice—somewhat cool from the ending winter, but sunny enough to feel like spring. The green hills stretch out before us, a view so lovely that it almost takes my mind off this disaster of a day.

Almost.

I swat away a stray fly. "Your mother is going to kill me."

"If you're lucky. I imagine there'll be a fair bit of torture first."

Now that my excitement and resolve have melted away, all I have left is an anxious tummy. Sweat slicks my palms and the back of my neck. I stop still, the grass pricking at my ankles. "Oh, dear. What did I just do?"

"You could go back and apologize. . . ." Livvie's voice trails off at my unamused expression. "Or. Not."

"You know I'm nothing if not stubborn. I only ask that after your mother kills me, you recite a list of my good traits at the funeral. No less than ten, twenty is respectable, thirty is preferable."

"Dunno if I can think of thirty good traits," she mumbles. "Here lies Stella Sedgwick, weaver of stories—"

I nod. "Very good—"

"Destroyer of men!"

"It was the *tiniest* shove—"

"Died a spinster at eighteen!"

I gasp. "And was quite glad for it!"

I pluck off her pretty shawl, and she chases me all the way to the river until we're both out of breath.

We arrive at the Witherson country house just after two in the afternoon.

"Afternoon, Father!" Olivia says cheerily, touching the portrait in the foyer.

"Afternoon, Uncle Edward," I add. My late uncle's pale face looks a bit grim against the floral wallpaper; funny considering that he was a most joyful man, especially for a vicar. Livvie looks just like him, only with light brown skin and darker eyes. While Aunt Eleanor, Olivia, and I are not the only colored people here in Addyshire, there are far fewer of us here in the country surrounding London than the city itself. Everything we have is because of him, really. This house, the little money he left, the goodwill his position in the village has granted us.

Olivia settles onto the sofa in the drawing room while I poke my head through the garden doors. Mr. Chapman is working at replacing the fence to the chicken coop, and I spot Mr. Townsend in the distance tending to our two milk cows.

"Good afternoon, Mr. Chapman!"

He lifts his head and peers at me from under his wide-brimmed hat. "Miss Sedgwick, aren't you back early? How is Mrs. Smith?"

My stomach flips, but I manage a nod. "She's well. Erm, is my aunt still at market?"

He grins, the wrinkles lining his dark brown face deepening. "Yes, haggling, I'm sure—you know how she likes a deal."

I return his grin. This is *perfect*. I'll be able to explain myself before Mrs. Smith gets to her.

I just need to come up with a story.

2

From my dress, I pull out a small notebook. I asked Olivia to sew pockets in the lining of my dresses—mostly for sweets—and they have come in quite handy. A few of my mother's old letters stick out of the pages. They're the most precious things I own, the only things she left me, the last pieces of my mother's memory.

Creativity runs in our family, you see. My mother, the utter gem that she was, once wrote the most notorious advice column to sweep the city. Under the name *Fiona Flippant*, she responded to the whims of the refined and wealthy. Rich people could be burdened by such mundane annoyances! They wrote to her for counsel on everything—the latest trends, surviving a coming out season, rooting out potential scandals, French kissing—*among other exercises of passion*—and how to react to finding your husband with his hand down his best mate's trousers. The column was money, excess, and the thrill of coveting the dashing lord who'd just rolled into town on the back of a majestic horse.

I've always wondered how those genteel society folks would react to Fiona Flippant's true identity. If they knew that they'd craved the advice of a woman they'd treat as lesser if they saw her in London, a witty Black woman descended from those that were enslaved.

It is true that honesty is a most noble virtue, says Fiona in issue three, *but a little embellishment never hurts.*

I pace before Olivia, wringing my hands. "Your mother won't be *that* angry with me, right?"

Livvie doesn't look up from her thread and cloth. "You asked me this already."

"But do you think she'll *very* be upset? As in throw-me-out-of-the-house upset?"

"Stop. My mother is tough, but not cruel."

"It's not like she even likes Mrs. Smith very much. I'll tell her that I've come upon my menstruation, and it made me irritable."

Olivia holds in a giggle. "That won't work, you're always irritable!"

I frown at her.

"Surely you can come up with something better."

"Fine. I'll say that the sun got in my eyes, and *I* tripped, and that boy was in my way and stumbled backward."

"And when my mother asks you why you were traipsing outside during lessons?"

I inhale deeply and plant my fists at my hips. "Fresh air, of course. Growing girls like us need—"

"*Girls?*"

The sound of Aunt Eleanor at the front door throws my heart into my throat. I freeze where I stand. "*She knows,*" I whisper.

"How could she know?"

"Your mum *always* knows."

Eleanor Witherson has all the cool severity that her daughter lacks. My aunt is a thin, pointy woman with dark brown skin, high cheekbones, and a blistering gaze that sends men running with one look—I swear, I've seen it happen to the baker's boy who tried to haggle with her at the market. Where Olivia is baby-faced, sweet, and sometimes naive, her mother is serious and sharp. I am immensely fond of her. Not that I have a choice— along with Olivia, she's the only family I have. And knowing what I've heard about orphans from town gossip, books, and horrifying bedtime stories, I will always be grateful that she took in her dead sister's child. While it seems like an obvious thing to do, not everyone is so kind, even to their own kin.

She looks at us, smoothing a few hairs displaced from the country winds. "Saw you two through the window. Heavens, did you walk all the way here? Olivia! Look at that mud!"

She doesn't bother commenting on the state of my dress, but gives me an exasperated sigh before taking the few steps into the kitchen to put down her basket and fix a pot of tea.

While I am fond of my dear aunt, sitting directly across from her in the small drawing room as she silently stirs sugar into her tea is quite unsettling.

✦ 13 ✦

I fidget. This well-worn blue sofa is my favorite seat in the house, but it now feels too soft, like I'm folded into it, unable to pull myself out.

Aunt Eleanor sips her tea.

I look to Livvie. She glances up from her needlework to shoot me a warning look. *You're on your own.*

I inhale slowly. "Aunt El—"

"*Stella.*" She sets her cup down, and my spine immediately straightens. "I heard the most peculiar story while at market today."

My heart thrums. "Did you, now?"

"Oh, yes. With that overactive imagination of yours, I want you to picture my shock when I overheard the grocer speaking of his nephew who'd been struck by a feral vagabond."

I swallow. "Why, how interesting."

"I didn't think much of it. Men like to embellish and brag; I thought maybe the true story was that his nephew got caught up in a brothel, treated a woman poorly, and got what he deserved. Except, Mr. Wilson—you know Mr. Wilson, he brings about the fruit deliveries."

"Mr. Wilson . . . Mr. Wilson . . ." I narrow my eyes. "Oh! I think I know him."

She doesn't bother commenting on my ridiculous feigned uncertainty. "Well, he pulls me aside and says that the feral vagabond was none other than my niece, Miss Stella Sedgwick. You can imagine my confusion. See, I've raised Stella since she was thirteen, and I've never once brought up a feral girl, have I, Olivia?"

Livvie's eyes snap up. "No, Mother."

Aunt Eleanor's smile goes tight, more of a grimace, really. "I nearly laughed in the man's face. Only, he described a dark-skinned girl wearing twin braids and a feather in her cap, a burgundy dress, and a face that seems prone to mischief."

I raise a brow. "Well, she sounds *gorgeous*."

Livvie snorts, and as much as I enjoy making her laugh, I instantly regret not holding my tongue. Aunt Eleanor sets her dainty teacup onto the saucer in her lap and glares at me. I wouldn't mind the couch eating me up now. I settle for looking down at my feet instead. "The boy spoke of us as if we were animals."

Aunt Eleanor sets her jaw. "And so he is a cruel and worthless fool. But *you* are no fool, and you need to learn when to let the opinions of the ignorant go." She pauses. Her expression relaxes. "Things are always changing, but most days I think their prejudices against us will never end." She leans in and whispers, "Did you at least get him good?"

Olivia inhales an excited breath. "Mum, if you'd seen his face! She practically threw him to the ground!"

"It was the apples," I mutter.

Aunt Eleanor winks at me, but her scowl returns. "I know Mrs. Smith, and she will not have you anymore, nor Olivia."

"Olivia didn't do a thing!"

"I know that. No matter, Olivia's skills have been refined, and I trust she'll make a nice match. A well-paid tradesman or a barrister, maybe an officer? She knows her duty and that the future of this family depends on her."

Next to me, Olivia fidgets. She's very good at hiding her emotions, but I see through to the pressure on her shoulders.

Aunt Eleanor continues, "You, however, cannot depend on Olivia's match to bring you good fortune as well. Father Mitchell has been nice enough to let us stay here, but who knows if the next vicar will, and your uncle's money will not support all of us forever. Stella, I've told you again and again, you must settle in the house staff of a good family, unless you'd rather become a barmaid, or *worse*?" She takes a breath. "I'd suggest you marry as well, but with little money of your own and your determination against it, I'd be wasting my time."

I feel cowardly, looking at my shoes like this. I lift my eyes to meet hers. "My mother——"

"Your mother was a nurse first, then a nursemaid; both good, secure jobs before she went chasing independence."

I chew on the inside of my cheek. She doesn't need to remind me; I was there during Mother's time waiting on the wealthy Fitzroy family, their children the heirs to a fortune. The memory of them—of us—chasing Mother through the garden tugs at my heart.

"And where did she end up?" my aunt asks plainly.

"In the ground. I have not forgotten."

Aunt Eleanor eases back into her seat, her eyes softening for a moment.

"*But* before she died, my mother found glory by way of the pen. That's not what killed her; an illness did. And who knows what she would have become if it had not! No, I won't do it. I won't be a servant, I won't be a nursemaid, and I will not be a wife. I have greater dreams than that, Aunt Eleanor."

"Dreams," she whispers under a scoff. It makes me feel even more naive that I already do. I brace myself for the fight, one that we've had dozens of times already. Aunt Eleanor is not one to yell, unless she's come across a lizard in the gardens. Instead, she's a sharp speaker. She knows how to cut deep with a few expertly placed shots to one's confidence. *Dreams are for men,* she'll say. *Rich men. Fair-skinned women, or rich colored folks. Not an orphan like you.*

But Aunt Eleanor doesn't argue this time. She simply places her teacup on the side table, rises to her feet, and smooths over her skirts. Her voice is level. "Then you will be nothing."

Somehow, this is worse than an argument. In many ways, I know she wants the best for me. But now it seems that she's given up.

I won't be nothing, I want to say, but my confidence is shaken. In this moment, I don't know that I truly believe it.

Finally, Olivia drops her needlepoint. "That wasn't so bad."

I glare at her.

"Well. It was a little bad."

I chuckle humorlessly. "Olivia, if you had the freedom to choose whatever path you wanted in this life, what would you do?"

Her pretty brow furrows in thought. "Oh, I don't know. I reckon I'd still want to be married, with loads of children and a house with a big garden. I'd spend my days looking after them, and playing piano, and planning parties. . . . Oh, don't give me that look!"

I laugh truly now. Not in a mocking way; they may not be *my* dreams, but I do think it's sweet that she essentially wants what she has now, but with a doting husband and kids in the mix. I'm a little jealous. While it might not be easy for a mixed-race girl to accomplish such things, her wants seem much more attainable than my dreams to be a novelist.

"You're lucky, Livvie. Proper ladyhood comes so easily to you."

There's more that I want to say. *You're lucky that your father had money, that he loved your mother, that he left you all this lovely house and money for your comforts in his untimely passing.* But the money won't last forever, and Olivia knows she must marry, and soon. I've tried to convince her that I'm far better company than some pompous gentleman from London, but she won't hear it. She *wants* to be married. I can't make sense of it.

She sighs. "Mrs. Smith's lessons were no stroll through the gardens for me either, Stella. I'm somewhat relieved to be done with them."

"I only mean that you want to be out—socializing and dancing and meeting people. Is there not a way to make a life out of scone eating and tea drinking? Why, I'd be set."

"And until there is?"

I pull the little notebook from my pocket once more, a force of habit. "I suppose I must make a fortune of my own."

3

Uncle Edward's study is my favorite spot in the house. It has the coziest, lushest little reading nook. A velvet chaise, fluffy pillows, the smell of old books. I curl against the large wide window, the green and pink of the gardens and hills stretching out before me, and the slightest view of downtown London in the distance. The reflection of my pleased face stares back at me, sunlight illuminating my dark brown skin.

I have a cup of decadent sipping chocolate and toast, burned to a crisp the way I like it. I'm spoiling myself, you see. I've had a hum of anxiety in the pit of my stomach since I mucked up the lessons with Mrs. Smith a few days ago. Though my aunt hasn't told me what I'm to do now, I must make myself scarce and enjoy the peace before she inevitably comes up with something.

While I refuse to give up on my dreams of writing professionally, Aunt Eleanor does have a point. Okay, many points. The world is not made for me, and I cannot change it. Even my mother worked two jobs, and I doubt the wages she earned as Fiona Flippant would've been enough to support us on their own. The little money she left me wouldn't last very long if I didn't have Aunt Eleanor. I need to eat to survive, and I need money to eat, and since no wealthy man will ever look my way, I have resorted to looking through the classifieds in the *Times*.

I sip my chocolate, scanning the words. Few listings specifically mention being open to colored help, though there is also a section of prospective employees advertising themselves for work.

West Indian nurse, handy with a needle, good character, excellent references.

Colored man, speaks French, available for valet. Fifteen years of work, good references.

Half-caste, young woman, Anglo-American. Excellent references for work as nursemaid, seven years of experience.

I sigh, dissatisfied. Nursing seems to be an honorable profession for a girl of my standing, but I'd be terrible at it. I'm not a *comforter*. Blood doesn't scare me, but the thought of bandaging up wounds makes me sweat, and seeing others get sick only makes me want to vomit alongside them.

Annoyed, I flip through to the serials, but reading other writers' stories always makes me eager to work on my own. It isn't long before I return to my notebook of half-written stories and the faded clippings of my mother's words. Perhaps her genius will rub off on me, and I'll write the most brilliant piece of fiction and fetch a wealthy patron with good taste. I'd much rather that than a husband.

I'm so distracted by this lovely daydream that I do not notice my nemesis, Cheswick, Olivia's tabby cat, coming up to me. With no warning at all, he *plucks* my mother's old letter from the hand I was dangling over the chaise.

I nearly throw the cup of hot chocolate into the air. "Cheswick, no!"

I give chase. Like the satanic beast he is, Cheswick scurries out of the room, out of the house, and—before I can yell at Mr. Townsend to shut the garden door—into the great willow tree.

"*Fiend!*" I screech as his fat orange legs propel him up into the branches. A tan sliver of paper hangs from the edge of his whiskered mouth. "How dare you? *And don't you dare chew that!*"

He purrs. I think he's laughing at me.

Before I can convince myself against it, my fingers are on the lapels of my red cardigan. I pull it off, fold it over a lower branch, and kick off my boots. I hike up my dress with one hand and reach for a thick branch with the other. Fiona Flippant always said that a lady should engage in light sport here and there. She likely meant a brisk morning walk, or heaving with fake laughter to please a suitor, but climbing this tree will have to do.

I am sweaty and out of breath by the time I reach the hefty cradle of branches that the traitorous Cheswick has cozied himself in. I wave a hand at him, and now, after chasing him through the house, only now when I'm teetering on this branch, on the verge of falling to my death, does he leap into my arms.

"Fiend," I whisper, gentler this time. I pull the letter from his mouth, and he even lets me scratch behind his ears, so I think I'll call a truce. "Where was I?" I mutter to myself, settling into a sturdy spot. "Cheswick, would you like to hear the dreadful story of Duchess Wits, wife of Duke Pea-for-Brains? Duchess Wits is hiding a horrible secret, you see. She's taking lessons in biology and chemistry from a professor at a local college, and her husband, Duke Pea-for-Brains, hasn't a clue. The horror!"

Cheswick nips at my finger, which I shall take as agreement.

Now the submission gets a bit more complicated. The writer's husband has assumed that—since no lady could ever be interested in the sciences—our witty duchess must be coveting a lover. And, as it turns out, the Lord of Chemistry is quite the dashing young man. He holds her heart, but Pea-for-Brains holds something even more important. Her purse. Her reputation. Her honor. What a horrible thing it must be to be married!

As Fiona, my mother responded as she always did—with grace and wit. She'd answered the so-called duchess by telling her to *follow your heart, but ensure you have the means to do so first! It is good for a lady to pursue her own needs, but don't throw yourself to the dogs, dearest Duchess.*

I feel closer to her, reading these letters. Sometimes I imagine my own responses. I don't know how Mother ever found the

❖ 22 ❖

patience, because my response to Duchess Wits would be as simple as it is scathing: *run away from the boring bastard.* Mother never hid her alter ego from me. I was around nine when she took up the job, and I immediately noticed how she spent her nights in Kendall Manor scribbling through pads of paper after waiting on Mr. Fitzroy's grandchildren.

"Why do you like to write so much?" I asked once.

Her brows were knitted in concentration. "Unlike you, I didn't have a nice teacher like Mrs. Marstock. A miserable woman taught me, and then gave up on me, told me I wasn't worth teaching. I thought, *I'll show her.*"

This was fascinating to me. My mother rarely talked about her past before coming to England, and certainly not her childhood. Aunt Eleanor was the same. So, I held on to this nugget of information like it was a precious gift.

"Do you really believe in all this advice you give? I never hear you talk about love and marriage, and all of this stuff."

I could tell she liked this question from the way her big, dark eyes lit up at me like I was the cleverest girl in the whole world. "Do I believe it? Well, that's complicated. Really, I just try to give the best advice I can. It is very important that Fiona Flippant doesn't coddle her queriers, but she also doesn't judge. But most importantly, my love . . ." She leaned in conspiratorially. "Fiona Flippant must *entertain.*"

"Why do you sign your letters as Fiona? Why not just Ginny Sedgwick?"

Her smile softened. "Stella, my love. I think you know why."

While this double life seemed so normal to her, I felt a jolt

✦ 23 ✦

of pride whenever I saw *State of London* folded up under some passerby's arm. Sometimes Mr. Fitzroy would give me a few shillings and I would buy a paper just so I could flip straight through to the culture section. I'd trace the words Mother had once scribbled on a rickety desk, now immortalized in neat, dark type. It didn't matter that the vague drawing accompanying the title of each column was so clearly modeled on a pale genteel woman with a button nose. My mother wrote the words. No matter the pen name, the picture; the column belonged to her.

"Comfortable up there, are we?"

I turn toward the voice so sharply that I nearly pitch myself out of the tree. "Oh! Livvie! Well, how nice to see you!"

She folds my jacket over her arm. "I've barely seen you all morning—why are you hiding?"

"Your wretched cat committed a most dastardly act of thievery, and I had little choice but to reclaim what was mine."

She giggles. "Will you come down?"

"I would, but poor Chessy's in a nap, and it would be cruel of me to—"

He leaps from my arms and into Livvie's.

I sigh. "Ah."

She waves me down. "Hurry, Mother wants to speak with you."

My stomach flips. "About what?"

"There's a letter." Her eyes are big with curiosity, her voice inquisitive.

"From Lady Tess?" I ask, making my way down the tree. My mother's old friend, Tessa Sinclair—who we lovingly tease as

Lady Tess for her proximity to the London elite—likes to check in from time to time.

Livvie shakes her head, curls whipping around her. "No, but it was hand-delivered by a courier, so someone paid quite a sum to ensure its receipt. Must be important."

Now I see why she's so restless. A mysterious letter was as much excitement as we got out here in the country, and while Lady Tess's father owns *State of London*, she's never called upon us in such an extravagant manner. Who is this wealthy sender, and what do they want with me? My anxiety only grows when I see the sleek, luxurious black carriage waiting in front of our country home.

We make our way to the drawing room, and I know this is serious business because Aunt Eleanor is sitting up perfectly straight, heels tucked together, full lips pressed into a line.

"Stella, finally." She waves the letter, a signal for me to come fetch it. Her impatience is so palpable, I'm surprised that she hasn't already opened it. "You've received a letter from Mr. Thomas Fitzroy."

My brow twitches with concern. That is a name I have not heard in years.

Aunt Eleanor folds her hands together. "His footman informed me that a carriage will return tomorrow. *For you.* You've been summoned to Kendall Manor."

4

"Kendall Manor?" My breath catches around the words. I hold the envelope in unsteady hands. In some ways, the home of the wealthy Fitzroy family was once my home too. But even saying those two words after all this time feels strange, like my tongue has forgotten how to do it.

My father left my mother and me when I was little, and there were not many opportunities for a young unwed mother, and certainly not one born of an enslaved woman from the West Indies. Thomas Fitzroy was the only one to give her a chance. We shared a bed in a tiny bedroom, but I never once minded snuggling up next to my mother, who sang me to sleep every night, however exhausted the day's work left her.

Though some of the servants stuck their noses up at me, I was permitted to play alongside the Fitzroy heirs. Their tutor, Mrs.

Marstock, taught me letters and numbers. The children and I became companions. There was Jane, the eldest and bossiest; feisty Gwendolyn, always getting chastised for some trouble; and Nathaniel, my best friend once upon a time. Thinking on my childhood now, these memories are hazy, like they belong to someone else. And yet I can't help but feel a sort of *longing*. A comfortable nostalgia unlike anything I've felt before.

This feeling subsides rather quickly. I was thirteen when my uncle died and we left Kendall to be here at Aunt Eleanor's side. Mother died a year later. The Fitzroys did not attend the funeral and never called upon me as the years passed. It was very clear then that as close as I'd grown to the Fitzroy grand-children, they didn't consider me with the same closeness. My mother was just a nursemaid, after all, so perhaps I shouldn't have been surprised, but since Jane, Gwen, and Nathaniel also lost their mother as children, I thought . . . Well, I expected some show of sympathy. And while Thomas Fitzroy's country estate, Enderly, is only twenty minutes from here by carriage, the family spends so little time there that I've been spared any awkward chance meetings. I'm not sure why the house is just sitting unoccupied—perhaps they simply prefer the liveliness of the city.

So here we are now, after years of silence. I run my fingers along the lush envelope. My name is written in an elegant hand, letters in beautiful swirls. It's thin, so I know it's not a lengthy letter. Perhaps it's an invitation to Jane's wedding; I'm sure she's made a fine match. Or perhaps Gwen's engaged. Or Nate.

Under Aunt Eleanor's watchful eye, I slip my thumb under

the wax seal of an eagle—the Fitzroy crest. Indeed, it is a short letter. I scan the text, and my heartbeat quickens.

"Well?" Aunt Eleanor asks, hardly hiding her impatience.

"It's not from Mr. Fitzroy; it's from his solicitor. He's ill, gravely ill." I swallow hard. There's a surprising pang of sadness in my chest. "I've been requested to come to his bedside. If I accept, a room will be prepared for my stay at Kendall."

"How awful," Livvie says earnestly. She squeezes my hand.

Aunt Eleanor stands. "I'll tell the courier to expect you. I'll inquire whether Olivia might go as well."

I spin to her, my heart racing. "What? You want me to drop everything and leave?"

My aunt raises her brow incredulously at me. "Of course. The man is dying! And Stella, dear, what is it that *you* have to *drop*?"

I bite my tongue.

"Don't make that dreadful expression; it'll only be for a day or two. I wouldn't want you to impose. There's too much to be done around here for me to join you, so I'll call upon Mrs. Sinclair to retrieve you. Now's as good a time as ever to take her up on her offer to tour you girls around London."

I feel a small rush of relief. I'd much rather spend time with Lady Tess than the Fitzroys.

Livvie scrunches her face like a child. "Why do I have to go to Kendall? I never even knew the Fitzroys! Can't I just go to Lady Tess's?"

Aunt Eleanor brushes the underside of Olivia's chin. "If you run into Jane Danvers, perhaps you'll learn something. I've heard she's engaged to a wealthy viscount."

I make a sound like a deranged gull, and flail my arms quite like one. "There's a man on his deathbed, Aunt Eleanor! This is not the time for social climbing!"

She sends me a warning look, though her tone is gentle. "Hush, now. I'm simply looking at this horrible situation from all angles so that I may find a more agreeable one." Before she leaves us, she shouts over her shoulder, "And be sure to pack your nice dresses! You know the ones I mean, Stella."

It sounds like a threat.

"The woman is so keen," I whisper once she's left. I plop down into her armchair and raise my feet to the ottoman, but Livvie smoothly pushes it away before I can settle them there.

"Don't get comfortable. You heard Mother. And if you don't start packing now, you'll put it off until the very last second."

I roll my wrists. "Ah. Yes. Well, I'm not going."

"Don't be silly, of course you're going. The man who took you and your mother in is near death!"

"He didn't take her in, he employed her."

"Fair, but he certainly didn't have to take *you* in!"

"Livvie, stop making so much sense. You're giving me a headache."

"*Stella.*"

I look her up and down, and a thought dawns on me. "You *cannot wait* to go to London, can you?"

She plays with the pretty bow on her sunshine dress.

"Praying you'll fall into some man's arms and be swept off your feet? Engaged by summer's end?"

✦ 29 ✦

"What's so wrong with wanting an engagement?"

"What's so wrong with a lifetime of boredom and servitude, you mean?"

Olivia is so used to my pessimistic musings that she simply laughs. "Stella, if you don't want to get married, then don't get married. But your insistence on your opinion being the *only* one is getting old."

I scoff, though it stings. Perhaps I deserve it. "Olivia, it won't be the same for you as it is for Jane Danvers. Having a grandfather like Mr. Fitzroy—"

"I know that," she says, a little edge to it. "I'm going to start putting my things together. I suggest you do the same before Mother sweeps back around and sees you lying about."

She leaves me alone to foster my quickly graying mood. I unfold Mr. Fitzroy's letter and read it once more. I imagine that Mother would've wanted to go, if she were here. And yet I think of what Fiona Flippant's sharp answer might be—*What a tragedy! That said, you might get a few days of fancy meals out of this, and that's worth it on its own, no? Even if it means returning to a house that you're not sure you'll recognize and a family who have forgotten you entirely.*

I swear, I'm not some heartless monster. I am touched by Mr. Fitzroy's wanting to see me before his last rites. My resistance is simple—I do my best to avoid uncomfortable or unplanned situations when I can, and this seems a horrible mix of both.

I push myself onto my feet and head up to my room. This trip must be done, even if my mind is already playing out the dozens

＊ 30 ＊

of uncomfortable situations that will surely come to pass. The anxiousness rises from my belly and into my chest. I bite down against it, tightening my hands into fists until the feeling subsides enough to ignore it.

As promised, the carriage returns the next day. Mr. Fitzroy is apparently "delighted" to host Olivia as well—an embellishment surely added to by the footman—though not nearly as delighted as Aunt Eleanor is at the prospect of her daughter rubbing elbows with his grandchildren. I give myself a last look in the mirror, ensuring that my dress is wrinkle-free. My thick hair is pulled into four plaits and pinned back at the nape of my neck. I've packed a few books, my notebook, and a stack of Fiona Flippant's best jabs. My wardrobe is nice enough, though, unlike Olivia, I have only a few lovely dresses, and it only took me twenty minutes to pack them. I certainly don't need three trunks and the footman's help.

The poor man is red-faced as he lugs her things to the carriage.

"Livvie, you can't be serious," I say.

Her eyes are bright with excitement. "Lady Tess will have engagements planed. I have to be prepared."

I try not to grimace. "Oh, you're going to abandon me for parties, I see."

Livvie pinches my elbow. "Well, I'd invite you, but I imagine you'd be awfully bored with suitors and parties and nice wine."

"Don't be ridiculous. I do like wine."

We find ourselves giggling as the footman opens the carriage door. Olivia slides into the seat, but I feel a tug on my arm before I can follow.

Aunt Eleanor pulls me back, putting some distance between us and the carriage. "This is an important trip, Stella. For you, and for your cousin."

I look back to Olivia watching us curiously from the carriage. "You can't truly think she'll be welcomed into society life with open arms? That some wealthy man will love her so much that he overlooks her lack of money, or the color of her skin? And would it be worth it to marry a man who found those things nuisances to be overlooked?"

Aunt Eleanor scoffs, her nostrils flaring. "I know you are inclined to believe the very worst in people, but believe it or not, I would *never* pressure Livvie to marry a man who disrespects her so."

I look away, a little ashamed of myself. "Of course. I apologize, Aunt Eleanor."

She smooths her skirts. "That said, I do hear Nathaniel Fitzroy is a proper gentleman just waiting for a match."

My entire body stills, though my heartbeat quickens.

She smiles. Oh dear, I can practically see the wheels turning in her head. "And you know him well, so it's perfect."

"I wouldn't say I know any of the Fitzroys very well anymore."

Aunt Eleanor lifts a brow. "I was thinking he'd make a handsome match for Olivia, no?"

Heat creeps up my face. "He could be aggravating, mind you."

❖ 32 ❖

"Oh?"

"Well. He was terribly quiet, and so serious, and annoyingly mild-mannered."

"Is that supposed to make me *not* like him?" Aunt Eleanor leans in, a smile widening. "Do your best to . . . *convince* them."

"I don't know that I'd do well at matchmaking."

"Not matchmaking. Just, well, ensure they have each other's attention." She winks. "What a fine betrothal that would be, and with Mr. Fitzroy sick—I hate to say it—"

Oh, but she will—

"Nathaniel will inherit a handsome sum."

Thankfully, I'm saved from crafting a response. Olivia sticks her head out of the carriage door. "What are you two scheming about?"

With a mischievous smile, Aunt Eleanor gives her daughter a last embrace and kisses the top of her forehead. My heart hurts for that feeling, but Aunt Eleanor also pulls me into a hug as well. I give her a good squeeze before scooting into the seat across from Livvie. The carriage begins to pull away.

"Goodbye, now!" I call out while Aunt Eleanor is still in view. "Be horrible and mean to Cheswick for me!"

"No!" Livvie shouts in earnest distress. "Feed him all the fish he wants!"

Aunt Eleanor, quite used to our ridiculousness, only cups a hand around her ear, shakes her head, and pretends not to hear us.

With a giggle, Olivia settles into her seat. "What was she talking your ear off about, Stella?"

"The usual. Demanding we be on our best behavior and that I watch over you."

She nods and fixes her gaze on the window.

I do the same, relieved that it's left at that.

5

Despite my dislike of carriage rides, the two-hour journey from Addyshire to London is much too quick for my liking. I am unprepared for the sight of the city. It's so odd returning to a place that exists only in my fuzzy memories. How it takes my breath away.

The Fitzroy estate is somehow both expansive *and* cozy. Olivia's eyes widen at the lush daisy bushes and hedges lining the walkway, elegantly carved into crisp edges and curves. Great oak trees cup the three-story manor in a perfect semicircle. It's all very pretty with the rosy vines curling around the windows. Kendall Manor is not nearly as sprawling as Enderly, which could likely house an army in comfort, but the coziness only makes it more charming. It's barely changed, though the same cannot be said for the surrounding land. More houses have been built around it—all just as lavish—and the sidewalks are busy with fine-dressed ladies and gentlemen. The streets are louder with curricles and hansoms, and I can see the tops of the shops and flats of downtown London in the distance.

"I can't believe you were raised here," Livvie says, her face pressed up against the window. She shoots me a playful glance. "It's a wonder you aren't more snobbish."

"Are you calling me unrefined?" I say, before using the window as a mirror and picking my pinky nail between my teeth.

Livvie laughs sweetly. There's nothing like that sound. It's comforting, like one of Mother's letters, a mug of mulled wine, or wrapping myself up in Aunt Eleanor's favorite quilt—the one I'm most certainly *not* allowed to touch.

She leans back. "What are you thinking, Stella?"

I part my lips to speak, but how can I describe the way every memory comes back to me in one heart-wrenching wave? Was it not just yesterday that I bested Nathaniel and Gwen at tending to tomato seedlings? Mine was the tallest of the bunch, and the gardener, Mr. Owens, had given me the promised prize of strawberry candy, making Gwen quite cross. Was it not just last month that my mother forced us all into the drawing room to perform a carol for Mr. Fitzroy? Even his stoic expression bore a smile, despite his proclamation that we were all quite off-key.

It was all here. I learned how lucky a person could be simply because of who their ancestors were and whom they married. A place where I roamed about during the day, but hid myself when guests arrived. Where I lived, played, ate, wept, yet I could not truly call it home, because it never belonged to me. I may have been treated well enough, but I was always the nursemaid's daughter.

"Stella?" Olivia pats my hand gently.

I smile at her. "What am I thinking? For one, I wish my mother were here. She always knew what to say."

"Well, what do you think she'd say?"

I shrug. "Something beautiful and sweet about life and its many gifts, and its many tragedies. How, perhaps, God never grants one without the other."

She nods. "And do you believe that?"

I turn back to the manor. "No, I think God does as he very well pleases. But Mum had a way of making skeptics into believers."

We are pulled into the circular driveway where no fewer than six servants wait to receive us. I don't recognize a single one. Shame; I'd wondered if I might see Mrs. Marstock, who was Mum's favorite as well as mine.

"A bit much," I mutter, though Livvie can hardly contain her excitement. Her brown curls bounce as she fixes her hair.

A pale middle-aged man opens the carriage doors. He looks me up and down, from my thick, coily hair to my polished shoes. I'm sure he's been informed that I was not some fair-haired maiden, but he still can't quite hide the flash of shock in his eyes. "Miss Sedgwick, I presume?"

"Yes."

He dips his head slightly. "Welcome back to Kendall Manor," he says. "And this must be Miss Witherson."

As they help Olivia with her luggage, I skip the pleasantries

❖ 37 ❖

and stride toward the door. Brisk footsteps trail after me, but I excuse the poor footman with a polite wave. "Don't trouble yourself, I remember the way."

Really, I just want to be alone with my thoughts for a moment. There's that painful nostalgia again.

I run my fingers over the cherubim faces embossed in the wooden side table by the door, like I always used to do. I'm just missing Gwen running in behind me and Nathaniel yelling at us to slow down. They've replaced the portrait hanging here— what was once a sweet painting of the Fitzroy patriarch with his wife and their young grandchildren has been aged up. This one must've been done recently.

Jane still possesses that discerning gaze that could either comfort or kill you, depending on her mood. Her skin is pale, her cheeks brushed red. Her brown hair is styled in perfect ringlets. She is elegance incarnate, a perfect illustration of a well-bred lady.

Gwen looks about a moment away from a scathing eye roll, and I almost laugh. Her blond hair is done in a tight bun, paper-stiffened curls framing her face, which I know she must've hated.

Then there's Nathaniel. I scarcely recognize him at all. He is the anomaly. Light brown skin, amber brown curls, dark— nearly black—eyes. His smile is faint, but he looks happy to be surrounded by a family one would think he didn't belong in at first glance. I see his grandfather's face in his, though Mr. Fitzroy is as pale as snow. They have the same sturdy chin, and Nate inherited the sharp cheekbones that skipped Jane and Gwen, and even his mother, judging from the pictures I'd seen of the late Emily Fitzroy, who became Emily Danvers after her first marriage.

The memory I have of Nathaniel is baby-faced, but the young man before me has lost that sweet, young touch. His fingers are adorned with rings and curled around Gwen's shoulder. I'm sure the painter had a fit, knowing what those rings were worth, knowing they'd been fitted onto the tawny fingers of a mixed-race boy.

The picture is a stark reminder that I'm not the only one who has lost their mother. Mr. Fitzroy's daughter died giving birth to Nate, a tragic ending to a most scandalous story. Mum used to tell me how lucky Emily was to have had a father who did not throw her out for falling in love with a colored tradesman after her first husband's death, for taking their marriage as legitimate, and for raising her baby boy as his own and giving him his last name, whereas his half sisters have their father's name—Danvers. If Mr. Fitzroy were a poorer man, he likely would not have kept his place in society after entertaining such an egregious scandal.

The lush strokes of paint compel me to touch the portrait. I remember sitting at the artist's feet as he constructed the original iteration of the younger family, watching the brilliant strokes of color from the palette to the canvas. How jealous Nate was—he'd much rather have watched the painter work than pose for him. I remember how, when it was done, Mr. Fitzroy had plopped me onto my mother's lap and had the painter craft us as well. My mother and me, a smiling pair, immortalized in brilliant browns and golds. I miss her, I miss her. Heavens, I haven't thought about that portrait in years. I wonder where it is now? Perhaps the Fitzroys simply got rid of it.

I hear a shuffle behind me. The servant clears his throat and looks perturbed to see that I have touched the elegant painting. His face is bony and grim, and I'm reminded that this place may have felt like home once, but that was long ago.

"Mr. Fitzroy will see you now," he says, gesturing to the stairs.

From above, there's a horrifying fit of coughing and retching. Quietly, I make my way up the stairs. The poor man's coughs rumble down the hallway, decorated by the same green floral wallpaper from a decade ago. I remember standing here in the hallway as Jane tugged on my coarse curls and Nathaniel slipping a newt down the back of her dress in my defense.

The servant follows the sounds to Mr. Fitzroy's room at the end of the hall and knocks twice.

"Yes?" an unrecognizable voice answers.

I play with my sleeves, my heartbeat ticking up.

The servant announces me. "Miss Stella Sedgwick is here, as Mr. Fitzroy requested, if he is well enough to receive her?"

There are soft voices, and then Mr. Fitzroy's unmistakably terse one. *"I said open the bloody door!"*

The door does open, revealing a cluttered bedroom that smells of mint, herbs, and perspiration.

A wraith lies in bed.

Illness has transformed the bullish Mr. Fitzroy into a shell of a man. He's lost most of his thick gray hair, and what remains is thin and spotty. His eyes are sunken, and his pale skin is slick with sweat. I bite back a gasp, but Mr. Fitzroy's weak, ashamed scowl is enough to beckon me forward. I want to be angry with him, and to ask how he could've said nothing after my mother died. But the sight of him softens my heart. He reaches out a hand, and I do not hesitate to take it.

Laboriously, he says, "I thought you might ask if I was contagious first."

"You wouldn't have offered your hand if you were."

"*Hmph.* There's Stell. Always thinks the best of me. When you were a child, you always defended me for the punishments I levied against Gwendolyn and Nathaniel."

"Well, only because you never had the heart to punish me with them."

I sit on the velour bench at his side. There are two nurses trying not to gape, and a stuffy man standing in the corner with a leather folio. He's gone white as a sheet at the sight of me. He looks impatient and important, and is much too far from the bed to be the physician. I turn to Mr. Fitzroy. "How are you . . . Erm . . ." I wring my hands. "How much longer?"

He winks. "Keen to be rid of me?"

I find myself smiling. "Never, Mr. Fitzroy."

He scoffs, though it sounds more like a wheeze. "The doctor has given me the dastardly prediction of three months—which I intend to fight, tooth and nail. I brought you here now so it isn't such a shock later on. Mr. Adams—" In one movement, he dismisses the nurses and waves the stuffy man forward.

The man does come forward, albeit reluctantly. There's an edge to his gaze that heightens my anxiety. He thrusts a neat pile of papers at me. "Mr. Fitzroy's will."

I blink, waiting for him to explain.

He fidgets. "You can read, yes? According to Mr. Fitzroy—"

"*Yes*," I answer curtly. "I can read."

"Well, then . . ." The solicitor waits until the nurses have closed the door behind them before adding, "Look them over carefully."

I try my best, but the legal language is difficult to parse, and my disinterest grows with every word. I don't really care how Mr. Fitzroy is chopping up his enormous fortune. I'd much rather get to pilfering a freshly baked lemon scone that I can smell from up here. "This looks, erm, agreeable."

Mr. Fitzroy raises a brow. "And on the matter of the estate here in Kendall?"

I wave my hand. "Sure, sure, I'm sure your grandson will be a fine keeper."

"Nate?" Mr. Fitzroy's face falls into confusion, and he looks up at Adams. "You made the changes, yes?"

Changes? I turn back to the papers. I look for his name, for Gwen's, for Jane's, and my mouth pops open in shock at the heir he's named to inherit this lovely home.

Why, my name does look splendid in shiny black ink.

6

I wave my hands incredulously, trying to buy time as I think of what to say. "Well! *This is absurd!*" I meant to sound firm, but it comes out more like a shriek due to my tight throat. It's hard, holding back tears. I wipe my nose messily.

"Stella—" Mr. Fitzroy starts impatiently, never one to stand a girl's crying.

I turn to Mr. Adams. "Sir, shame on you for abetting Mr. Fitzroy's antics."

Mr. Fitzroy grumbles in annoyance. "Do you think I'd be so cruel as to jest about this?"

I don't, but it's difficult to cut back my skepticism. "Anyway, even if it were true, it wouldn't hold."

"And why not?"

I sputter a laugh. "Oh, just the unavoidable fact that I am no relative of yours."

Fitzroy pauses, then shakes his head. "No, no, it's my money, my property; who should tell me what to do with it? Adams, you see that I am of clear mind, yes?"

Mr. Adams hesitates. "Well, yes, but it's unheard of, to say the least—"

"Besides, who would stop me?" Mr. Fitzroy interrupts. "Jane has her grandmother's jewels, a handsome allowance, and soon, a husband wealthier than I. Gwen has her own allowance, and will marry well—*well*, if I could get the girl to hush every so often. She will be taken care of. Only Enderly and Duberney are entailed, and seeing as Nathaniel has not yet mastered the art of existing in three places at once, I think he'll do just fine there." He pauses to take in a ragged breath. "The boy's only concerns in life are his silly paintings."

I nod slowly, if only because it's the one reaction I can manage. Mr. Fitzroy seems serious about this. I try to imagine having Kendall, a home, all for myself and in my keeping. And an allowance too, enough to change my life tenfold. Hell! With this money, not only would I be able to freely pursue my dreams of writing, I could start my own press!

I see my future opening up before me in ways I'd never dreamed . . . and so, there must be a catch. I find it quickly, the text blurred in my teary vision.

There it is, the clause that crashes my daydreams. A blank space precedes my name, followed by the word *husband* in parentheses. But of course. I cannot truly inherit Kendall Manor, and couldn't even if I had Fitzroy blood. Only a man can hold property.

I've spent my whole life disregarding the idea of marriage. I have no reputable family name, no money for a dowry, and according to *absurd* societal rules, undesirable genes. Just as I am not like Jane or Gwen, I am not like Livvie or Nathaniel, with one white parent who came from some fortune that might be enough to overshadow the last bit. With Enderly and Duberney in his keeping and a handsome yearly allowance, I imagine a few genteel families might be willing to dismiss the color of Nathaniel's skin and the scandalous circumstances of his birth.

"Why are you doing this?" I ask in a stunned whisper. "I am grateful, but I must admit that I don't understand."

Mr. Fitzroy turns away, exposing the gray spots dotting his wrinkled neck. "Because Ginny deserved better."

At the sound of my mother's name, I sit upright. "What about her?"

He sounds wearier now than when we began. His gaze becomes unfocused. The solicitor steps away to call in the nurses.

Mr. Fitzroy speaks like a sinner at a pulpit, his voice shaking with desperation. I never knew him as a staunchly pious man, but I suppose being so close to death changes a man. "I should have protected her, I could have done so much more." He lunges for my hand. "Stella, forgive me."

I'm frightened, but I press on. "Protect her from what?"

He coughs so violently that I have to lurch away. His body rattles, and the bed shakes. The nurses rush in to tend to him. I'm shooed away—rather rudely, I must say—and suddenly find myself in the hall behind a closed door once more.

I linger for a few moments, but I can hear the nurses

discussing giving him a sleeping draft, so I suppose there's no point in waiting for this to pass.

Adams slips out of the room. He peers at me from behind his glasses. He still has the folio in hand. "Miss Sedgwick." He offers a polite nod. "It seems as though this great fortune comes as a shock."

"Yes."

He examines me. "Are you feeling faint? I know young ladies have delicate constitutions."

I bite my tongue against a hundred rude responses. "My *constitution* is quite formidable, I assure you."

He gives me an uncertain look before continuing. "I should mention that Mr. Fitzroy discussed your inclusion in his will long before he fell ill."

My chest squeezes. "And did you advise against it?"

He adjusts his spectacles. "I'll tell you the same thing I told him—you may face opposition. The entailment of Kendall Manor ends with Mr. Fitzroy, so he can do with the land as he pleases. It helps that he has no siblings, and the late Mrs. Fitzroy's family has remained distant, on account of . . ."

His voice trails off, and he does a fumbling motion with his hands. I have no patience for this. "On account of Nathaniel Fitzroy, yes?"

He shuffles uncomfortably. "Right. Still, that does not mean that you will not have a fight ahead of you. I suggest that you marry, and soon. The sooner, the better, really. Not to be crass, but we'll need your husband's name in the will ready when Mr. Fitzroy passes on."

❖ 46 ❖

I can't help but grimace. "Is there no way I could inherit without marrying?"

Adams's amused pity makes my skin crawl with embarrassment. "Better yet, marry the young Fitzroy himself. That would keep the vultures at bay."

"*Or*, I could throw myself over the railing, die, and haunt Kendall Manor for eternity—yes, I do believe that would truly make it mine."

Awkwardly, Mr. Adams plays with his hat. "I must be going, though I suspect we'll meet again. Good day, Miss Sedgwick."

He descends the stairs rather hurriedly.

From Mr. Fitzroy's room, a nurse's hushed voice drifts to me. ". . . I'd throw a fit if my grandfather was as wealthy as he is and gave my birthright to some—"

I turn away from the door sharply. I do not need to hear the rest. I have half a mind to defend myself, but my heart's anxious. I'm not up for a fight. I wonder where Gwen, Nathaniel, and Jane are. I wonder what they think of all this.

Perhaps I'll find some comfort in Livvie's company.

From the sound of it, the staff has settled Olivia into our guest room. I poke my head in and find her twirling in the wide-open space. Between her pretty dress billowing out around her and the last slice of sunlight pouring in from the open windows between rain clouds, well, she looks like she belongs here in a way I never did. She flops onto the lush white bed with a giggle, and I duck away before she notices I'm even there.

I patter down to the first floor, past the kitchen—I'm quite proud of myself for resisting the urge to nick a piece of treacle off the counter—and through the doors of the great room at the back of the house. My favorite one. The shamefully underused library.

My breaths are still unsteady, but seeing that every book is in its place, the sculptures are the same, and the pillars have not been painted eases me a bit. Nothing has changed.

When I was a child, this estate felt like a princess's castle. I'd pretend I was one, spinning around Gwen's room as Mum played the pianoforte. And I'd felt like an explorer, too. I know all of the house's hidden secrets, of the latch behind the bookcase that opens up to a secret pantry where Jane sometimes gossiped with her friends. When I think of Kendall Manor, I think of sitting by the fire, my head in Mum's lap as she plaited my hair and hummed a sweet tune. I think of the gardens where Nate, Gwen, and I acted out scenes from books as Jane looked on with delight.

It's their childhood home.

But I suppose it's mine too.

I must force myself out of this thinking. Mr. Fitzroy might truly mean to grant me this great fortune, but I've read enough of Fiona Flippant's letters to know that riches can be easily spoiled. Am I prepared to fight for this? I have no plans to marry, and I'd rather cozy up in the study at Aunt Eleanor's than open myself up to whatever confrontation might be waiting for me in the future over this inheritance. But, *heavens.* Uncle Edward, devout as he was, used to say that wealth is no substitute for the true happiness of love, companionship, and piety. With all love and respect to the pastor, I think being born into wealth would have made me a much happier girl.

Rain bursts in the gardens, and a squeal erupts behind me. *"Stella!"*

I don't get a chance to react. Pink-faced, Gwendolyn Danvers propels herself at me, arms open wide. I can do nothing but plant my left foot behind my right, catch her, and hold her as tightly as she holds me. I'd know it was Gwen without even seeing her or hearing my name in her musical, sweet voice. I'd know her from the flash of yellow hair and the smell of blueberry tarts on her breath.

"Oh dear," I manage through tears of my own. I don't know what else to say. I wasn't expecting to cry at the sight of her. Every memory of the childish games we played and the mischief we got up to comes rushing back to me. I thought I was still angry with all of them, but here I am, blubbering.

She can't be comfortable in her damp shoes, but she is delighted. Eyes closed, fists tight, *delighted.* "What a perfect surprise on such a miserable day!" She swats her hand in front of my face like a fan. "Don't waste your tears on me. Sit, sit!" She pulls me to the couch. "How have you been?"

"Oh, well. *Well.*" I reach for something else to say. "I'm still horrible at the pianoforte."

Gwen beams. "Good; that makes two of us. You know I was only ever so diligent at causing trouble during lessons."

"Please, you have natural talent! I, on the other hand, still can't seem to command my pinky to move with such abandon." I wiggle the useless thing, and she laughs. Gwen always had such an easy laugh. I could get her to snort up her tea with little

✦ 49 ✦

more than a dirty joke. I used to live for that.

She sighs. "If only your mother were here, too."

I fidget. I'd hoped we wouldn't be doing this so soon.

Gwen drops her eyes and focuses on rotating her pretty silver bracelet around her wrist. "She was such a lovely woman, and far warmer to me than she needed to be. I hope you received the flowers."

I nod, biting back the rising anger I'd often felt at Gwen's family's sudden distance. "Yes, and thank you."

"What is it with mothers and abandoning us?" Gwen laughs, shaking her head. "At least mine can't interrupt my plans for the summer. My grandfather would like to see me engaged before he's *covered in dirt*, as he put it. Just horrid of him to use his sickness like this. Well, fine, but I'll dance with all the gentlemen I can before settling down." She drops her voice and narrows her eyes into a conspiratorial wink. "And the ladies, too."

I grin with her. I missed keeping Gwen's secrets and hearing of her schemes. "I imagine your grandmother is jolting in her grave at such a declaration. What a scandal!"

"Oh, it's only a scandal if you get caught. Besides, all the boys get to have their fun. Even Nate—" Her gaze lands behind me. "Oh, hello. And who is this young woman?"

Even Nate, what? I want to ask, but I'm not sure I want to know what was coming next. The thought of Nate *having his fun* sends a wave of unease through my core. I feel silly for it, but it's not as if I can help it.

I turn to Livvie, standing sweetly in the doorway. "Miss Witherson, my cousin. *Don't flirt.*"

❖ 50 ❖

Gwen offers an amused—and admonishing—glare. "Come, now, I wouldn't dare flirt with a lady before properly introducing myself."

"Please, call me Olivia." She settles next to me on the couch. "You must be Miss Gwendolyn Danvers."

"Sometimes, but *Gwen* most often."

I lean back, relishing the comforts of being tucked between them. "As my mother once said—Gwen when she's behaving, and Gwendolyn when she's cross. And I prefer Gwen indeed."

She pats Livvie's hand. "It's nice to meet someone who has also known the triumphs and perils of being at Stella's side."

I huff. "Never mind, I'd rather you flirt. Olivia's skills need refining, her first time in London society and all. Her mother would love to see her engaged as well."

"Oh, thank heaven! We'll weather this together." Now Gwen's eyes are wide with excitement. "Can you imagine, the three of us—"

I shake my head. "I'm only here to pay my respects to your grandfather, Gwen," I reply sternly. "I've no desire to show myself off like a prized bird in the hopes of catching some man's eye." *Besides*, I want to add, *I do not think there is a place in London society for a girl like me.*

I haven't spoken to Olivia about the inheritance yet, and if Gwen knows the details of her grandfather's will, she says nothing of it.

Gwen squeezes me gently. "Well, obviously it sounds horrible when you put it that way. Really, it's a lot more fun than you'd think. The parties, the dancing, and yes, *the flirting.*"

Livvie is buzzing with excitement. "Oh, I can hardly wait!"

Gwen rises and holds a hand out to her. "We shall discuss what I learned from my sister, Jane, and perhaps convince stubborn Stella in the meantime."

I watch as they make for the sitting room, giggling arm in arm. I look around at Mr. Fitzroy's library, feeling as small as when I was eight, a little piece in this massive house.

7

I only manage two or three restless hours of sleep before I jolt awake. I'm not sure what's awoken me; maybe a thunderclap, since it's still storming. But here I am, vibrating with energy in the dead of night. My mind is fretful; my thoughts are running wild. I try everything—counting to ten, blocking out the moonlight from my eyes with a pillow, and even reciting the alphabet, but nothing seems to help. On the other side of the room, Olivia is sound asleep, so I can't even ask her to list Mrs. Smith's silly *genteel commandments*. That would've knocked me right out.

When I was younger, my mum would curl up beside me and hum lullabies. At Aunt Eleanor's, I always sleep like a rock. Here, I can't feel the faintest touch of fatigue in my eyes.

I swing my legs over the edge of the bed. I figure a good

dosing of Shakespeare will bore me to sleep. I slip on my bed jacket, grab my spectacles, and head for the library.

I take my lamp, but I don't bother lighting it. My feet still know the way, and I'm in the library without sounding the squeaky bits of the stairs or the creaky sliding doors. The moonlight is plentiful, so I push back the curtains and forget the lantern altogether.

The Fitzroy collection is impressive, and seemingly untouched. The spine of his copy of *Midsummer* is still uncracked, and the pages feel fresh. I sweep away a healthy layer of dust before settling comfortably onto the couch, my ankles tucked under my bottom.

It takes only eight pages for my eyes to feel heavy. My spectacles are sliding off my face; I'm very nearly about to fall asleep with my head against the armrest, but I'm roused by steps in the foyer.

I don't think much of them—it's probably one of Mr. Fitzroy's nurses, or house staff. I hear the housekeeper, Mrs. Phillips. She sounds startled, but there's laughter too, and more footsteps tottering about.

My curiosity gets the better of me. I tiptoe over to the sliding doors and push them open a smidge.

A sopping wet Nathaniel Fitzroy steps into the house, waving away the very fussy servants. His voice is low and slow, laden with exhaustion. "Apologies for the late arrival, we got caught in the storm."

Mrs. Phillips is red with worry. "You'll take ill!"

She's rushing him up the stairs to change, but he's already

* 54 *

making quick work of his shirt, his pale brown fingers fiddling with the buttons before pulling it off entirely.

I'm not watching, I swear. I'm simply not fast enough, for when I realize, his gaze flicks to the left—*to me*—and I frantically slide the door shut.

Hell.

Hell.

Quickly, I throw myself onto the couch, procure the copy of *Midsummer*, rest my feet on the ottoman, and place my elbow against the armrest, surely looking *very natural*—

The sliding doors creak open.

"Oh!" I jump, as if not expecting this at all.

Water drips steadily from Nate's dark curls onto his face. He doesn't seem to notice this, or that the damp shirt he'd hurried back on is only half buttoned at the top, revealing a rather delicious sliver of slick brown skin that I am trying my best to ignore.

He stares at me, dazed, and blinks as if I'm just a spot in his vision.

"Miss Sedgwick?" he whispers, more an exhale than a word. His voice is marked with the same rasp of his grandfather.

"So formal," I mutter sardonically. "Hello, *Mr. Fitzroy.*"

He fixes his mouth to speak, but is interrupted by Mrs. Phillips scampering into the library with a large towel in her arms.

Fitzroy ignores her. He shakes his head a little, still questioning his own eyes. "I just—I wasn't expecting you." He gestures vaguely to the hallway. "There was mention of a guest—"

"Your grandfather sent for me. Did you not know?"

❖ 55 ❖

He shifts his weight between his feet. "He'd mentioned you, yes, but I didn't expect to see you so soon."

Unlike Gwen, who came at me with tears of joy and the fiercest hug I'd ever felt, Nathaniel regards me with no such warmth. His mouth opens. Then closes. He thinks for a moment, then turns to Mrs. Phillips and graciously takes the towel. He turns to me with a lifted hand. "Don't move."

Mrs. Phillips shoots me a curious glance before they both leave the library.

I return to the sofa, my heart stuttering. It should be against the law for a young man like Nathaniel Fitzroy to sneak up on innocent ladies such as I! Particularly when I'm in an embarrassingly frilly shift and bed jacket, and especially when they've just come in from the rain that, might I add, would've rendered me a drowning cat, and not a dashing beauty.

The sliding doors creak again. Nathaniel has returned in dry clothes—a linen shirt and trousers—and still-damp hair. He's balancing two small glasses of brandy, their rims lined in gold.

I can only stare. He has *changed*, so fully. Not even the portrait in the foyer has done him any justice; not his chiseled face or the perfect dimple in his right cheek as he admonishes himself for dripping water onto the sofa. There is a boyishness in his round, dark eyes, but his shoulders are broad, obviously so, even in the loose dress shirt that is much too formal for this time of night.

I wrap my bed-jacket tighter around myself. "What are you doing?" I ask with a questioning laugh.

He doesn't look up at me. "Mrs. Phillips claims it's an old

family cure for warming up after being caught in the rain: a fire, and brandy." He offers a cup. "Alas, I have never been fond of solitary drinking."

I look back to the closed parlor doors, waiting for Mrs. Phillips to return. This isn't proper, the two of us alone like this.

I accept the cup. "Don't tell me *you're* going to attempt the fire."

He doesn't look at me, but sure enough, his eyes are already assessing the firewood that must have been left over from a previous night. "Don't you trust me?"

"I grew up with you. I've seen how you are with flames. You used to get so distracted by what was going on around you that you'd end up with scorch marks on the side of your trousers."

Finally, he looks up at me from beneath long, dark lashes. "You remember that?"

I shrug. "Of course I do."

I can't make sense of the curious expression on his face. With steady hands, he uses a flint to light the tinderbox, then tends to the fire. "Easy enough."

"Well, the wood was already collected."

I catch the hint of a smile on his lips, though I can't be sure, it's gone so quickly. "Be nice to me, I brought you a drink."

The firelight flicks over the sharp edges of his face. My God, I mustn't stare, but my eyes won't obey. It's so strange to see a face I know but hardly recognize. It's as if my gaze has been starved of this sight and must take in all of Nathaniel that it can in case I go years without seeing him once more. He examines me with the same careful consideration. I wonder what he thinks. How do I look to him? Years older, familiar and unfamiliar at the same time.

"How have you been?" he asks quietly.

I mull over a thousand answers, and not one feels right. "I've been well enough." I sigh a laugh. "Sorry, I'm so tired of this question."

He raises a brow, humored by this. "Forgive me for asking; it's only been four years."

"Five. I left just after Gwen turned fourteen."

His brow furrows now. "Oh, yes."

"She hasn't changed at all, and neither has this house. Though, where has everyone gone, like Mrs. Marstock?"

He shakes his head. "It was so long ago. I think Mrs. Marstock left just after you did, and Grandfather sent everyone else away some time after that."

"I hope whoever you have in the kitchen now is as good with shortbread."

He offers a small smile. "Yes, she even tops them with lemon curd."

There's silence suddenly, and though it feels a little odd on its own, it's made all the more awkward by his intense staring at me.

"What?" I laugh, trying to play off my nervousness.

"What?"

"You're staring, Fitzroy."

"Well," he whispers. "I was wondering about those *ghastly* things on your face. They're falling apart, Stell."

I push up the slanted spectacles. "Oh, hush. I haven't had the time to get them fixed."

+ 58 +

The ghost of a smile on his lips, he presses his fingers to his forehead, as if fending off a growing headache. "I just can't believe you're here. Did you speak to my grandfather?"

I swallow. "Yes."

He sets his cup atop the ledge of the fireplace. "So you know of his intentions to bequeath this very house to you."

"I do."

Fitzroy turns from me. He watches the fire flicker as he considers my response. *This is a boy you no longer know*, I remind myself. I thought I'd wanted to know how he felt about all this, but now I'm terrified. After all, what am I but a servant's daughter? My body tenses. My heart thrums.

But then he *smiles*. Why, he nearly laughs! "Then why do you look so miserable, Stella?"

I exhale. It's like a boulder has been lifted from my chest, but I don't bother unfurrowing my brow. "I don't mean to sound ungrateful, but having this great fortune—that I'm not sure I have the ability to accept—bestowed upon me without any sort of warning has made this quite a stressful day."

"What do you mean? You loved this house."

"Also, I was training to be a servant—"

"And it ended poorly."

I shoot him a worried look. "Has the gossip traveled this far?"

"No, no. But that's not your calling." He tugs on his bottom lip with his teeth. "It's been some time, but I still know you, Stella."

I drop my gaze to my hands and fiddle with the book in my lap. "My cousin, Olivia, and I will be spending some time in London with a friend of our family. Perhaps we can keep each other company, what with Gwen and my cousin being so busy with society life."

Fitzroy goes rigid. The hint of lightness I'd coaxed out of him disappears. "It will be a busy time for me, as well."

I try not to frown, but it's impossible. I should have known he'd be in society, surely looking to court the perfect wife. I hear Aunt Eleanor's voice in my head. *Do your best to convince them.* I wish I hadn't remembered that.

"I'm excited for you to meet Olivia. She's very sweet. Talented, too. Piano, and needlepoint, and all. Makes a fine pudding." It's all I can manage before the pounding in my chest becomes too much to bear. Livvie and Nathaniel really would be a handsome couple, and I should be happy at the idea of my two worlds coming together. And yet, hard as I try to be pleased by the image of the two of them at the altar, it only sours my mood.

Nathaniel smiles politely. "I'm sure we'll all enjoy her company. Jane won't be in for a few weeks, however. She's spending some with her fiancé's family."

My shoulders loosen, though I don't remember when they got so stiff. "How is the baron?"

"He's a viscount, actually."

I feign a swoon, and he smiles. "Well, forgive me, I've heard nothing about him except that he's very rich. Is it a good match?"

"It must be. He's very rich."

"*You're* very rich."

"No, my grandfather's very rich. And the viscount's *impossibly* rich—it's different."

❖ 60 ❖

I scoff. "I forget that there are ranks in how one avoids starving."

"What a point to be made by someone who stands to inherit an estate and two thousand pounds a year."

I shoot him a look of warning. "Right, because this is all going to work out just fine, without any troubles, whatsoever."

He smiles stiffly. "You're in such a mood."

I feel restless, and jump to my feet to pace. "I'm being practical. Realistic."

"*Pessimistic.* I think you deserve a piece of the family will as much as any of us."

"You'd feel differently if your grandfather were a poorer man without several properties to split."

"Well, thankfully, he's a very wealthy man," Fitzroy says with a dark laugh. "I don't deal in what-ifs, but you're less of a disappointment to him than I am, so it makes sense."

I stop pacing to look at him, but he's relinquished my gaze in favor of the fire. I hope he'll fill the silence, because I don't want to prod, but he does not.

We stand in a stagnant silence, only the crackling fire between us.

"I need a husband to receive Kendall, Fitzroy!" It comes out of me in a frantic, breathless stream of words. "So, yes, perhaps I am being pessimistic."

He wears an undecipherable expression—brow slightly raised, lips a little tense. "Oh. I see. Is there not a male relative who could hold the property instead?"

"My only relatives are my aunt and my cousin."

He looks down to his hands. "Will you pursue a match, then?"

I sigh, half laughing. "Truthfully, I've been asking myself the same thing. I couldn't even sleep; it's why I came down here, to quiet my thoughts with reading."

"*Ah.*" He clears his throat. "That's why you're up at such an hour. Sometimes Grandfather yells in his sleep. It's the medicine, I suppose. Gives him horrible nightmares. Anyway, I thought he'd awoken you."

"He wasn't at supper. Gwen says he doesn't feel up to it most of the time." I think back to the switch in his behavior when I spoke with him, and the way he mentioned my mother. Nate seems to already have experienced this. I return to his side. "Nathaniel, has your grandfather spoken about my mother at all?"

"Not that I know of, no. But I've been away traveling. Why?"

I wave my hand. "He mentioned her briefly, but perhaps it was only the medicine talking."

"The doctor says that all we can do is give him comfort as he goes."

"Comfort, then. I suppose I should rethink my plan to fill his socks with mud, like you used to."

He brightens, he *grins*, revealing the snaggletooth that always made him self-conscious as a child. Oh, the lengths I used to go to to see it! I always felt so accomplished when I made him laugh so hard that he forgot to hide this insecurity. That thrill never died—even now it warms my heart to know that I have that power to ease his worries, if only for a moment.

I pull away from him, and instantly miss the warmth of his presence, and for that, perhaps the distance is for the best. I place *Midsummer* back on the shelf. "Well. We should go to bed."

His brow twitches with mischievous curiosity, a trouble-making expression that knocks the air out of me.

"I mean! You should—" I lift a finger. "You should go to bed. And I shall go to bed. I shall go to *my* bed."

Goodness, Stella, what in the world are you saying?

Slowly, his lips curl into an inviting smile. His voice drops a touch, as if he's going to tell me a dark and horrible secret. "I missed you."

Then why did you forget me? I think, the old anger rising to the surface. If I could speak, I'd say it. But Nathaniel's admission is so unexpected, I can only blink a few times in response.

He swallows hard. "We all did. Immensely. And we're happy to have you back—"

"I missed you, too," I blurt out. "Even if you only ever got on my last nerves."

"*Liar.*" The corner of his mouth ticks upward in a small, crooked grin. He runs a quick hand through his still-wet curls and starts to snuff the fire. "Good night then, Miss Sedgwick."

"Night, Fitzroy."

And I *flee* from the room as fast as my feet can take me.

8

I wake to Olivia thrusting two dresses in my face. "Stell! Wake up! Which one?"

I try to blink away my fatigue. "Erm." I squint. "Livvie, they're identical!"

"What? No!"

"They're certainly both pink."

"This one's peach!"

I pull a pillow over my head. Olivia has always been an early riser, but I forgot how much of a torment she could be, since we don't share a room back home in Addyshire.

Thankfully, she retreats. "I know it's under strange circumstances, but are you happy to be back?"

I sigh. I know she means nothing by this innocent question, but I was hoping to stave off conversation about *feelings* until

I had at least three cups of tea in me. "I don't know how I feel. Being picked up and dropped into a place I haven't known in five years is giving me vertigo."

"I'm sure this massive inheritance isn't helping," she says under a giggle. I much prefer this to the squeal of shock she let out when I told her about Mr. Fitzroy's intentions for Kendall Manor last night. She'd taken my hands and spun me around with no mind for my unease.

I sit up only so I can give her the most exasperated glare. "Am I the only one that has any sense around here? You can't really believe that this will come to pass. I am not a Fitzroy heir, nor a man, and"—I lower my voice—"I know you saw how the footman hesitated to take your bags, Olivia. This is not a life that accepts us."

"Thankfully, the footman's opinion is irrelevant in the matter. Besides, the Fitzroys are all so well off, who's going to complain?"

I adore Olivia, but she's not the best when it comes to serious conversation. She likes her world to be surrounded in sweetness, and I blame Aunt Eleanor for it. Not that I had a miserable upbringing in the least, but I am well aware that most ladies of my coloring are not afforded the comforts we've been given. Olivia doesn't like to dwell on such things.

She's still looking at her two dresses in the mirror. I point to the one on the right. "That one. The orange one."

Her reflection glares at me. "It's peach!" Still, she removes it from the hanger. "You ought to get up already, one of the servants came by and said breakfast was nearly done."

I fling off the sheets and tug the satin scarf from my head. "Oh, you might have said so earlier!"

"I was trying to let you sleep! Seems like you didn't get enough of it."

I wait for her to ask me where I went last night, but she doesn't. Olivia sleeps like a sack of bricks and must not have noticed me leaving bed. I think of how to bring up Nathaniel, but I don't know what I would even say. Is there anything *to* say? We simply caught up the same way I did with Gwen. It was nice.

I pull a day dress from the wardrobe. It's powder blue and simple, but has embroidery of birds in the neckline. I received it as a gift from a farmer's wife back in Addyshire after I'd helped her write a few letters. I move to Livvie's side and begin undoing the thick plaits that she put in my hair before bed, and she undoes the ones I did in hers. While she slips her loose curls behind a scarf that matches her dress, I oil my much thicker curls, pull them into two tight braids, and pin them at the back of my head. On the way downstairs, I spare a look at old Mr. Fitzroy's room. The door is closed. Perhaps he's already at the table.

But the small dining table is occupied only by two and set for four. We walk in just as Gwendolyn is stealing a triangle of toast off Nathaniel's plate, though there's plenty to choose from on the spread. He notices, but pretends not to, and I am hit with a distinct memory of little Gwen once placing three beans into each of Jane's fine shoes during supper and Nathaniel immediately volunteering himself up for the blame—though of course, Jane was not convinced.

✦ 66 ✦

"Good morning," Olivia says cheerily.

Nate rises from his seat. "You must be Miss Witherson. Welcome to Kendall Manor. I hope you've found it comfortable."

She smiles, ducking her eyes under her long lashes. "Thank you for having me. It's been lovely to see where Stella grew up."

He smiles proudly at this. Again, Aunt Eleanor's request haunts me. I will those pesky thoughts out of my mind, not wanting to feel that irritating twist of jealousy once more.

Quickly, I take my seat next to Livvie. "How is your grandfather?"

Gwen doesn't look up from her plate.

"He's taking his breakfast in bed this morning," Nathaniel says plainly. "He has his good days and his bad ones."

I want to ask what exactly the nature of his illness is, but I know it's not pleasant breakfast conversation. "I'm happy you both didn't wait. Olivia was taking forever to decide on what to wear."

She immediately stops spreading strawberry preserves on her roll and smiles up at me. It probably looks amused to the Fitzroys, but I have the distinct feeling that I'll be getting an earful later.

"Did you sleep well?" Gwen asks. "I detest sleeping in beds other than my own." She winks at Nate. "Unlike some of us."

Nate rolls his eyes, the slightest blush on his tan skin, and looks like he wants to throw his roll at Gwen's head. His eyes flick to me for the briefest second before returning to his plate. I feel a twinge in the pit of my stomach and a reluctant curiosity that warms my face. Of course, young wealthy men are known to partake in, well, lustful behaviors. It's none of my business, and I should be laughing along with Gwen, the two of us teasing him like old times. I only manage a stiff chuckle before focusing my attention on cutting up my bacon.

"I won't see my own bed for quite some time, since we'll be staying in London for the summer," Livvie says, missing the crass joke.

"And perhaps never again, if your mother's wishes come true," I add, a bit sharply. "Married at seventeen, how splendid."

She ignores that very sharpness. "Enjoy your jokes, dear cousin. Once Lady Tess arrives, you'll be outnumbered."

"Thankfully, I am blessed with a temperament that grows even more determined when the numbers are against me. Pass the jam, please."

Gwen beams at Nathaniel. "You see, our Stella has been well taken care of. Though I admit, it's difficult to keep from turning jealous."

"You may have her," Livvie mutters, to which I grant her a rather childish show of my tongue.

"Are you leaving already?" Nate asks me softly.

"Our chaperone, Mrs. Sinclair, should arrive this afternoon," I reply. "She has a town house in Primrose Hill."

"Oh, good." He smiles, relieved, dimples on display. "Not too far, then."

That smile should not have the power to give me gooseflesh. *And yet.*

Gwen gasps. "You must join us at the opera this week! Grandfather is a patron, and we have plenty of room in our box."

"Oh! An opera!" In her glee, Olivia nearly knocks aside her glass of apple juice. I do wonder how she'll make it through society gatherings with such excitable tendencies. She'll likely have a fainting spell if some suitor does indeed ask for her hand.

But I do share this joy with her. A few months after Mother passed, Lady Tess took me on a holiday to Paris. I hadn't seen any theater outside of a crude adaptation of *Twelfth Night* in the Addyshire community hall . . . which I am no longer allowed to frequent as I may have let out a few loud critiques. At the Paris Opéra, Lady Tess took me to see *Les Huguenots*, which might be the most thrilling thing I've ever witnessed. In all my anxiousness about this trip, I didn't once consider that a summer in London offered such opportunities.

"I'm assuming by the look on your face that it's a yes?" Nate says quietly, under Gwen's and Olivia's more vocal excitement. "It's called *Aurora* by a man called Otofsky. Apparently, it's the most sensational opera to land in Covent Garden, if you can believe the critics."

"Such high praise; I suppose I'll have to see for myself."

"I imagine you'll have much more interesting things to say. Remember when Gwen and I used to put on plays for the house staff, and you never wanted to join—"

"Hold on; that was before I convinced Jane to let me write them. She always created such boring parts for me!"

"And so, you'd sit in the audience, in your mother's lap, watching us carefully. It was nerve-racking—"

"Nerve-racking? I was about eight!"

"And you always had a full *list* of criticisms for us the second we stood from our bows." He laughs into his hand. "It's a wonder you don't write a review column of your own."

"I—" I pause, forgetting what I was going to say. My thoughts have snagged on his words.

A column of your own. I never saw myself pursuing anything but fiction, never saw myself writing pieces like my mother. But thinking on it now, perhaps I should ask Lady Tess if she could put in a good word for me like she did with my mother.

I reach for my little notebook of stories, but it's up in the room.

"What's that look?" Nathaniel's brow furrows as he laughs. "Heavens, what have I done?"

I smirk at him. "I think an opera sounds like a lovely time."

9

After breakfast, Nathaniel leaves us to check in with his grandfather. Though Mr. Fitzroy has enough energy to loudly scold the nurse for her cold hands, his presence in the room above us is like a phantom haunting the halls. Perhaps that is why Gwen beckons us to the sitting room and immediately takes to the piano. She sets her fingers to the keys before saying, "He'll make a trip to Enderly at the end of the month. The doctor thinks it's a poor idea to travel, but he won't be swayed." She plays a high note.

"Stubborn man," I say gently.

"He says if he's going to die, he wants to die at Enderly, where he was raised, and where his father and his father before him died." Quickly, she eases into a lovely tune.

I turn to Livvie. "Fancy a dance? Let's see all the things you learned from horrible Mrs. Smith."

Luckily for her, I don't get the chance to sabotage her dancing skills with my own. A servant enters and announces the arrival of Mrs. Tessa Sinclair. She appears next to him, wearing a silken green hat with two dove feathers sticking from the lapel.

Livvie and I share a brief look, and like children, we bolt to her, nearly tripping over ourselves to get to her first.

"Girls!" she squeals, half shock, half delight. Though her opinions are like Aunt Eleanor's, her sensibilities are different. Lady Tess is eternally cheery, always just *delighted*, and can't understand why the world around her doesn't match her sunny moods. Her pale skin is dabbed with pink blush, matching her pink lips. She has quite a severe face—sharp, catlike—but it's only intimidating if you don't know her. She wears her dark hair styled in paper curls like most fashionable ladies. My mother's old friend could pass for a girl my own age if she wanted to, and with her nice—and by *nice*, I mean *encumbering*—dress, she'd likely be taken for a new girl of the season rather than a widow.

She extracts herself from our embrace and holds Livvie and me at arm's length. A proper inspection is in order, clearly. Gwen laughs at our excitement, and Lady Tess peeks over at the bench. "Oh, my apologies. You must be Miss Gwendolyn Danvers."

She rises. "Gwen's fine. Pleasure to meet you, and welcome to Kendall Manor." She nods at us. "I shall leave you to catch up while I check on my grandfather. Tea, Mrs. Sinclair?"

"Yes, thank you."

"Gwen's invited us to an opera!" Olivia says excitedly. "*Aurora* in Covent Garden!"

Lady Tess's eyes seem to jolt with lightning. "How splendid!" We gather on the sofas, the same that Mother used to assemble us children on to inspect our scrapes after roughhousing in the gardens.

She removes her luxurious gloves. "So what's the news? How is Mr. Fitzroy? Your mother always spoke so well of him."

"Well," I begin softly. "About that . . ."

I tell her about the inheritance, and one might've thought that I just spoke of seeing Jesus Christ himself in the streets from the way she chokes on her tea. Her eyes are as wide as moons. "Stella! He means to leave Kendall Manor to you?"

"My husband, more accurately."

"How generous of him!" Glee radiates off her, and I feel a little guilty for not being able to match it. "Stella, this is incredible news. Your mother would be thrilled at such good fortune."

I chew on the inside of my cheek. "Speaking of Mother, did she ever mention anything about him, other than being a fair man?" I lower my voice should any nosy servants be hovering in the hallway. "See, Mr. Fitzroy looked a little guilty when I spoke with him, and he said something about making things up to my mother before he passed."

She thinks for a moment, then shakes her head. "No, I don't think so? My understanding is that she liked working here well enough and only left after your uncle passed, may he rest in peace. I'm sure he just appreciated her work and laments her death, as we all do. He was likely fond of you as well."

I watch as she sips from her cup, not quite meeting my eye. I have a feeling that there's more to the story, but it looks like Lady Tess won't be much help.

She claps her hands together. "Oh, Stella, when people find out, you're going to be the talk of the town."

My expression goes so frightful, Olivia has to turn away to keep from laughing.

"Don't look so glum! Your life has just opened up in ways that many only dream of!"

Lady Tess, God bless her. I may not know everything about life in London society, but I do know that she is considered *new money*. My mother used to say as much, and often advised such families as Fiona Flippant. Lady Tess is certainly wealthy by many standards, but she is not one of London's elite. Unlike them, her grandfather and his before him worked to earn money so that their sons could afford school. Her father, Richard Elmhurst, made a few smart investments, and now his paper is sold on every block in the city.

I love Lady Tess dearly, but I wonder if some of her excitement comes from now having a real connection to an old-money family. I also wonder now if this separation from the upper echelon of the elite is what makes her unbothered with being seen with Olivia and me. I wonder if she would drop us if she were ever truly invited *in*. I would ask, but a small part of me doesn't want to know the answer. The disappointment would be too much to bear. I know that Lady Tess cares for us, and I do believe her friendship with my mother was genuine, but I can also see Lady Tess giving herself a righteous pat on the back for doing the good deed of helping a Black family. Can you blame me? People like her make the rules, and I have a hard time believing that a white woman raised in this society is immune to its effects.

"Can't I just stay here?" I ask. "I'd much rather work through Mr. Fitzroy's collection of boring nature guides than entertain London society."

She scoffs impatiently. "It's obviously not clear to you, so let me say it plainly—liking books over balls does not grant you a moral high ground."

Livvie mutters, *"Thank you."*

Olivia Witherson, the traitor!

I shrug. "Well, it does grant me poorer eyesight, so I've won at something."

Lady Tess laughs. "Oh, I pity the man who marries you."

"Yes, pity the man, for he does not exist."

"Careful, you'll jinx yourself."

"Unlikely. Really, why should I spend my life suffering the whims of a man?"

"My dear, do you think that marriage is only pain and suffering?"

"Yes, and I wonder what sort of love would be worth it."

Lady Tess softens. Her green eyes go wide and full at me. "Stella, believe me when I say this with the best intentions. Your harsh judgment may be your undoing one day. And when you've realized it, I hope those caught in your path love you enough to forgive you."

I unfold my arms and loosen up my shoulders. "You can just say, *Stella, you're being a total arse,* you know?"

Livvie claps her hand against her wide smile while Lady Tess only rolls her eyes. "Besides, what could be more fun than having your pick of eligible young men? How else would you spend your summer?"

I want to answer truly—*by plucking out my eyelashes?*—but I bite my tongue. Lady Tess is vastly overestimating how this so-called fortune might affect people's reaction to me in their lily-white social circles, but I know that prejudices are not forgotten so easily. Even Aunt Eleanor had never intended for Livvie to snag a wealthy man of high society. Before we received the letter from the Fitzroys, her hopes were for a man with enough money to take care of Olivia in relative comfort, but not *luxury*. Lady Tess loves us, but she is the well-to-do daughter of a wealthy white man and will never *understand* us. I don't want to be London society's shiny spectacle.

Still, I enjoyed the last opera I saw. And I like nice food. Music can be fun, I suppose. It's the *socialness* of the matters that makes me nervous, even at the small balls in Addyshire. I feel like I never say the right thing, and being in a room full of people is enough to make my stomach roil. If it were up to me, I'd spend my summer in near isolation, creating something like my mother did. Making my mark.

Like a spark set aflame, an idea forms in my head. "Mrs. Sinclair, I would like to come to an agreement. I shall let you lead me into society on one condition: I want your father to publish me, like he did with my mother. Put my work in *State of London*."

Lady Tess's brow rises. "Oh, I knew this day was coming.

Ginny's girl through and through. Well, you are quite young, Stella—"

"But she's ready," Livvie adds quickly. "You should read her diary, her poems, her short stories. She's very talented."

Olivia Witherson, my dearest darling cousin!

"And I suppose if she's ready to be married, I daresay she's ready to pursue her dreams." Though her words are encouraging, Lady Tess looks a touch skeptical. "And what would you like to write about? My father's paper doesn't accept fiction. Did I ever tell you how your mother got the Fiona Flippant job?"

I smile. "Tell it again."

"Well, we kept running into each other on our walks around Hyde Park. You were just a girl, and those Fitzroys! Your mother had her hands full with the four of you. One day I sat beside her, and we overheard the most absurd conversation between two lovers." She smiles warmly. "Oh, the dramatics. Anyway, Ginny said something under her breath that I thought was so funny. She said, 'Everyone needs a good friend to tell them when they're being so lovestruck that they cannot see straight, or a good shake of the shoulders when all else fails.'"

I grin as my heart squeezes.

"We became friendly, and I always thought she had such strange, but insightful, things to say. Later, when my father was trying to come up with ways to reach new readers, I thought of her. He had an idea for a column that blended the excitement of scandal sheets with societal commentary. He wanted a new and unique perspective, and I didn't think it got more unique than a colored nursemaid in a house of high standing."

"And Fiona Flippant was born."

"Yes, well, after some convincing on both ends. Your mother was even more stubborn than you, and my father wasn't sure about hiring a total novice."

"But he did," I say, perking up.

She lifts a finger to temper my excitement. "Your mother was well accustomed to London society before she began the column. Seeing as you've just arrived, your path may be more difficult. And I want your full effort in all social events."

"I will be on my best behavior. In return, I ask that I have final say over the man who earns my hand—if any. If there is not one whom I find agreeable, then I reserve the right to continue on as a single woman."

She wrenches her mouth in contemplation. "But Kendall Manor!"

"This is nonnegotiable. Trust that if I were to become engaged, it would be to someone I really adored."

Unlikely to happen, but better to give the woman some hope.

"Fine," she concedes. "But while I can get you to my father's desk, you'll have to convince him on your own. Is that fair?"

"Mrs. Sinclair, I do believe we're in agreement."

Olivia claps giddily, and even Lady Tess can't keep from grinning.

I can't help feeling like I've run away with treasure here. I won't need Kendall if I manage to get a real, paying job. I can help Aunt Eleanor keep the house while building my portfolio.

A few months attending events, rubbing elbows with the wealthy, and entertaining suitors? How difficult could it be?

10

It's easier settling into and sleeping in Lady Tess's chic townhome. I don't feel out of place here like I did stepping back into Kendall. The housekeeper is away for a family visit, and while Lady Tess asked us to excuse any mess, I quite like the look. Lived in, and homey. The noise of the bustling city streets will take some getting used to, but I find it fascinating to watch the people hurrying to their destinations.

A letter arrives after luncheon, one that I've been dreading.

"It's from Mother!" says Olivia, shooting me a knowing glance. "Would you like to read it, or should I?"

I look at her over the top of last week's issue of *State of London*. "Go on, get it over with."

While my letter to her was a bit of a rambling mess, Aunt Eleanor's response is quite short. *Don't muck this up*, essentially, just in a more proper way.

"'. . . and, Stella, remember that while society is not built for us, you are no less deserving of space than any other young woman in the room.' How sweet! She also sends love from Cheswick—"

"Which I politely decline—"

"Who has been most sorrowful since our departure. Poor Chessy!" She refolds the letter. "I can't wait to tell her all about the opera tonight."

"And I cannot wait to write my piece." I dramatically snap the newspaper with flourish. "I may not be Fiona Flippant, but I'm hoping a well-written review will impress Mr. Elmhurst. Their current arts critic is so safe with his reviews."

She tries to peek over my shoulder, and I push the notepad away from her so that she doesn't see my scribbles and doodles.

"There'll be many handsome men at the opera tonight, I'm sure, all fighting over your lovely hand," Lady Tess says, coming in from the hall. "Our dear Stella will soon have her own line of suitors as well."

With a chuckle, I settle back on the sofa. "Oh, you'd just love that."

She sits across from me wearing a peculiar expression of delight that can only mean trouble. "Stella, you're the talk of the town. With just a few strokes of Mr. Fitzroy's pen, you have become the most eligible lady in all of London."

"You're . . . *jesting.*" It's a struggle to get the words out.

"Never. I was just at the dressmaker's, and your name came up a few times, and never by *my* prompting." A servant returns with tea for her, and she takes a long sip. "Everyone is dying to know when Miss Stella Sedgwick is going to make her first appearance."

"They know my name?"

I narrow my eyes at her, but her delighted expression is steadfast. I imagine what was actually said—*Did you hear? Mr. Fitzroy is leaving his fortune to some wayward colored country girl!*

"How could anyone even know?" I ask. "Why, I only just found out myself!"

"People talk. Servants, valets, cooks, nurses. It's not every day that a young colored woman is named the inheritor of a great fortune."

More like misfortune. Tonight will be a real test of my mettle. With Aunt Eleanor's encouragement and years of my mother's advice guiding me, let's see if I can keep up with the most genteel of them.

"Now, this is the place to be seen!" Olivia squeals.

She and Lady Tess are brimming with girlish joy as our carriage bounds down the perimeter of Hyde Park. All sorts of people are out and about—newsboys hawking papers, wealthy ladies strolling in their finery, well-dressed gentlemen eyeing them. It all feels a little ridiculous, everyone putting on a show to catch an audience's eye.

"Oh, I just adore London!" Livvie says, watching the little performances as we pass by.

Next to me, Gwen exudes a cool sort of blasé allure; she's seen this all before. I'm happy that she offered to pick us up in this fancy carriage. She turns to me, on the verge of a laugh. "Are you not impressed?"

I laugh. "That's not quite the word I'd use, no."

"What words, then?"

"Astounded. Fascinated. Disturbed."

"Disturbed?"

"Did you not see the lady with an entire flock's worth of peacock feathers in her headband?"

Lady Tess sighs. "You'll get used to the displays of excess."

"Excess I understand. It's the desperate need to be noticed that I do not."

Gwen says, "Lucky for you, with your inheritance, you won't have to try so hard."

She means to tease me, but I frown. Yes, I will be noticed, though not for the reason she thinks. I swear, I'm not some spoiled twit. I understand how lucky I am to be sitting in this carriage, in a nice dress, with a chaperone like Lady Tess and a friend like Gwen Danvers. And even more so, to potentially be inheriting a piece of a fortune. "I don't mean to sound ungrateful. I'm simply . . . out of sorts."

Lady Tess pats my knee warmly. "You've always been a stubborn girl—no, don't pout—but you'll come around in time. I think a night at the opera will be exactly what you need. With your bookish sensibilities—*Stella, dear, I asked you not to pout*—it'll be the perfect introduction into society life."

I don't argue, though the pit of my stomach feels like a twisting tangle of snakes.

We arrive at the theater, and my nerves are temporarily

+ 82 +

abated by the magnificent structure ahead of us. I can't resist a gasp to rival Livvie's. "Oh—it's beautiful!" The theater might as well be a miniature castle. I nearly miss the footman holding out his hand for me, I'm so enamored by the statues carved in the stone, the majestic pillars, the radiant light shining out from the windows.

Inside, there's a healthy crowd milling about and socializing. Everything seems so dazzling, from the people to the lush sofas and decadent paintings on the wall. I take in a deep breath and remember my aunt's words. I must remember that I am no less deserving of space here than the woman with an ungodly number of jewels around her neck.

That small confidence doesn't last. People begin to stare. There's a particular type of look that's being employed here. Not quite shock, not quite disgust, but a fascinated curiosity that verges on disbelief. The double takes when they see Livvie and me in nice dresses rather than the clothes of a servant. The furrowed brows, the whispers. They might not be acting downright cruel to our faces, but it is discomfiting all the same.

Olivia manages to smile through it, but I am not so strong. Panic rises in my chest. I take a reflexive step backward, but Gwen slips her arm in mine and moves us forward, fully shepherding me into the opera house.

A server comes around with a tray of sherry. I'm happy to be here with Lady Tess, who only warns me to have one glass, instead of Aunt Eleanor, who would have glared at me for even looking in the server's direction. I'm mostly grateful to have something to focus on other than the people around me. I inhale.

I exhale. I force a conspiratorial giggle with Olivia, touching my glass to hers. "Cheers, then. Our first social drink in London."

Gwen waves to someone over my head. "Nathaniel!"

I spin at the sound of his name.

As Fitzroy steps away from a group of sporting young men to approach us, I think, *Well, this is exactly where he belongs*—in an elegant coat, his dark curls slicked into a coiffure. There's an effortless confidence in his saunter and his smile is somehow both roguish and inviting; these things seem like a talent to possess so genuinely. Any other man would look like a rake posturing for attention, but he wears it well. Against a backdrop of stoic men of proper parentage in fine clothes and stiff backs, he's the one who pulls the eye. Is it his handsomeness? The brown skin? Either way, he doesn't seem to notice. He's used to running in these circles.

Fitzroy gives his sister a peck on her cheek. "I see you managed to buy a new dress."

She beams at him, then me. "It is a special occasion. Stella's first night in London."

He looks to me, that smile going from chastising to sweet. He smooths his jacket. "This night suits you, Miss Sedgwick."

A silly heat creeps up my neck. "You only think that because you're not the one in an extremely tight pair of shoes," I mutter. He laughs at that while Lady Tess's smile goes stiff. I surrender to her displeasure. "I mean, thank you, Nate. Nathaniel. *Fitzroy.* This night suits you as well."

Gwen turns to Lady Tess. "Mrs. Sinclair, this is Nathaniel Fitzroy, my brother."

+ 84 +

Lady Tess bows her head. "Pleasure to meet you, Mr. Fitzroy. I visited Kendall yesterday, but we didn't get a chance to speak. What a lovely home!"

Of the group of young men that Fitzroy had excused himself from, one turns toward us. He's blond, pale, a full head taller than Nate, perhaps a touch older. Our gazes connect for a moment. While his expression is pleased, if not curious, I turn away for the awkwardness of it.

As Olivia and the Fitzroys continue in conversation, Lady Tess turns slightly so her mouth is nearly flush against my ear. "Don't slouch."

"I'm not!"

"You are. And somehow have still managed to catch the attention of a very fine man."

I take in the room once more. As my gaze falls past Gwen's shoulder, I see Nathaniel's friend doing the same. This time, when he meets my eye, he smiles, and I return it for a moment before looking away.

I sip my drink. "You know him?"

She grins a *scheming* grin. "Bernard Ogden." She looks at me expectantly, as if that's supposed to mean something to me. "Of Grantchester—Earl of Grantchester, now. His father just passed a few months ago . . ." Her voice trails off as he finally makes his way over to us.

Gwen gasps. "Lord Grantchester! What a surprise!"

He chuckles. "I'd much rather be at home, but your brother is hard to say no to."

Nathaniel claps his hand on Grantchester's shoulder. "Your

father wouldn't have wanted you holed up alone in that dark estate. It is better that you are here with us."

Blue eyes beaming, Lord Grantchester smiles sheepishly. It's awfully dimply. And handsome. I suppose.

He turns to me. "You must forgive me for staring, I don't believe we've met."

Gwen takes my hand. "This is our dearest friend, Miss Stella Sedgwick, her cousin, Miss Olivia Witherson, and Mrs. Tessa Sinclair."

"Sinclair?" Lord Grantchester asks.

"Her father, Mr. Richard Elmhurst, owns *State of London*," Olivia adds proudly.

"Ah, yes. *State of London* is quite the accomplishment," he says.

I smirk at Livvie. "And shall only get better with my words in its ink."

Grantchester levies an inquisitive glance at me. "Are you a writer, Miss Sedgwick?"

I pause. I didn't think he'd have paid attention to my little aside. There's not even any amusement in his voice, which is surprising. I try my best to sound confident. "One day."

"One day?" Nathaniel laughs. "I used to read her stories all the time when we were kids. I thought they were exceptionally clever." He adds, rather quickly, "We all did. Gwen, Jane, and I."

I feel a strange little thrill at the way Fitzroy averts his gaze and takes a long draw of his drink.

Lord Grantchester raises an impressed brow. "And how would you write of this night, so far?"

I grin, if only because Lady Tess's face has taken on a nervous sort of pinching. "Well, I haven't seen the performance yet, but I suppose I'd start with an impassioned description of the theater, and then of the guests." I clear my throat. "In all their finery, the waiting hall resembled less a refined evening at the theater, and more of a randy herd of male peacocks showing off their—*ow!*"

"Are those tarts?" Lady Tess interjects and eyes a server, ignoring my accusatory glare for the poke she gave me.

But this fellow, Lord Grantchester, only laughs. "Fitzroy, where have you been hiding this fascinating young woman?"

I know he doesn't mean much by it, but I dislike the phrasing, as if I am Fitzroy's to be hidden as he pleases. "Oh, I've been locked away in Addyshire, writing stories."

"But we're here for a few months!" Lady Tess exclaims, ignoring my sardonic quip. "Perhaps one day you might take a break from the bustling ways of London and join Miss Sedgwick and the Withersons in the country."

Expertly, she leans out of the way of my own warning pinch.

Lord Grantchester doesn't seem to notice. In fact, he's blushing a little, which feels absurd. What could make an earl blush? "I'd find that agreeable, yes, if you'd have me, Miss Sedgwick."

Lady Tess doesn't let me answer. "Oh, she would!"

I manage to hold in my grimace. Why are they speaking of me like I'm not standing right here between them?

"Well, doesn't that sound grand?" Nathaniel says cheerily. He pulls another drink off a server's tray.

Ahead of us, a footman begins ushering people to their seats.

Nate seems thankful for it, and nudges his friend. "We should go on." He nods politely at us. "I'll be in the Grantchesters' box, but I do look forward to hearing your thoughts."

"It was a pleasure to meet you both," Lady Tess adds.

"The pleasure was mine." Grantchester waits with a hand toward me, and I see now that he means to take mine. I let him, and he kisses it before leaving us.

"Oh, how *swoony*." I try to laugh after he goes, but it comes off with more nervous energy than sarcasm after taking in the giddy curiosity on Gwen's and Olivia's faces. "Come, now," I say, feeling a sudden heat crawl up my neck. "Don't give me that look!"

"What look?" Olivia's voice is high-pitched, and her smile is infectious.

We take the side stairs leading up to the boxes and join a small line of guests, shimmering in their dresses and jewelry.

At the top of the stairs, the porter eyes me, then Olivia. I brace myself for the inspection, for him to ask Gwen and Lady Tess if we're in their party, even though it's quite obvious that we are. But, mercifully, he simply steps aside without an inquisition. Still, I hate the way shame blooms in me, because I know rationally, I've done nothing to deserve it. Nothing but stand here. Livvie gives me an understanding look, a hundred similar thoughts passing between us.

She slips her hand into mine and squeezes. Ahead of us, Gwen and Lady Tess share a laugh, utterly oblivious.

Aurora is somehow both dazzling and disappointing.

As the heady, elegant music blares through the seats, I can't help but wish the story were different. The heroine, Aurora, is currently belting a crescendo while teetering dangerously close to the ledge of the tower she's been trapped in since she was a girl.

"Don't tell me she's going to jump?" I mutter to Livvie, who shushes me instantly.

I fold my hands in my lap. Oh, Aurora's abandoning hope now, for her love has forsaken her for a princess in a *different* tower. "Who in bloody hell wrote this?"

"Shh!"

It's far more interesting to look around the theater and watch the audience's reactions—fear, excitement, rage, even glee. I suppose a proper production does just this—elicits passion rather than just pleases. In the mezzanine, a woman dabs her eyes with a handkerchief while a young man yawns with boredom a few seats over. In the box opposite us, an old man strokes his younger companion's knee before kissing her gently. The music swells into Aurora's death knell, and the woman swings her head around for one last look.

Fitzroy is in the box over. He's laughing about something with Lord Grantchester, though Aurora's just sung of her intentions to cut out her lover's heart, which is the most I've liked the character.

The audience gasps, and I turn back to the stage. Ah, Aurora's lover has returned, and she's setting her castle on fire. Though I can't quite parse my feelings about the plot, the production is astounding on its own, with thick flames engulfing the tower, the heat wicking toward the audience. Olivia quickly reaches for my hand in fear.

✦ 89 ✦

My eyes flick toward Nathaniel once more. He and Lord Grantchester are silent, each considering the ending bouts of the drama onstage. Nathaniel has on a more intent, serious face, while Lord Grantchester looks lightly amused, mouth tucked into his fist. I want to know what Fitzroy thinks. I have a good idea of what Olivia and Gwen likely think of this production, but he's a mystery to me.

Livvie clears her throat. "The play's being performed in *front* of us, Stella."

I turn, straightening my gaze. "Then why are *you* looking at *me*?"

She bites her lip against a laugh.

Aurora belts an impressive wail as she and her lover burn, and the tragedy is finally complete. My thoughts are turning. I wish I'd brought some paper to jot them all down.

After the show, Lady Tess leads us outside to the crowds waiting for their carriages or mingling with their companions. "Wasn't that, er, dramatic!" she says, holding her hat against the breeze. "And a touch violent. Girls, I worry you'll have nightmares."

I scoff. "Oh yes, Livvie nearly broke every bone in my left hand."

Olivia wrings her hands together. "Well, there were a few shocking moments, that's all!"

Gwen chuckles. "I must see to an attendant about the carriage. Wait here."

"A truly interesting show," says Lady Tess. "Though I'm not sure what that dastardly Ignacio was thinking, challenging Staud to a duel."

With Lady Tess and Olivia discussing the sword fight in *Aurora*'s first act, I'm distracted by familiar laughter from around the corner. I peek around a pillar to see a small gathering of young men drinking and smoking, lounging on the steps surrounding a statue of an angel. Elegant but relaxed, they look like they own the place—the statues, the steps, the whole sky. Lord Grantchester and Fitzroy are among them, Nathaniel leaning coolly against the stone base of the statue. He laughs openly, pale brown cheeks flushed from the drink.

I catch the end of a jest.

"... At this point, Fitzroy's bested us all! And she was *French*." A young man says this last bit with a wag of the brow.

Another boy, with sleek red hair, chuckles. "I think that's a disqualifier, no? French girls are just so much more *willing*—isn't that right, Fitzroy?"

Nate winks.

My stomach turns.

"A gentleman does not kiss and tell," he says coolly, lips curving into a smirk. "And luckily for the countess, I am a true gentleman indeed."

There's more laughter on their end and some stomach turning on mine. Nathaniel hardly looks like himself with this new bravado, but what do I know of it? He seems at home here, with his top button undone, his hair a mess, a cup of brandy in one hand and a cigar in the other. The Nathaniel Fitzroy I know is only thirteen years old. I haven't known him in his most formative years, and clearly, I don't know him at all anymore.

Lord Grantchester squeezes Nathaniel's shoulder. "A pity to

think that someday soon, our dear Fitzroy will be tied down. Let us wish strength to the woman who tries to capture his curious, indecisive, and ever-hungry heart. Miss Chen, is it? Ah, she'll have her hands full with this one."

What *drivel*. There's a part of me that wants to say, *Well, this is just how young men talk in each other's company*—but it hurts to hear it anyway.

And who in God's name is Miss Chen?

"I do wonder about Miss Sedgwick."

My ears warm at the sound of my name on Lord Grantchester's tongue.

Nathaniel turns his glass in his hands. "What of her?"

Grantchester shrugs. "I find her interesting—"

His friend butts in. "Oh, he must be serious—dear Grantchester has no need for her inheritance." He elbows Nathaniel. "How wicked, to give such a girl *your* home."

"You must be mindful of social climbers." The redhead winces dramatically. "You two have been mingling in some interesting company. That daughter of the man with the newspaper, for example, my God does she reek of new money. My sister always sees her around the shops, sniffing out the latest trends and buying them all up."

"They're not so bad," Nathaniel says, so softly that I nearly miss it.

My skin goes alight with embarrassment and with rage. *Not so bad.* Is that all he can say? He might not know Lady Tess well, but she doesn't deserve to be gossiped about so unkindly. And is that all he can say about me? *Not so bad?*

❖ 92 ❖

The others snicker, but Nathaniel eyes Grantchester. "Are you inquiring after my opinion of Miss Sedgwick?"

"Why, yes. I am not blind to the attention my father's inheritance has given me, and for once, I am intrigued by her utter *lack* of interest." Grantchester shrugs. "You find her agreeable, yes?"

After a few moments of consideration, Fitzroy says, "I find her agreeable in the way I enjoy the company of an overexcited parrot—entertaining for some time, yes, but tiresome soon after." He shakes his head, pulls from the cigar. "I give you my best wishes and wish you the best of luck."

There's a bit more laughter, and I spin on my heels, not wanting to see him and all the rest laughing at my expense. My heart falls into my stomach, but unlike the shame and anxiety that grew in me when I walked into the theater, I only feel anger now.

What a fiend! I've spent so little time in his presence since I left Addyshire, and this is what he thinks of me? *An overexcited parrot?* As if he's so perfect, with his humorlessness, his arrogance, his pretension! The insult wounds me. There's not just anger, then, sadness too—as much as I hate to admit it—so much that I can feel tears pricking at my eyes behind the rage.

"Stella!"

Olivia's waiting for me while Lady Tess makes her way down the crowded steps. Gwen waves a hand at as from the bottom curb, the elegant carriage waiting behind her.

I run over to Livvie, eager to get away from the boys. "What an awful night. Let's go."

"Well, I was looking for you! One second you were beside me, and the next, you'd disappeared." She wants to admonish me, but I must look properly annoyed because she softens instead. "Hold on, what's happened?"

"Nothing, I'm sorry for wandering off." I lock my arm with hers as we make our way toward the carriages. "Come, let's not keep Gwen waiting."

11

I wake under the light sheets of the four-poster bed in Lady Tess's guest room, utterly content. It's a blissful moment. There's a bit of lovely sunlight streaming through the lavender lace curtains. Olivia's bed is already made, and she's sitting at the vanity, humming sweetly to herself as she runs oils through her curls. She doesn't see that I'm awake, and something about the stillness, the quiet, makes me feel at ease.

It doesn't last. The sound of Nathaniel and his friends laughing rings in my head.

Olivia turns as if sensing my sudden discontent. "Good morning!"

Hissing at the sunlight, I bring the covers over my head.

Roughly, the blankets are pulled back from me.

One look at me, and Livvie can hardly hold in her laughter. "City life agrees with you, Stella!"

I fix my mouth to argue, but she raises a finger.

"As much as I enjoy your banter, it will have to wait. Breakfast is ready—and it looks like you're in need of a strong cup of tea."

"I think I'll need the whole pot."

"*And.* There's some news I forgot to tell you last night."

The pause between the two statements raises my suspicions. "What is it?"

She's practically shaking with excitement. "We've been invited to a ball!"

"A ball?" I blink. "Is that all?"

She clearly wants to hit me for being so unamused, but thankfully, she is not the hitting sort of girl. "To prepare, Gwen wants to go shopping. With us! Lady Tess said it'll be her treat."

"I think you have a good number of dresses already, no?"

She sighs. "Stella, this party is being generously hosted by Mr. Samuel Désir." She waits for the name to register, but gets impatient. "He's French! His father is on Paris's chamber of deputies, he's a very well-connected man. Gwen says that this is his first social event in all of England, though he's known for throwing only the most exclusive and lavish balls in Paris. Nothing I have now will do!"

I say, "Hopefully you'll find a nice man at this ball considering Nathaniel's not single."

She turns to me, her entire face wrinkled in confusion. "Nathaniel?"

"Yes."

"*Fitzroy?*"

❖ 96 ❖

I wave a hand. "Sorry, I never mentioned it—your scheming mother wanted me to play matchmaker, but he's occupied with another."

"Stella." Her eyes widen. "Are *you and Fitzroy*—"

I nearly choke! "Not me! Heavens! No, there's some fine lady named Miss Chen who will become his very lovely bride."

"Oh. I see."

We lie there for a few moments just staring at the ceiling. The silence here is worse than her initial surprise. It's nearly unbearable. I want to tell her about the conversations I overheard, but it's painful enough to think of it, and I know that saying his words aloud will make it worse.

Olivia says, "Well, perhaps we will *both* find nice young men—and don't you dare groan."

"He'd have to be absolute perfection to catch my attention, I think."

"What about the earl? Lord Grantchester? Goodness, he's so handsome."

For her sake, I do hold in my groan. Not that he's done anything groan-worthy; it's simply hard to picture him without Nathaniel standing there, ruining the image. "He certainly was nice."

"And seemed taken with you."

And he asked about me. In all my annoyance with those haughty young men, I'd forgotten that point. It does give me a little thrill, I must admit. "I suppose he did."

As Olivia leaves to freshen up, I pull out the pad and pencil I'd stashed under my pillow last night. Needing something to steer my mind away from Fitzroy, I'd made some notes on *Aurora* to practice my writing skills. I have to squint at the words. Has my handwriting always been so atrocious? I suppose it doesn't help that I'd been half asleep. All I can make out is *foolish lady! A fire! Really?*

I sit by the window and start on a fresh page. By the time Livvie returns, I have three pages done.

She says something about me preparing for breakfast, and I scribble on while she speaks. "I can't—I must finish my essay while the opera is still fresh in my mind. I'll need samples to impress Mr. Elmhurst with when the time comes."

"You're writing about *Aurora*?" She peers over my shoulder, and I resist the urge to swat her like a pesky fly. "You could stand to be a touch more sympathetic to our heroine, I think."

"Hush, I can't concentrate while you're talking at me."

I wave her away, and she mimes biting my fingers before retreating with a laugh.

After jotting down a few more notes, I force myself away from my words and into the washroom. In front of the mirror, I make a promise to myself—from this point on, I am only entertaining London society so that I may uphold my agreement with Lady Tess. These wealthy families may have more money than I do, but their prejudices and judgments put them beneath me. Assuming that nothing can be done on the matter of Kendall, at least I'll have fostered some connections for my writing career. I'll be on my best, sweetest, most charming behavior to get through it. I will support Olivia, laugh with Gwen, ignore the stares and quips, and most importantly, I'll not spend another moment thinking about Nathaniel Fitzroy.

I feel a bit better after neatening my braided crown and changing into a simple cream-colored day dress and shawl.

As I walk back into our shared room, I announce, "I was promised a strong pot of tea!"

But Olivia's not alone. Lady Tess is here, *beaming* at the end of the bed. "Stella, there you are. Nathaniel Fitzroy is here to speak with you."

My face must show my displeasure, for Olivia raises a brow and Lady Tess's face goes stony. Oh, it's just like him, showing up out of the blue a whole five minutes after I've vowed to avoid him!

Reluctantly, I tread downstairs. I stop on the second to last step and catch Fitzroy in the small, minimally furnished sitting room. He looks *ridiculous* in his elegant waistcoat and polished boots, particularly considering how bare Lady Tess's sitting room is compared to the ones at Enderly and Kendall. Where theirs are draped in velvets and decorated with statues, busts, and an obscene number of crystalline trinkets, Lady Tess's is furnished only with a nice sofa, two lovely armchairs, lace curtains, and a simple floral arrangement on the low center table. Nate looks uncomfortable. He turns the teacup in his hand so that the handle is facing to the right, then to the left, then sets the cup and saucer down altogether. He rubs his palms against his nice trousers and sighs.

"You called for me?" I say curtly.

He jolts, then rises to his feet. "Yes. Good morning." He smiles. I hate it. "I hope this is not an inconvenient time."

I say nothing as a fresh wave of anger flickers in me. Just looking at his face is upsetting.

To my silence, he awkwardly clears his throat.

I feel Lady Tess appear at my side. "Oh, please sit, Mr. Fitzroy!" She nudges me to the seat across from him. "To what do we owe the pleasure?"

He looks at me, pausing to gather his thoughts. "There will be a ball tomorrow night at Lord Grantchester's bequest, hosted at my grandfather's villa, Duberney. Gwen's been pestering the good earl to host one for months now, and he's finally acquiesced, though, considering his father's recent passing, he would rather not have it at his home." He tries a small smile, which I do not return. "As Grantchester is handling some business matters this morning, I offered to extend the invitation to you all in his stead. I can send a carriage, if you like."

There are so many things that I would like to say, none of which would be appropriate here in front of Lady Tess. "Wow, two invitations in just as many days." From my tone, you'd think I was invited to a funeral. "You Londoners sure do like to drink and be merry, don't you?"

"How kind of you to come all this way to invite us!" Lady Tess says cheerily, doling up the praise to make up for the lack of mine. "Now, where are those biscuits? Let me check—"

I frown as she rises and leaves us. Leaving a young woman and a young man alone, without a chaperone or attendant, is not done. I know this because Mrs. Smith once said that an unwed woman who seeks a private audience with a man must either be a family member or a prostitute. Olivia had gasped so hard she nearly pitched herself out of her seat. I'd only scoffed. A man who would do the same was obviously a rake, which sounds so much more fashionable than prostitute.

Fitzroy fiddles with the teacup once more. "Did you enjoy the opera?"

"It was fine."

He nods. "A bit much, I think. I hope you will enjoy tomorrow's festivities more than the show."

"I must admit that I am surprised at this invitation." I let the words wash over him, relishing the small twitch of discomfort in his posture. "Why, I didn't think Lord Grantchester would want the presence of an inelegant girl like me. Hopefully, I won't ruin the celebration. See, sometimes, I can get overexcited, a bit like a parrot, and I talk and talk and talk—"

Fitzroy's face goes rigid. "Stella."

I bat my eyelashes and put on a sweet tone. "Yes, Fitzroy?"

He offers half a shake of the head, then closes his eyes for a moment. "Look, I don't know what you heard—"

"Oh, I heard quite enough."

"Well, I don't want you to get the wrong impression."

"My impression is mine to make and mine to keep—if you were so concerned, perhaps you and your companions should have chosen kinder words."

He clenches his jaw, and when he speaks, his voice is steady and hard. The initial shock of my jab at him seems to have worn off rather quickly. "Perhaps I did not expect to be spied upon—"

My mouth pops open. "*Spied?*"

"Yes, what were you doing?"

"What was *I* doing?" Oh, I want to shake him! "What were *you* doing? I don't know what you've done with Nathaniel Fitzroy, but the boy I know would never be caught dead all, well, *hobnobbing*—"

He laughs sardonically. "Hobnobbing?"

I punctuate my words by jabbing a finger at him. "With such dreadful company like that, and appearing to enjoy it!"

Well, one thing hasn't changed. Fitzroy still relays frustrations by scoffing and shaking his head. "They were just being daft boys, I'm sorry you had to hear it."

"And what is your excuse? Daftness as well? We used to laugh at haughty men like that, Fitzroy."

His lips part, but he says nothing.

I look away. "Who's Miss Chen?"

He keeps silent, and when I turn to him, he anxiously runs his fingers through his hair and finds a nice spot away from my eyeline to look at. "Miss Katherine Chen. Everyone calls her Kitty." He fidgets with his sleeve—another thing to look at that isn't me. "If the powers that be have their way, we will be engaged by the end of the year, if not the summer."

It's curious, the way he says it, as if it's just going to *happen.* "You're going to propose?" I ask, rather pointedly. His eyelashes flutter. I don't understand why he won't just say *yes.* "You could have mentioned that sooner."

"I didn't think it was important."

"You didn't think your upcoming wedding was important?"

He exhales sharply through his teeth. "Her family comes from new money, but—"

Fitzroy catches himself, but it's too late. The dread in me grows.

I laugh. "Only a complete dolt would find less worth in money because it has the shame of being acquired *recently*. I wonder what you think of me. No money at all, pitied by your grandfather, slinking around and digging my claws into your fortune."

His expression goes stark with pain. It's maddening. Why is he acting as if *I've* insulted *him* after all the things he and his friends said about me? "You know damn well that we don't think that about you."

"Do I?" I ask plainly.

In the silence, I enjoy the color draining from his face.

I stand from the sofa. "Fitzroy, do forgive me, but I'm feeling a bit ill and would like to retire to my room now."

He rises to meet me. "Stella, please, I didn't mean—"

"Time for biscuits!"

Fitzroy and I both snap toward Tess, her pleasant and sweet tone barely cutting through the tension between us.

"Apologies, Mrs. Sinclair," I say, attempting the very same sweetness. "Fitzroy was just leaving." I don't look at him, but I do my obligatory bow. "Do send my love to Gwendolyn and your grandfather for me."

I walk away, and I know it's poor manners, but I don't care. I find Olivia in the kitchen arranging biscuits on a tray. We share a look. I don't even exhale until I hear the front door close and the rattling of the carriage outside.

Lady Tess comes in after us, and the cozy kitchen now feels cramped. "Stella, would you like to explain yourself?"

"No. I wouldn't." I nibble on a biscuit. "And I will not be attending this party."

"Oh?" Lady Tess says. "I think our agreement dictated your presence at social events." She cuts me off before I can answer. "I ask you to consider what it would look like for you, a girl who has been written into the will of a dying man—such an unconventional thing, such kindness—to then turn around and deny an invitation offered by his very own grandchild. It would be badly done." She claps her hands together, signaling the end of the conversation.

Reluctantly, I hold my tongue. As we sit down for breakfast, Olivia whispers, "And it will be good experience for your writing on society, won't it?" She's pleased, smiling to herself as she spreads fig jam on her roll. I feel a little guilty. She must be tired of me making such fusses over everything she's excited about. I will try, just for Olivia, to be more agreeable tomorrow night, even if it means playing nice with Nathaniel Fitzroy.

Heavens, *I hate him.*

12

I thought that maybe I'd been to the Fitzroy villa called Duberney as a child, but I have no recollection of it. I think I'd remember the simple elegance of the large lakeside house, or the massive gardens which have been trimmed into gorgeous mazelike hedges, bursting with roses and peonies. The spacious sitting room has been transformed into a dance floor, and by the time Tess, Livvie, and I arrive, there's already a graceful set of couples dancing to the lovely music. It's all rather decadent, from the six chandeliers above us to the lacquered oak tables lining the walls.

Olivia swoons at the rich floral arrangements. "Isn't this lovely?"

"Yes," I agree, giving her my full attention so as to ignore the glances and stares. I swear, one woman looked like she was about to hand me her empty glass before I turned. "You can expect nothing but elegance from the Fitzroys."

I seem to have successfully hidden the edge in my voice, for Olivia sighs happily and links her arm in mine. She is a vision in her delicate pink dress. Her curls are pinned back into two flat twists on either side of her head, feeding into the dark brown curls at her nape. I'd done those twists and she'd done mine, though the five twists running down the crown of my head lead to a large puff of black hair, a cloudlike halo. My dress is light blue, adorned with a deeper blue silk under the bust and through the sleeves. It was my mother's dress, and is a touch fancier than Livvie's, but I think she looks so much more sophisticated than I do. It's the air about her.

Lady Tess adjusts her headdress. It's a bit, erm, *louder* than many of the other ladies are sporting, and I think she's just noticed. With her milky skin, she fits in with the sort of people here. But I think of Fitzroy and his friends. *New money.*

Looking around, I catch sight of Gwen, pretty as a rose, surrounded by suitors. Young men, older men, all standing by for their moment of acknowledgment. The mere thought of holding so much attention makes my palms sweat, but Gwen is in her element. With fluttering eyelashes and demure smiles, she's got them all eating from her hand.

Lady Tess stops fiddling and squeezes our shoulders. "I'm going to say hello to an old friend. Feel free to mingle."

Before my stomach has time to drop, I am saved. Gwen approaches—without her admirers, thank the heavens. She gives me a hug. "Stell, thank the heavens. I've been stuck in a conversation with my dreadful cousins."

"Cousins?" Gwen and her siblings didn't have cousins—or rather, they didn't speak with them. What I knew of the Fitzroys' extended family I learned from hushed conversations between my mother and Aunt Eleanor. While both Gwen's mother and grandfather were sole children, their late grandmother did have a sibling or two. Those family members wanted nothing to do with the Fitzroy side after Emily Danvers bore Nathaniel.

Gwen leads us around the room, her perfect blond curls bouncing with every step. "Yes, my cousins. Allison, Mary, and Imogen. Turned up at Kendall to visit my grandfather, and now they're here."

I raise a brow, but hold my tongue. I wonder if Gwen's thinking what I am—that it is awfully nice they're trying to patch things up before Mr. Fitzroy passes and that it's certainly a convenient time to seek his good graces.

The pace of my heart goes up a tick. Mr. Fitzroy's solicitor had mentioned that a fortune as massive as his would attract errant family members.

I must look distressed, for Gwen hands me a cup of blueberry cordial. "Anyway, who will you be dancing tonight with, Stella? Well, me, of course, but who else?"

I laugh. "If you want them, you may have all of my dances."

Olivia is looking about the room expectantly. "I hope I'm asked before the sun goes down. It all looks so pretty in dusk."

"Oh, that reminds me, I must take you through the gardens before the night is done. Jane had arranged to have them done since she couldn't be here . . ." Gwen's voice trails off. "Oh no."

Olivia spins to look behind us, but I keep my gaze on Gwen. "You've gone ghostly pale, Gwen," I say.

She exhales sharply. "Quick, let's have our dance!"

"No, no, I wasn't being serious! I'm a *horrible* dancer. Ask Livvie!"

"Olivia!" With an overenthusiastic smile, she pulls my cousin into the fray with the other dancers.

Finally, I peek behind me. The brown-haired boy standing there stares helplessly at Gwen. He's got a round face with pockmarks—he can't be more than fifteen.

He turns to me, considering. For a horrible moment, I wonder if he's going to ask me to dance. Instead, he clears his throat and walks away—with a bit of a sneer, I think, so that I'm aware that even he is not so desperate.

No matter. I pick at the small tray of nuts Gwen left at her table. There are four empty chairs—I assume for her and her cousins, and I can't help but wonder where Nathaniel is.

I get an answer quickly. The music softens, and at the garden entrance, there he is at Lord Grantchester's side.

I hardly recognize Fitzroy. I'd seen him all dressed up at the opera, but this is certainly a more elegant getup. In a full dashing waistcoat of deep green silk, he seems taller now, and more broad chested. Strong. *Humorless.* His slight tan renders him golden in the candlelight, which flickers across his high cheekbones. He has qualities that even I envy—thick, darling lashes and a perfect full mouth that seems set in a permanent scowl. His curls are coiffed neatly, and he brushes away the one that managed to fall onto his dark brow.

❖ 108 ❖

Who is this?

Nathaniel Fitzroy is no longer the spindly, silly, affable boy who used to chase me around Kendall gardens, brandishing a terrified newt. He is an heir. To court, to covet, to wish for.

If only he weren't so cruel.

As if reading my thoughts, he looks about the room and sees me. He blinks, and to my horror, makes his way over.

It is all so much worse up close. The lush clothes, the scowl, his cheekbones, his rich amber eyes.

"Miss Sedgwick." He nods. "Is the evening to your liking?"

I glance around. "I've found nothing objectionable about the evening, no."

"Finding nothing objectionable is not the same as enjoyment."

I smile tensely. "You needn't force displeasure into my words, Fitzroy. Take the compliment for what it is, the night is well done."

He shifts his weight from one leg to the other. "If that were true, you'd be dancing with an upstanding gentleman rather than doing your very best to avoid them."

"I have looked around the room and found no such men in my vicinity." I pause. "Or even next to me."

He exhales slowly. "Might I just—" He looks back toward the entrance. A girl has just entered the room. Her presence seems to be an interesting one, judging from the way the other girls turn to their cliques and whisper.

I don't have to ask. This must be Katherine Chen.

Fitzroy swallows the rest of his sentence. He looks away,

then finds my gaze again. Steely, serious Fitzroy has returned. "Do try to have a pleasant evening."

I shrug. "I'll try my best."

His mouth twitches. He leaves to welcome her.

Katherine Chen's dark hair is pinned up in an elegant bun, a crystalline butterfly clip holding it in place. Her skin is a pale tan, her deep brown eyes are lined with black, and her lips are a lovely shade of pink. She is beautiful, and though she does not immediately stand out as I do, I feel a pang of endearment in seeing another face in the room that doesn't match the white English puzzle.

Fitzroy holds out his hand, prompting yet another flurry of conversation.

His back is to me, so I can't see his expression, but Miss Chen lights up. Her face is tilted up at him as she drinks in his every word. A giggle bursts from her lips, and she takes his offered hand. Even Gwen is interested in this exchange. Despite dancing with Olivia, she's watching Nathaniel and Kitty like a hawk. Some childish jealousy, I suppose, Gwen seeing the young woman who will whisk her brother away. I often feel the same thinking of Livvie getting married and suddenly having a family of her own that doesn't have room for me.

"What has happened to England?" a voice somewhere near me says. "Is this the sort of people we're letting into society?"

I turn to find three young, blond ladies tittering about. They look rather like wraiths—pale skinned, with faces scrunched up in smugness.

The oldest one, the one with the yellow ribbon in her hair, fixes her mouth into a pout. "Stella Sedgwick, is it?"

＊ 110 ＊

I nod reluctantly. "Yes."

"Ah, so you're the baseborn girl come to claim Mr. Fitzroy's home."

A chill creeps down my back. "I have not come to claim a thing. I was summoned, actually."

"*Hmm.*" She looks me up and down. "Sedgwick, well. That's an aristocratic name."

I shrug. "It came from the man who enslaved my grandmother, I suppose."

The middle one lets out a ragged breath like the cake she's been delicately nipping on won't go down.

I blink in her direction. "Forgive me, I forget that it is unladylike to speak of your kin's horrors."

The youngest shakes her head as if my voice is a pesky fly. "Mary, Allison, we must seek out more agreeable company."

I pout. "Oh. So soon?"

They wander away, throwing displeased looks in my direction. That interaction may very well cause a hit to my reputation, but no matter. I'm not here to be loved or accepted; I'm merely entertaining such trivialities so that I can go to Lady Tess when this is all over and be given the connection to *State of London.*

I peek at the dance floor. Olivia is dancing with a young gentleman now. She looks *radiant.*

I move out of the ballroom and toward the back door. My intention was to see those lovely gardens, but a room to my left steals my attention. The door is half-open, and I catch the edge of a bookcase lit by candlelight. I look around twice before slipping inside.

The reading room is small, and between the candlelight and

the glorious moon shining through the wide arch-top windows, it has a dreamy, cozy feel. The fire isn't lit, but it smells smoky, and I wonder if there were men in here with their cigars, and if they will return.

What a *perfect* place to hide out.

I decide on a plan. I will stay here for five songs. Then I will feign an ill tummy, find Tess, and ask to be taken home. I run my fingers across the neat books tucked into the shelves, smiling to myself as I pluck one at random.

There's a loud burst of giggles and whispers nearby, and they stop right outside of the door. Feeling like I'll surely be scolded for entering this room, I fling myself behind the sofa.

Thankfully . . . and *unfortunately* . . . there is another person there to break my fall.

I practically land in Lord Bernard Grantchester's lap.

"Oh!" he sputters in shock, blue eyes wide at the sight of me.

"*Oh!*" I repeat in pure and utter embarrassment.

We stare at each other in a moment of disbelief before I quickly right myself. I settle on the floor next to him against the back of the sofa. "What are you—?"

He places a finger to his lips, and I have to stifle a laugh for how absurd this is. He flashes me an apologetic look, gesturing back toward the door. I peek over the couch. The couple who stumbled in are doing a bit of flirting, and the girl—the eldest of Gwen's horrible cousins, seems eager to have her companion to herself.

I turn back to Lord Grantchester. He's wearing spectacles, his blond hair is messy, and there's a spent cigarette in the ashtray at his side. He looks less like an earl and more like a merchant's son at a local college.

"Needed a bit of quiet," Grantchester whispers, also taking his own peek at the pair.

"Sorry," I mutter.

He smiles, waves the book in his hand. "I guess we had the same idea."

Under the moonlight, I notice a heaviness under his eyes, the redness around them. I remember what Lady Tess said about his father dying. Imagine trying to celebrate only a few months after such a shock.

We go silent. Thankfully, the pair are startled by someone calling for Allison outside. The door opens and shuts once more.

"Too loud in there for you too?" Lord Grantchester asks.

I sigh. "A bit. The balls in Addyshire are more restrained."

"Well, my apologies."

"No, no, I know this was Gwen's doing." I wink at him. "I've fallen into trouble at her requests as well."

He smiles. "I'd been wondering when I'd see you next," Grantchester says.

My face warms. "Were you?"

"I wanted to ask your thoughts on *Aurora*."

I resist grinding my teeth. When I think of that night at the opera, my stomach flips in an awful way. But Grantchester looks genuine. He studies my face in anticipation of my answer. "I found the play to be entertaining," I reply. "And the rest of the night lacking."

And as I look at him, I remember him there, speaking with Fitzroy. I was so hurt by Nathaniel's comments that I forgot it was Lord Grantchester who mentioned me at all. He'd asked after me.

Grantchester, oblivious to my knowledge of his inquiry, runs his fingers through his hair, and I can see how it got so messy. The gesture gives me a fuzzy sort of thrill.

"It's your ball, I'm sure they're all missing you out there," I say.

"I think I'd rather stay here." He huffs and loosens his cravat. "And I think a good number of people would miss you as well."

"Ah." I wave his words away. "People like new, strange things. They don't want my company, they want to gawk at me, examine me, pet my hair." I shiver. "I won't have it."

He relaxes against the back of the sofa. "Well. I won't tell if you won't."

I smile. I may be new to London society, but I know what a scandal it would be if we were seen together like this. Heavens, I think of what Lady Tess would say. She'd scold me, even if she was secretly thrilled at the prospect of me having an earl's attention.

It's odd. I don't know Grantchester, but I feel utterly content sitting beside him. The quiet is peaceful rather than uncomfortable. He reads his book, and I read mine, though I catch him peeking at my pages more than once, and I wonder if he catches me examining his dimples. At one point he laughs, and I smile too, though I have no clue what he's found so amusing. Just the sound of it raises my spirits.

I'm not sure how long we stay there like that, which frightens me a little. I have a sudden vision of Lady Tess screaming through the garden maze for me. *How embarrassing.* "It's probably time to return to your guests, Lord Grantchester."

"So soon," he says with a smile, but then closes his book. "Perhaps we shall brave the ball together."

He stands and offers his hand to help me to my feet.

The party is not as boisterous as it was when we left it. It seems to be winding down a little, the ballroom occupied more with young girls spinning with each other than potential courtships.

"Guess we missed the fun," Grantchester whispers.

I smile. "Shame, that."

We walk around the room together. I look for Livvie. She's with Lady Tess and some other gentlewoman. Even from here, I see the glee radiating from her. At least one of us had a good night. Gwen and Fitzroy are a few steps away from them. It looks like they're arguing over a last strawberry tart. He relents, throws his head up in annoyance, and as his gaze comes back down, he's just about to catch my eye—

I turn back to Grantchester. "I'm sure I should be going. My chaperone will wonder where I am. Thank you for tonight's invitation, Lord Grantchester."

Much like the night at the opera, he offers his hand. This time, when he brings my hand to his lips, I do not mind at all. "Until next time, Miss Sedgwick. And I hope it does come soon."

13

With one ball hardly over, I must prepare myself for the next. No one seems to know much about the mysterious French businessman Samuel Désir, but his party calls for new dresses, and there is no time to waste. After a rushed breakfast—Olivia practically shoved the food into her mouth—I am forced into a bustling Covent Garden.

"Here we are!" Lady Tess says, leading us to a dressmaker's shop. Even from the storefront, I can tell that this is a pricey place. The dresses on display are delicate and fine. I don't have to touch them to know that they'd feel much different than even the nicest dress I've worn in the past. Everything is so lovely that I feel out of place.

Gwen is waiting on the steps, thankfully. She cackles menacingly at the sight of my wide eyes before pulling me in.

We are not the only ones with a mind to acquire a new dress. The shop is humming with young ladies and their chaperones. Within moments, Olivia is gliding through the room, inspecting gowns and shyly making charming conversation with everyone in her path. I turn to Gwen to comment on her ease at this, but she's off inspecting a string of pearls of which I do not want to fathom the cost.

I decide to look at the shoes, which are all so undeniably beautiful. I hold a lavender pair embellished with a white floral embroidery. The velvet is fine, and the heel is short and sturdy.

There's an attendant at the end of the row of shoes with her head down as she arranges them. She clicks her tongue at herself, and doesn't look up at me as she asks, "Shall I pull a pair for you, miss?"

"Oh, no, I—" Quickly, I put the shoes back on the display. "I was just looking, thank you."

"It'd be no problem at all—" Finally, she looks up, and her words catch. "Oh, sorry, are you . . . retrieving an order for your mistress?"

I narrow my eyes. "Am I what?"

Lady Tess is there suddenly, her hand on my shoulder. "Miss Sedgwick would like this pair, actually." She aims a withering smirk at the attendant. "*Quickly*, Flora. I know how Mrs. Jessup values my patronage, and I'd hate for her to learn of your dallying."

The attendant, Flora, turns an awful shade of pink. "That won't be necessary. One moment, Mrs. Sinclair."

I play with my hands, unsure of what to do with them. I don't know what to say, but Lady Tess quickly lifts my chin with a gentle nudge. "Don't you dare drop your head, Stella. I won't allow it."

My eyes feel hot, though I'm not sad. I'm annoyed, and a touch angry. I hate how weepy I can get when I'm uncomfortable. "You don't have to buy those shoes."

"Nonsense, it's my treat! And those shoes are the only thing I've seen you look at without derision in the past week, so I think I do."

I manage a smile, and she leads me to the dresses, where Gwen and Livvie are comparing fine gowns.

Livvie immediately senses my discomfort. "Stella, what's wrong?"

I strike all of the disdain from my voice. "Oh, nothing." I nod toward the dress. "This one would be lovely on you, Livvie."

Before she can press me further, there's a gasp from the other side of the shop. "Gwendolyn, is that you?"

The voice is dreamy and light, and touched with an accent I don't quite recognize. I turn to find Katherine Chen holding up a stunning green dress. The sunlight perfectly highlights her sharp cheekbones and brings the amber out of her dark brown eyes.

Gwen instantly goes over to take her hand. "How nice to see you here, Kitty!"

Livvie and I glance at each other. I nod to the silent question I know she's asking.

Kitty is pretty, poised, and judging from her finery, supremely wealthy. Even ignoring the small pearls around her neck and the glittery lace in her dress, everything about her seems regal. Her posture, her voice, the way she holds her hands in a delicate fold. If I didn't know she was an heiress in a wealthy family, I'd assume she was *actual* royalty. This is a bride to snap up.

Gwen stretches her hand toward us. "Kitty, meet—"

"Yes, of course!" Kitty muses with a sweet smile. "You must be Stella Sedgwick." She takes my hand. Her gloves are sumptuous. "Jane's told me so much about you."

Really? Odd, as I haven't seen Jane at all since arriving in London. Now I wonder what the eldest Fitzroy heir has said of me. She always felt more like a stern governess than an older sister or confidant. "Lovely to meet you as well," I reply politely.

She turns to Gwen. "How is your grandfather? Your brother doesn't want to discuss him with me at all."

Gwen smiles tightly. "It's hard to say. Some days he has his strength, and others, he can hardly stand to be awake for more than a few hours. The doctor says there's not much he can do aside from giving him some comfort."

"I'm sure you're all giving him just that—and to be reunited with his ward, how sweet!"

I realize here that she's speaking about me, and I don't know how to respond to that, so I simply present Livvie. "My cousin, Olivia Witherson."

They exchange some pleasantries, but Kitty's attention turns to me once more. She rests her hand on mine. "Why don't you all come over for tea? We're renting a beautiful town house just a few minutes from here!"

Lady Tess, having purchased my shoes, appears behind us.

＊ 119 ＊

She's beaming. "That sounds lovely!" Ignoring the silent pleas of distress that I'm levying at her by way of wide eyes and a slightly shaken head, she hands off Gwen's and Olivia's choices to Flora. Then she holds up a yellow dress. It is *perfect*—pretty without being too showy. "How's this one, Stell?" I cannot lie, and she knows she's done well. Even before I say, *It's very nice*, she angles it toward Flora. "You all go ahead, I'll handle this and meet you all later."

Katherine Chen's London town house makes Lady Tess's look like a dollhouse. I'm rendered speechless within moments of stepping inside, and my wonderment only grows as Kitty leads us toward the back sitting room. There's even a garden— nothing like Aunt Eleanor's in the country, of course, but well trimmed and bursting with rosebushes.

"It's small, but cozy enough," says Kitty. With a tired, satisfied sigh, she unties the ribbon around her chin and pulls off her hat. "Tea?"

Before we can answer, she calls out for a servant. Three come running, and they take the request with speedy diligence.

"You'll have to pardon the mess and the wait. We're short on house staff."

There's no mess that I can see, and the tea is brought out not a second after we take our seats around the shaded table in the lovely garden.

"Imagine if we had three servants," I mutter to Livvie. "I'd actually get my tea hot."

Livvie releases a quick laugh.

◆ 120 ◆

Kitty eyes us with an amused raise of the brow.

Gwen smirks. "Don't mind them, they're likely only giggling at our expense."

I open my arms to her. "Is this where you finally duel Livvie for my attention?"

"Of course, and for the title of Stella's Right Hand. Olivia, how are you at badminton?"

Olivia smiles. "There's no need to compete—as I said once before, *you can have her.* I need a break from soothing the cynic."

Kitty looks between us, her amusement growing. "Aren't you three fun? It's so boring being shut up here with my parents; thank goodness for the social season. I relish any chance I can to converse with well-bred ladies."

I know what she means by well-bred, and yet it calls back the uncomfortable moment in the shop with the attendant. I sip my tea as Kitty tells us more about herself. I learn that she split her time between Shanghai and London as a child until her father moved them here permanently just two years ago. She and Gwen seem extremely close for such a new friendship. They share secret jokes that me and Olivia don't understand, but giggle at nonetheless. Kitty relays the who's who of society ladies making their debuts, watching Gwen grin or frown depending on her opinions of the person. "Hattie Dover? She's only fourteen!"

Kitty replies, "Her oldest sister's a spinster. I imagine her mother wants to take no chances."

"I can't imagine being fourteen and married," Olivia says quietly.

I want to tease her—*you're only three years older!*—but I decide against it.

Kitty gives a casual shrug. "Her mother has her eye on some wealthy baron with an impressive collection of jewels. As Fiona Flippant would say, *There is no love worth as much as an enormous diamond.*"

I nearly choke on my tea.

I nearly fall out of my chair!

"Fiona Flippant?" I sputter.

"The columnist?" Gwen asks vaguely.

Kitty giggles. "Oh, she was only the most ludicrous gossip in all of London!"

I cock my head at her. Olivia wrings her hands—I can feel her telepathic plea to *be kind.*

"Well, I was bored one day and found a pile of old papers in the library, and a few had the column," Kitty continues. "My mother would have a fit if she knew I'd read all that drivel, but between us, I thought it was entertaining, if you can tolerate that lowbrow sort of thing."

"Lowbrow?" I chuckle to hide my nervous anger. "It wasn't as if she made up stories. And readers wanted advice; that's why they wrote her."

"Oh dear, you mustn't misunderstand. I just think it's not the sort of talk ladies should take part in." Kitty has a very soft and agreeable way of speaking that makes me want to dunk my head in water. "Such coarse, unsavory language."

"Isn't that what makes it fun?" Gwen adds. "Personally, I believe a lady deserves a little unsavory treat every so often."

She winks, and Kitty flushes red before recovering with a tight smile. "How is it that the same household that bore Jane's and Fitzroy's good manners also gave way to your poor ones?" She means to tease Gwen, but it comes out a bit sharp. For a moment, I can't tell if they enjoy each other's company or despise one another.

"*Furthermore*," I interrupt, "Fiona Flippant's column was more than *salacious drivel*. She spoke of injustices in society, like the oppression of women, like you and me, forced to marry to make our ways in the world. Meanwhile, men will do as they very well please! The lady's goal wasn't to hurt people. She simply wanted society to change. And, well, I think that if a man intends to take lovers, then he bloody well might expect me to do the same!"

"*Stella*," Livvie warns.

I quiet, and find that they're all looking at me with a curious sort of apprehension, well, except for Gwen. She bangs a fist on the table. "Hear! Hear!"

I reach for my tea, if only to have something to do with my hands. There's a part of me that's ashamed for this outburst, and there's another that desperately wants to keep shouting until someone—*anyone*—hears me. "Apologies, I just . . . Frankly, I don't know how you all can bear it!"

"Bear what?" Kitty asks.

"This!" I splay my arms wide.

"Sunshine and biscuits?" Gwen offers with a little laugh.

"All the teas, and parties, and balls—I mean, is this really all there is for us?"

Livvie stirs her tea. "I like parties. Would you rather have none of this?"

I shake my head. "I don't mean to say I'd rather be scrubbing floors or turning beds. But Fiona Flippant had a life in her letters. She had purpose, an audience, and must have found joy in those things. What will we have besides marriage and motherhood? What will we have for ourselves? I don't mean children or husbands, I mean in actual interest and passion."

Kitty only shrugs. "I'm quite looking forward to a life of being taken care of." She places her hand on mine. "And once you find the right suitor, I know your mind will change. Now, who's up for a rousing game of whist?"

Oh, they're unmovable. I don't know how to make them understand.

My thoughts are still reeling when a footman informs us of the arrivals of Lady Tess and Kitty's parents. We follow him back into the house. Lady Tess's voice drifts out from the sitting room, and I'm happy to hear her decline Mrs. Chen's offer to stay for supper.

We move inside to the sitting room where a handsome couple are sipping spirits and laughing away, the way carefree wealthy people often do.

"My parents," Kitty says sweetly.

They turn to us, and we bow our heads. Looking at Mr. Chen now, I realize that I recognize him from the opera. He was in the box across from us with a younger woman . . . who is certainly *not* the wife sitting beside him now.

What kind of man would risk being spotted at such a large

event with his mistress? Well . . . a man who doesn't care about being caught, I suppose. I want to think of a better explanation, but she said herself that she only had brothers, and the way they were sitting together, well, let's just say it wasn't in the way of familial love.

Kitty's voice pulls me out of my thoughts. "Stella, a word?" I follow as she leads me to a magnificent painting of a garden on the wall—signed with her name, *bloody hell*—but I imagine she's got something else in mind, judging from the way she's twiddling with her thumbs.

"I'll just come out with it. Has Fitzroy mentioned me at all?" she asks sheepishly. "I thought I'd ask, since you are his closest friend."

My words stick in my throat. Closest friend? Did he tell her that? Maybe accurate once, but certainly not now. "I'm sure he has friends that are closer. The Earl of Grantchester, perhaps. Or, erm, Gwen?"

"Well, I don't have the earl at my behest, do I? And I can't ask Gwen. Every time I mention him, she changes the subject." She glances down to her feet. "Has he not mentioned me once?"

I attempt a smile, as odd as it feels. "He did mention that you—Well. You two would be engaged—"

Her expression and posture change in one jolt. Her eyes widen, and her voice lowers to a tense whisper. "He's going to propose?"

I don't understand her shock—Nate spoke as if this were a well-known fact! So why does Kitty look so pleased? Surely she must've known?

❖ 125 ❖

Her surprise and delight are so stark that I have a terrible feeling I've made a mistake.

I stutter my attempt to correct my error—though I have no clue how exactly I've misstepped. "Oh, well, isn't it obvious? You two—well, I've heard—"

"What did he say, *exactly*?"

"Well!" I look around, trying to catch Livvie's eye so she might save me, but she's too busy perfectly playing the pianoforte to help her only cousin. "Something about the end of the summer?"

I think if Kitty widens her eyes any more, they'll likely pop right out of her head. "He's going to propose by the end of summer?"

Foot in mouth, Stella, *foot in mouth*! "Oh, I'm not sure about that—I may have misheard—"

She throws her arms around me, obviously hearing nothing of my attempts to get out of this.

Bollocks.

14

With Livvie and Lady Tess still asleep, I rummage for a pencil and a few sheets of paper in the study.

Gwen invited us over for breakfast, and though I woke up much too early, I can't go back to sleep. I'm too inspired. I don't know why. I must've dreamed of success at *State of London*, for my thoughts are buzzing with excitement. I pace for a few moments, thinking of having my words in the London papers, read by all types of people in society. For the first time in all my life, I feel like I have a purpose.

I take the seat at the desk and sharpen my pencil. I feel fairly good about my review on Otofsky's *Aurora*, but I'd like to write a general opinion essay for Mr. Elmhurst as well. While my heart is in storytelling, I think it would be best to stick to non-fiction that fits *State of London*'s tone.

The blank page is daunting. Quickly, I head it.

A Young Woman's Thoughts on Society
Issue One.

There. Aunt Eleanor always speaks on the importance of setting intentions and goals, so here I am. Issue One.

I wish my mother were here to guide me. I wish I'd asked her about her writing process. I wish she were here to see my attempt at following in her footsteps.

Mindlessly, I start scribbling flowers in the corners. I'm annoyed with myself. Obviously, I didn't think this would be easy, but I assumed the words would at least flow a little quicker. It's like all of the feelings and opinions I've been fostering have disappeared right out from my own mind. With every passing second, my mettle dissolves bit by bit. I can't explain it; every word feels inadequate.

Above me, the house creaks with life. Perhaps I need a change of scenery. I think Gwen wouldn't mind if I arrived a little early? I just want the view of Kendall Manor's glorious garden where Mum used to write. I want to sit up in my favorite tree like I used to do when I was small, watching Jane analyze plants with Gwen and Nathaniel.

I leave a note for Lady Tess and Livvie and set out on my way. Lady Tess's footman offers the carriage, but I decline. It's a half hour walk from Primrose Hill, but the air is cool, the sun is just rising, and the sweet smell of last night's rain is a welcome scent.

When I arrive, Mr. Fitzroy's butler, Mr. Edison, regards me with a tense grin. "Miss Sedgwick. You're quite early." He looks behind me. "Did you walk here on your own?"

"I did."

The smile thins. "Miss Danvers is still asleep, as is the rest of the house—"

"I won't be a bother," I say quickly, taking the next step. "I only wanted to sit in the garden, like I used to." I pause, letting that reminder that I know Kendall Manor as well as he does settle into the conversation. "I'm sure Mr. Fitzroy won't mind, seeing as he'd invited me to stay here if I didn't have my own lodgings for the time."

I don't mention the inheritance of course, though I'm sure Edison knows. He acquiesces. He even takes my coat and offers to bring tea. I wonder if he's envisioning me as the new mistress of this house and wondering if he'll want to keep his job with me at the helm. Or my husband, I suppose.

I go past the library and the sitting room and toward the back doors. Kendall's gardens stretch out before me, a picture of vivid green hills, lush and full fruit trees, the sound of birds twittering in the air, all cupped in the lovely morning light.

I start for my favorite shady nook, only . . . it's occupied.

Nathaniel Fitzroy stands there, hands on his hips. He's staring angrily at a poor rectangle of canvas drenched in the bright colors of a gorgeous sunrise. He looks like he wants to chuck the whole thing. He holds tension in his shoulders as if he's staring at a particularly difficult puzzle rather than his own art.

"You're painting?" I blurt out. I think of his grandfather's sneer when he mentioned Nathaniel's love of art.

He whips his head around. Without so much as a smile, he

❖ 129 ❖

immediately picks up the easel and turns his work away from me. "Stella—no, no—don't look, it's not done."

I'm upset with him, yet I can't help but laugh. "Surely you aren't serious. Fitzroy, it's beautiful."

His frown softens a little. "*What it is* is unfinished."

Well . . . I understand the feeling.

His eyes flick up at me from over the canvas. He's obviously still cross with me, which is silly, considering *he's* the one yet to apologize for his insult. I should be upset, and I am, and that makes me *more* upset, and I want to snatch back the compliment I granted him.

"You're early," he says.

I step backward. "Pardon the interruption, I was only looking for a place to . . . write a letter."

He raises a brow. "And you came all the way here?"

"Well, yes. This is my favorite spot in all of Kendall's gardens. I thought it might be nice to see the sunrise here. And why are *you* up so early?"

"I couldn't sleep." He pauses, then adds. "Grandfather wants me well versed in all the matters of overseeing an estate. I'll be spending the day under his careful eye as his advisors sneer at me." He furrows his brows. "*This* is your favorite spot?"

I nod toward the east, where the sun's coming in. "You see how the light hits this tree? It's bright, warm, and quiet. But I will have to find a replacement for today."

He raises a hand nonchalantly. "Nonsense, it wouldn't bother me if you wrote your letter here."

"Oh, it wouldn't bother you, would it?" I mutter sharply.

Even simple things sound presumptuous from his mouth.

He puts his brush down and begins shuffling his belongings. "Then it's yours."

"Oh, don't be a child." It's a touch meaner than I meant, but he deserves a bit of meanness, anyway. I pull on the tree branches to test their sturdiness. There, that's good. I hook my arm over one and plant my foot against the knotty trunk.

Fitzroy gapes at me. "Stella! *Careful!*"

"Well, don't look! I'm not so fortunate as you—to be allowed to wear trousers."

Face flushed, he turns back to his work. Now, I've long mastered the art of climbing trees in a day dress, but I like making him uneasy.

Once I'm settled, he adjusts his easel once more so I can't look at it. I scoff. "Fitzroy, I have much better things to do than peek at your unfinished painting."

He grunts.

I tap my pencil against my bottom lip. I could write about my experience in London so far, or about the ball, or dress shopping, or high society in general. Part of me wants to admonish it all in a searing critique, while another wants to test my ability to appeal to the genteel woman without scaring her.

I catch Fitzroy in my peripheral vision. He was looking up at me, but quickly turned away. "Is all the mumbling necessary?" he asks, whipping his paintbrush across the canvas.

I frown. I didn't realize I was speaking to myself. If the garden was as it was supposed to be—*empty*—then this would not be an issue. "Yes, yes it is."

I manage some vague notes about the pomp of Covent Garden and how the theater enables people-watching that is just as entertaining as a show on the stage before putting my pencil down once more. I can't focus with Fitzroy's gaze constantly darting toward me. "What is it now?"

This time, he doesn't look away. "Who's the letter for?"

I pause. He knows that my only acquaintances outside of my family and Lady Tess are the Fitzroys. I look down to my page. "An old friend of my mother's."

He mumbles just loudly enough so that I may hear it. "Not gossiping, I hope."

"Not that it's any of your concern, but no."

His face is stiff with annoyance. "Miss Sedgwick."

I exhale, putting down the pencil once more. "Yes, *Fitzroy*?"

He wipes his hands on the towel hanging from the easel, ignoring my sardonic tone. "I'd love to know what you were thinking when you started spreading the rumor that I'm engaged to Miss Katherine Chen."

I jolt, and have to grab the tree to remain in it. "Pardon me? I did no such thing!"

"No? You didn't tell Kitty that I was going to propose to her by the end of the month? The rumor seems to stem from that."

Oh, shite! "I—" The words catch, and I make a sound like a croak. "I said by the end of the summer, actually."

He throws down the towel and steps around the easel to levy a fierce glare up at me. It'd compel most people to shrink, but I won't be cowed.

"Why are you so upset?" I ask. "You told me yourself that it

❖ 132 ❖

was to be. Your friends teased you about it, even—I'd assumed everyone knew already. It's not as if I was yelling to the masses about your French countess, is it?"

This strikes him hard, and he jerks back as if I'd physically done so. "How poor of you to speak of things you know nothing about. Will you hold that discussion over my head for eternity? I'm not upset because of your unseemly eavesdropping—"

"*Eavesdropping!*"

"—but because of your quick tongue! Mr. Chen has inquired when I plan to ask for his daughter's hand!"

"And what does it matter if it was already to be done? You're going to marry her, yes?"

"Well, of course!" he sputters. There's an odd twinge of defensiveness in his voice. "She's exactly whom I'm supposed to marry!"

I want to grab him by the shoulders and shake him. "Then why are you so vexed?"

"Because it's none of your business, Stella!"

"Of course, it is! It's everyone's business! That's why you all have your balls and your chatty luncheons! Have I ever proved myself to be some incessant gossip to you? I was stung, Fitzroy, by the brashness in your words, but I had no desire to speak of them to anyone. Believe me, I wanted to forget the whole thing. But Kitty asked me herself, and I didn't know what to say!"

He looks at me. A hint of regret plagues him, I think. "The countess . . ." He scratches at the spot between his brows. "It was nothing but a drunken—"

"Heavens! I don't need to know!"

❖ 133 ❖

I gather my things and begin climbing down the tree. Coming here was a *horrible* idea.

He steps forward. "No, Stella—"

In all my haste, I miss a step and go fumbling down in a rather inelegant manner, my hat slipping from my head. I don't quite *fall*, but for some reason, Fitzroy reaches out and grabs my forearm to keep me steady.

I look at his hand on me. He does the same, then lifts his eyes to find my gaze.

I pull away from him hard.

He shakes his head. "Oh, you're welcome, only very nearly fell from the tree you had no business climbing!"

"Well, I——" I snatch my hat from his other hand. "I assure you, I've climbed many trees in my life and have managed just fine without you!"

He watches me gesticulate with amusement that only makes me more furious. Only he could make a smile so condescending. And yet I cannot help feeling prideful at the sight of that snaggletooth.

"Am I amusing you, Fitzroy?"

"Yes."

I have an intense need to wallop him in the arm like I might have when we were children, but I tamp it down and settle for a withering glare.

He throws his hands up and stalks back to his painting. "Good day, Miss Sedgwick."

"It will be, thank you. For me, because I am going to write the most splendid letter in letters' history, and for you, because you won't have to spend any more time with a girl whose demeanor so offends you! Good day, Fitzroy!"

Once I'm inside the house, I quickly make for the study.

I don't think. I just write, filling the page up with all of my frustrations with so-called gentlemen, with the inherent oppression of the male-headed peerage, and the utter absurdity of pursuing their approval.

By the time I'm done, I've got six pages full to the brim and graphite down the side of my wrist. I'll have to edit them heavily—it reads exactly as what it is, a stream of thoughts delivered breathlessly. Still, I'm satisfied. It's a start. A damned mess, but certainly a start.

I hear footsteps behind me. Bless Gwen, still in her sleeping clothes. She's even got a cup of tea for me. "There you are—I thought I'd seen your ghost flying across Kendall gardens. Why are you here so early?"

I shake the papers before her. "I had a bout of inspiration that I could not ignore. And you?"

"Well, you gave Mr. Edison quite a fright." She smiles. "I was half-awake anyway. Too excited for the ball tomorrow. I hear Mr. Désir is planning a debaucherously fun night."

"I hope you have a fabulous time with many dances."

"And won't you dance?"

"With who?" I realize I don't want her to answer, so I add, "I'd rather cheer you on with the rest of the spectators."

"You'll have to dance with someone. Like Lord Grantchester, perhaps?"

I frown, though it actually doesn't sound *too* awful, the more that I consider it.

"Or . . . my brother?"

The frown deepens. "I think there's as much a chance of me being asked to dance by Nathaniel Fitzroy as that hogs will fall from the sky tonight, he finds my company so disagreeable."

Her brow wrinkles. "What are you talking about? He adores you—"

Quickly, I gather my papers. "I thank you for the tea, and now let's have a proper breakfast. I'm sure Olivia and Lady Tess will be here shortly."

"Yes, of course." She's examining my face, looking for hurt. I turn away quickly, praying she doesn't find it.

15

"Oh, it's absurd," I blurt out with a wondrous laugh. "To think, this is merely a vacation home for him!"

Trinity Hall, the London house of Samuel Désir, seems to have been duplicated from a small girl's favorite fairy tale.

We arrive well after many others, and the house—*castle* seems more suitable here—is bustling with people. Ladies linger by the staircase, sipping daintily from crystal glasses, their chaperones trying to keep one eye on them and one on every potential suitor that passes by. A group of older gentlemen smoke their pipes and laugh, eyeing the young ladies as well, and look awfully presumptuous doing so. All about, people drink and mingle. Jaunty music fills the air as we step toward the outdoor veranda where couples dance on its pristine marble floor.

From a gaggle of girls, Gwen points at me with her wine flute and immediately rushes to greet us. "Thank the heavens, have you seen this place?"

Even I can't help but feel flush with excitement. I watch the dancing pairs, taking in their smooth, synchronized movements in line with the orchestra's song.

Livvie squeezes my hand. "What a party, Stella! Imagine, if we were back in Addyshire, we'd be doing something boring, like playing whist or cross-stitching, or teasing mother for her baking!"

I can picture it—a chocolate biscuit in hand, Cheswick warming my feet. "How lovely, let's go home!"

Gwen pinches me. "Oh, stop. Do try to have some fun!"

I fidget in my pretty new shoes. "I will, I promise."

I reach for two flutes from a server's tray, which Lady Tess promptly slips from my fingers and places back onto the tray. "Why don't we take a walk around the room first?"

"Rooms, you mean," I add. "Stay close, Livvie, we could get lost here."

I stay on my best behavior as Lady Tess introduces us to some of her acquaintances. I humor them—let them ask me the most absurd questions and make comments like *have you heard music before*, and *you've read* State of London? *I didn't realize your kind* could *read . . . how extraordinary!* Even Olivia, who would much rather complain in private than start a confrontation, looks exhausted by the end of it. Her well-practiced smile has a crazed edge to it. Well, I do draw the line at one Mrs. Evensway's attempt to touch the small poofs at the end of my plaits, using the nearby serving boy as an excuse to crane away and pluck a lemonade from his tray. All the money in the world and still thick in the skull, truly.

There's a sudden excitement behind us, at the front of the room. Girls run in pairs to the windows, mothers and chaperones craning around to see. We find ourselves moving with the surging crowd, back toward the steps we'd walked in from. There are a few footmen waiting with lanterns held up in the dark night.

"What's happening?" I ask no one in particular.

A girl I don't know leans in from my side. "Mr. Désir is here!"

"What do you mean? He's just arriving to his own party?"

My question is answered immediately.

I hear falling hoofbeats. A rider comes in from the darkness, like a valiant knight atop a noble steed.

The footman raises his voice over the murmurs. "Presenting— Mr. Samuel Désir!"

In one elegant stride, the man dismounts from his horse, adjusts his hat, and levels a steely look at the audience gathered before him. Coolly, he nods. "Good evening, and welcome."

I am left *speechless*, as is Livvie, as is everyone around us. The mysterious Mr. Désir is just a young man, perhaps a year or two older than I, with a sharp face cut from marble, and smooth, dark brown skin. His thick black hair is trimmed close at the sides, his curls lush atop his head. He is tall and stately, with broad shoulders that give him an effortlessly commanding posture. It's hard to look away from him.

"*That*," Gwen says softly, "is an entrance."

❖ 139 ❖

The guests seem just as shocked and stricken as I. A few revelers move to make his acquaintance, but others make their way *out*. I notice red-faced chaperones escorting their wards to the door, this lavish and elegant party now too pedestrian for them.

I turn to Olivia. "Hold on, did you know—"

I'm interrupted by the feel of something at my feet. It's Olivia's ribbon, slipped from her fingers. She is staring at this young man with lush eyes. Her gaze is unbreakable, her skin dotted with visible gooseflesh. Oh, she is lost to me now! I think I could scream out that the estate was on fire, and she'd stay rooted right here in this very spot.

"Livvie!" I giggle wildly. "Don't look so smitten!"

She snaps from her reverie, brown eyes popping open. "What! Smitten? What are you talking about?"

I roll my lips together to keep from laughing. Her face is *red*, for heaven's sake.

"Shall we introduce ourselves?" Gwen hooks her arm in Livvie's, a grasp from which she immediately slips.

"No, no, I'm fine here!" Livvie retreats backward into the party quickly.

I shoot Gwen an amused look before going after her. "You said you wanted to dance, Livvie!"

Gwen turns toward something behind me, and whispers, "Speaking of dancing—"

I look as well and find Lord Bernard Grantchester strolling toward us. "Good evening, ladies."

Quickly, Gwen moves from my side. She says, "Lord Grantchester, my dear friend, you'll have to excuse me, I have

❖ 140 ❖

a shy girl to catch and force to dance—oh, that sounds *wicked.* Pardon me." Honestly, it would've been less subtle if she'd held a giant sign over our heads that said *dance, you fools!*

I curtsy. "Good evening, Lord Grantchester."

He smiles, and I'm reminded of how lovely a smile it is. I haven't thought all that much about him since his party at Duberney, but now that he's in front of me, I realize that I'm pleased to be sharing his company once more.

"I'm pleasantly surprised to see you here, Miss Sedgwick. I thought maybe you might find it awfully overwrought."

"I will admit that I was skeptical, but I have enjoyed it so far. No need to hide out in a study yet."

He winks at me, and my stomach flips against my will. I do feel a little silly, but I don't hate it, either.

Mr. Désir is now dancing with the girl who informed me of his arrival. There's an eager group of ladies waiting for him. It's fascinating—and unsettling—to watch. They don't seem to treat him with outright disrespect, but it's certainly not *respect* either. They regard him like a new species, a rare find, something to gawk at. And there's that horrible Mrs. Evensway again, marveling at his hair.

Lord Grantchester clears his throat. "Might I be granted a dance, Miss Sedgwick?"

He offers his hand. I can't *not* take it of course; that would be rude. But . . . it's the strangest thing . . . I actually don't want to refuse. Suddenly, a dance doesn't seem all that intimidating. I place my hand in his, and when he rests his thumb atop my gloved fingers, I feel at ease.

✦ 141 ✦

He leads me onto the veranda. The night is beautiful, the full moon and radiant stars piercing the inky sky. I'm mesmerized by it for a moment. Grantchester and I take our places across from each other in the dance. He flashes me a sweet, shy smile that I can't help but return. I've always been well aware of Lord Grantchester's handsomeness, but being this close to him makes it all the more obvious. If there are whispers, I do not hear them.

Just before the music starts, a girl rushes to my other side to join the dance. I don't immediately recognize Kitty, but Fitzroy I know instantly from the flash of brown curls in the corner of my eye. It's instinct, the way I would recognize him anywhere, across any room.

His eyes find mine briefly before we turn back to our partners.

The spirited music whips my mind straight to the task of not falling over my own two feet, which requires all of my focus.

Grantchester and I move toward each other, pausing with the beats of the music. His shoulder lands against mine as we fall into a line. "It's a lovely night," he whispers as we pass each other.

"Reminds me of home," I say. "I could lie in the gardens and stare up at the sky for hours."

"London has its disappointments," Grantchester says diplomatically. "I much prefer the country."

"The stillness of it can be comforting," I offer softly.

He nods thankfully.

"Tell me about your home—Grantchester, is it?"

"It's the most peaceful place on earth, and with the most beautiful gardens this side of Paris."

I laugh. "A grand claim."

"Perhaps you'll have to judge them for yourself."

He turns to me with a smile, revealing a soft dimple in his right cheek that I can only savor for a second before we separate, and I am forced to partner with Nathaniel Fitzroy.

We snap our heads forward quickly. Though I'm happy enough trouncing forward silently—heavens, these dances are unnecessarily complicated—he says, "Are you enjoying yourself?"

There's a presumptuous edge to it that stokes a fresh flame of anger. "Yes, actually. And here I thought a ball would be a miserable thing. I suppose the company matters." I flick my gaze at him. "I *was* having a lovely time, at least."

His jaw twitches like he's grinding his teeth. "I'm sorry to have disrupted it."

"Ah—" I curtsy, though far from as low as I could. "So you do know how to apologize."

We turn back to our partners after six counts. I feel a faint accidental touch in passing—Fitzroy's fingers brushing against my knuckles. Like I've burned him, he flexes his hand before taking Kitty's.

It's odd to think I feel more at ease at Lord Grantchester's side than Fitzroy's. This man's a stranger, but he looks upon me with considerably more care than Fitzroy's afforded lately.

At the end of the dance, Grantchester's pale skin is slightly flushed. He still has a hold on my hand from the last spin, his thumb pressing gently in the space between my knuckles.

He smiles shyly. "I hope that was not so bad."

"Oh, you were perfect—it was my clumsy steps that should

have worried you." I laugh. "Really, Lord Grantchester, it was lovely."

I'm a little out of breath, and he is not, which makes his reddened cheeks only more peculiar. "I can't imagine I've ever been called perfect in any regard." He brings my hand to his lips. "Perhaps I will be granted a chance to receive such a compliment again, if you'd allow another dance tonight."

I think of Livvie falling over herself with glee. *Two dances!* "I would be happy to."

He grins wider, which I appreciate. He nods over my head. "I shouldn't keep you from your next partner, as much as I'd like to. . . ."

It is easy to expect that I'll turn and find Nathaniel Fitzroy waiting, so easy that I'm a little embarrassed by it.

Except it's the host—the handsome Samuel Désir—who bows his head and offers his hand.

16

"I'm surprised you asked me to dance," I offer. "You've hardly had a moment alone since you arrived."

"I could say as much for you," Mr. Désir counters, voice low, his words tinged with a French accent. There are a few seconds where we're separated and I'm forced to do a twirl that I can only hope doesn't look as awkward as it feels.

"It seems we're both shiny new playthings," I continue. "Though you're likely better equipped to receive such attention than I am."

"How so?"

"Perhaps you haven't heard. I am an unlikely heiress—I have unexpectedly come into the opportunity to receive a great fortune."

He smiles. "I think you and I may relate to each other still.

A fortune helps. But in some ways, we might never be fully at comfort here."

I am keenly aware of the eyes on us, and I'm sure it's not only because of our perceived wealth. I concede a nod. "To that, I agree."

Olivia swirls by us at the hand of Lord Grantchester.

I watch her for a moment, but when I turn back to my partner, I see that I am not the only one looking at her.

Mr. Désir exhales softly. "I believe I had the pleasure of speaking with your cousin. Miss Olivia Witherson?"

Oh?

Oh!

Olivia is just going to faint. And perhaps I'm not the cold-hearted skeptic I've always believed myself to be, because the thought of Mr. Désir and Livvie catching each other's eye makes my heart burst with glee.

I have to bite my tongue to keep from smiling. I must keep coolheaded. I think of Lady Flippant and what she might advise at a moment like this.

I smile sweetly. "Yes. She is a beauty, is she not?" We separate again, and when I return to place his hand against mine, I do not let him speak. "And far lighter on her feet than I. You should ask her to dance."

The corner of his mouth ticks up in a smirk. "Her beauty is unparalleled, as are her talents in dancing, I'm sure, though I think both are family traits."

I know that young bachelors can have poor intentions when courting young women, but Mr. Désir feels softer. More genuine. His compliments don't seem to be quite as driven by expectations of politeness.

"I wondered if . . ." He pauses, and it is so acutely obvious that he is nervous. "If your aunt would agree to a tour of Paris."

"I do think her mother would be happy for that. Olivia, however . . ." I let my voice trail off, and he turns to me. I let him stew in anticipation for a few moments as the line dance leads us away from each other. "Well, she has been noticed by many fine young men tonight."

Olivia, despite not being the murderous sort, would *kill me* if she heard this, but I know from mother's columns how unseemly it is to be overeager. She'll thank me later.

Indeed, Mr. Désir does seem a little stung. "I see."

"Still, I can't imagine any are quite so memorable as you." The song ends, and I give a small curtsy.

He chuckles, and it brings boyishness into his stoic face. It feels like a treat to savor. Politely, he dips his head at me, and instantly, no fewer than five ladies appear behind him to be his next partner.

I am horrified to see that I have somehow conjured my own little gathering of curious young men, but thankfully, Olivia is so dizzy with excitement that she forgets her good manners and pulls me out of the fray.

"Stella!" she yells once we're safely on the fringes of the group. The music is livelier now, the sound amplified by laughter and clapping. "Did you just? I saw you! You talked to him!"

"You're so lovestruck that you can't even speak!" Laughing, I spin her around until we're both out of breath. "Livvie, my dearest friend, don't scream, but he is *smitten* with you. Absolutely, heart-strickenly smitten!"

She claps her hand over her mouth as if that could stop the delirious giggles from escaping. "Oh, please, please don't tease me."

"I'm not!" I link my arm in hers and walk her away from a particularly attentive crowd of nosy society mothers. "He couldn't wait to ask me about you. He wants to take you to Paris!"

I wish I had told her this later, because now she's so happy that she's nearly skipping, and my feet are much too sore to keep up with her, *hell.* "He said that?"

"And he was such a gentleman—well, anyone with their sights on you must be a fine one, so I know he must not be as half-witted as the other men here—"

A voice starts behind us. "There's Stella, always with a jab on her tongue."

We turn.

Fitzroy bows his head to Livvie. "You look lovely, Miss Witherson, as usual."

She bows her head. "Thank you, Fitzroy."

"Miss Sedgwick," he says with a click of his tongue.

I raise a brow. "Is that all I get? Am I not lovely, too?"

I say it in jest, but he doesn't laugh. He's wearing a strange sort of distress on his face, like he's been out in the sun too long and is on the verge of fainting. "You crave compliments? Oh, Stella, if only you knew."

My face grows hot instantly. With a polite goodbye that I

hardly hear, Olivia quickly excuses herself. I turn toward the dancers. It's easier than looking at him.

He steps close to me. "I came to ask you to dance."

I laugh. "You know I have no skill in the matter. I'd sooner pummel your feet into dust with my own!"

"You danced fine with Lord Grantchester and with Mr. Désir."

I get a little hitch of satisfaction knowing that he was paying attention. "They were both such fine dancers that my clumsiness went unnoticed. I'm afraid you're not so skilled, and we'll both look silly."

I think it's obvious that I'm teasing, but his face remains hard. "Who better to share embarrassment with than your oldest friend?"

I walk down the edge of the dancers. He follows closely, stopping only to politely nod his head at a few acquaintances. I do see the eyes on us. On *me*. "Are you my friend now?"

He touches my elbow gently to stop me. "Stella. You must forgive me."

I hate him. I hate that with one look in his pleading brown eyes, I'm suddenly softhearted. I think he might be a little drunk— there's a vulnerability here that I know he wouldn't let me see otherwise.

He runs his hands through his curls, which only makes them messier. He can't even look me in the eye. "I've been sick knowing that you're upset with me."

Any attempt to harden my heart is quickly interrupted. *Sick?* I didn't think him the wallowing sort, but the earnestness in his voice is too much to ignore. But even more impossible to ignore

✦ 149 ✦

is the sound of his voice chiding me to his companions. I feel a little spark of anger from the memory, far from a flame, but still burning on. "I'm tired of dancing."

He inhales sharply. We're shoulder to shoulder, watching the dancers spin. He dips his head slightly toward me in a way that makes me feel as if he's even closer to me. "I'm a complete and utter fool. I deserve nothing but your contempt and your disdain, but I could not let you walk away from our friendship without apologizing. I'm sorry, Stella. I . . ." He shakes his head, lowers his voice. "I don't know why I said it. I don't know how to make this right."

I turn, just enough to get a peek of him. "Do you find my company so tiresome?"

He sighs a breathy laugh. "Your company is perhaps the only thing I find myself in want of."

He keeps his head bent toward me, and it feels so intimate that I know I should take a step back. I can't hear the music over the blood pounding in my ears.

"As for the French countess—"

I roll my shoulders uncomfortably. "Fitzroy, you have no obligation to defend yourself to me." It's the mature thing to say, as much as I hate it.

But Fitzroy is insistent. "Listen, Stella, it was a drunken *lie*. I did nothing more to her than lose miserably at a game of whist and offer her my shoulder on which to cry over her sickly corgi!"

"Her corgi?"

"*Ruffins*. He'd been attacked by a feral duck."

✦ 150 ✦

I bite the inside of my lip to keep from guffawing. I want to ask why he lied, or at least let the lie be believed, but I think I understand. "It's not always easy to be yourself."

"No, you were right to criticize me. I don't mean to be different when I'm with them. It was too easy to slip into their likeness—"

"Well, I should've known you weren't so like them when I've known you for so long—"

"It's been years, how could you have—"

I laugh freely, the relief nearly knocking the breath from me. "Goodness, we can't even apologize to each other without fighting about who is more wrong!" I grin up at him, and it's the most natural thing in the world. "What happened to us? I feel like we've been complete strangers, and I don't know how to weather it."

Finally, he lifts his head to look at me, and now that we have each other's gaze, neither of us can let it go. "You're right, and it's *absurd*, and I'm miserable." He swallows, then laughs, and I realize how little I've heard that laugh. I would like to avoid being without it for so long again.

"I hereby declare our quarrel ended, Fitzroy." I present my hand to shake.

He doesn't even look at it. "Nate. I want you to call me Nate."

I flash him a warning look. "That would be improper. People would talk."

"So call me Nate when no one else can hear." He gestures ambivalently to the crowd and whispers, "Be proper with other men, but not with me."

I feel a stunning jolt in the pit of my stomach. It's *horrible*, but it's perfect at the same time. "Nate?"

He smiles, snaggletooth and all. "Yes, Stella?"

"Promise me we will never fight again."

He takes my hand, but instead of shaking it, he presses my gloved fingers to his lips, brushing the silk against them. "I promise, but only if you grant me a dance."

My heartbeat is unsteady. "Are you still going on about dancing?"

"It's a *party*."

I shrug as if it's nothing to me. "Fine, if you insist!"

As I turn to join the dancers, I knock into someone. I didn't think I'd turned so sharply, but we collide hard, and the man at the other end spills his drink all over his nice clothes.

I'm instantly embarrassed and apologetic, but the immediate disgust on the man's face makes my stomach roil. "Oh! My apologies, sir!"

He looks at me, and I know he sees me, but it's as if he doesn't *really* see me.

The man snarls. "What are you standing around for? Go fetch me a towel, girl!"

He sees me, but not my fine dress, my neat hair, my jeweled neck. He sees my face and assumes I must be part of the staff. Or maybe he sees it all and decides that I'm nothing, anyway. Pretty clothes don't change a thing.

Nathaniel puts his hand out to the man, but is ignored. He continues, "Can't you hear? Or are you simply daft? I've known your kind to be inept, but—"

I swing my hand to my left, grab a poor woman's cup of wine, and throw it in the man's face.

I know without turning that everyone is in this moment, staring.

I don't care.

I want to run away. I force my feet to stay. *Stella Sedgwick is no runner.*

The man sputters. "*You*—"

Nathaniel steps between us. "I think it's time for you to take your leave, Mr. Royce."

He turns to Nate. "Have you lost your senses, Fitzroy?" he spits. "You have no authority here—"

"No, but I do." Mr. Désir has a gentle evenness in his tone that feels more powerful than this Royce fellow's booming threat.

Royce stills, blinks. "This girl—"

"Is my guest. The same cannot currently be said for you." Désir looks bored by him, and this is a coolness I can only hope one day to perfect. "As I strive to be as polite a gentleman as I can, I won't ask you to leave. I'll spare your dignity, and you'll elect to do so on your own."

Even Royce's pretty companion steps away from him. A serving boy finally brings him a towel, which Royce snatches ungratefully. He shoots me a last stormy look before stomping through the parted crowd behind him.

Nate gives me an apologetic look. "Let's delay our dance for now. Why don't you and Olivia take some fresh air." He holds my gaze for a second longer than feels appropriate. "And don't you dare pay him any mind."

❖ 153 ❖

The next moments happen in a blur. I pull away from the gawks and whispers, Olivia appearing at my side, her hand on my arm as she leads me up the steps to the balcony. "Goodness, you really just . . ." Her voice trails off, and she slaps her palms on either side of her face.

I don't know what comes over me, but I *laugh*. I can't stop laughing, even as a few tears form in my eyes. "I did. I just did that."

"Wretched man." She throws her arms around me and wraps me up into a hug.

The disillusioned joy wears off quickly, and now my tears are real. "Every single person in there who thinks that our people are uncivilized is likely foaming at the mouth in smugness."

"My dear cousin, I hate to see you weepy." She wipes my tears with her own kerchief. "Who cares about them? You are stunning and clever, and they should be jealous of all of us that love you."

My heart lifts a little, but our conversation is splintered by raised voices below us. From here, we can see a carriage is departing, and a boy is running after it.

"Is that Fitzroy?" Olivia whispers.

It is. And he seems to be pleading with Mr. Royce, who looks unamused in his carriage seat. They speak tensely for a few moments before Fitzroy offers his hand, and Royce shakes it.

My stomach twinges. "What is he doing?"

Olivia loops her arm through mine. "We should get back to the party."

I desperately do not want to, but I feel like I must. There will undoubtedly be sneers and whispers, but let them whine.

Let *them* be uncomfortable.

I am here.

And I have endless cups of wine to throw.

17

"Heavens, Stella." Lady Tess has not stopped rubbing the spot between her brows all morning. "He deserved it, but, *heavens*."

I'm curled up in a blanket on her couch, tea and toast in hand, utterly unperturbed and perfectly content. "Oh, if you had seen his face! Mr. Désir made it very clear that his behavior was unacceptable—oh, you should have seen it!"

"I certainly chose the wrong time to tour the gardens." She shakes her head. "Aside from that horrible incident, well, it's so nice to see you having your fun, finally."

I shrug. Stubbornly, I don't want to give her the pleasure of being right, though she is. "It was an agreeable night, well, *mostly*." I think of Nate, and finally feel a bit of comfort rather than anger. But I can't get that image of him and Mr. Royce out of my head.

Lady Tess smiles smugly anyway. I can see that she's quite proud of herself, which admittedly, makes me happy. "And Mr. Désir?"

I wait, listening for Olivia's footsteps, even though she's not the nosy sort. For once, she's sleeping late. "He is enamored, Lady Tess. Obviously, it's too early to say, but the way he watched her? I could hear his heart beating with admiration for her. He's a good man, I can tell; if you'd seen the way he demanded that Mr. Royce leave the ball! And Nate did what he could—"

"Nate?" She stumbles over the unfamiliarity of his name. "Mr. Fitzroy was there for this?"

"Well, we'd been talking—he was badgering me for a dance, you see."

Lady Tess sets down her teacup, which means I'm in for it. "Stella, I must be frank with you."

My body stiffens.

"I have heard of some . . . closeness between you and Mr. Fitzroy."

I can't help but laugh, though I feel that awful dread growing in the pit of my stomach again. "Funny. I'd only just thought that he despised me all this time."

"I have a hard time believing that."

"No, I—" I fumble for a way to explain, and that just makes me more nervous. "I mean it. We hadn't spoken since we were children. Then, when I arrived, we couldn't see eye to eye." I skip over the bit about the opera, not wanting to dredge that up again. "I think we've reached an understanding now, but believe me, it's *nothing* like what you're implying."

"Then, you shouldn't be addressing him as anything but Mr. Fitzroy, or Fitzroy in his grandfather's presence, or the like."

"I call his sisters Gwen and Jane—"

"Come, now, you know there's a difference. There will be more talk than there already is."

I cross my arms over my chest, even though I know it makes me look like a petulant child. Of course, I noticed the eyes and whispers, but now that I'm out of those critical gazes, it's hard to care about the opinions of people that I don't even know.

"I already warned you that you had people's curiosity and attention," Lady Tess continues. "You have to understand, if it were anyone else, I would be so full of joy that you had found a young man to capture your attention—"

"He doesn't capture my . . . anything!"

"But there are already plans in motion for Nathaniel Fitzroy, and it does you no good to be hanging by his side. You'll look like second best, pining after a man who is promised to another."

"Thank you, Mrs. Sinclair," I reply sharply. "I understand now."

She means to reach for me, but I don't move forward to meet her halfway. Her hand settles on her teacup instead. "Now, don't be cross with me. I'm only trying to help you. It's your first foray into society. How would you have known?"

The image she's painted of me hanging on to Nathaniel's side while he's off making eyes at Katherine Chen is stomach turning. "I also danced with Lord Grantchester," I blurt out.

At this, Lady Tess raises a brow.

❖ 158 ❖

"We were meant to dance again, but—"

She nearly drops her cup. "He asked you for *two dances*?"

"But all the business with Royce made a mess of the evening."

Lady Tess doesn't respond, but I do see the calculation running in her head. Oh, *shite*. I'm sure she's drumming up a way to get Grantchester and me in the same room once more. I shouldn't have even mentioned him, but I wanted so badly to move on from being chastised about Fitzroy. That said, if I am being honest with myself . . . I do like Lord Grantchester's company. He's good-natured and funny. It's just so easy to be around him.

I try to shrug off the thought. "Will you let us go to Paris?"

She beams, even happier now that we've moved on to Olivia's prospects. "Well, of course!"

"Good morning!" Just then, my cheery cousin drifts down the stairs and floats over to us. Though she has always been a morning person, she is particularly radiant this morning.

Lady Tess and I share a conspiratorial smile. "Did you sleep well, dear cousin?" I ask. "I've never seen you stay in bed past the birds' sweet songs. I was beginning to wonder if you'd taken ill."

"Not at all!" She pours a cup of tea and tops off ours. "Why, I don't think I've ever felt better."

I wink at Lady Tess. "What did I say? She's out of her mind, struck with love for Mr. Désir!" I sigh and dramatically faint onto the couch.

"Love?" Olivia laughs, but it sounds a bit *stressed*. "Absurd, I've only just met the man. But he is handsome, and kind—oh, the way he handled that horrible Mr. Royce! He may be the most honorable gentleman I've ever met!"

"Wow. Many words to use for someone you just met." I mutter.

"Hush, now." She makes room under the blanket next to me for herself.

Lady Tess regards us fondly. "There's something else. My father has sent word that there are a few remaining letters to Lady Flippant at his office."

I raise a brow. "Really? The column ended so long ago."

"I suppose there are some old readers who still take comfort in writing away their secrets—and it's not like they know your mother has passed on." She sighs deeply. "I know it's not exactly in the terms of our deal, but I think you should go retrieve them. My father is expecting you."

My eyes widen. "He wants to speak with me?"

"I only told him that I was sending a young acquaintance to fetch the letters, and that this young acquaintance had a knack for writing. I didn't tell him you're Ginny's daughter. You'll have to stand on your own."

"Couldn't you have said young, *brilliant* acquaintance?"

She laughs. "A warning, Stella. My father is a tough man to amuse."

Livvie sucks in through her teeth. "Shouldn't have said that; you know our Stella loves a challenge."

"He'll have his hands full, then," she replies with a wink. "I do have some appointments today, but I will take you tomorrow."

"Can't I go today?" I'm nearly bouncing on my toes. "I can handle myself, I promise!"

❖ 160 ❖

She looks me over and relents. "Fine. I'll have a carriage take you over this afternoon. Be on your best behavior, Stella."

I end up outside the offices of *State of London* just before two. The sidewalks are busy, and I'm nearly pushed aside by a parade of wealthy women making their way toward the shops. I must say, for all the importance placed on refinement and manners, well-bred ladies can be so rude.

I take a deep breath before stepping into the office.

It's slightly cooler inside, and I'm keenly aware of the beads of sweat forming on the back of my neck. The floor of *State of London* consists of rows of white men at their desks, scribbling away. A few turn in their seats to look at me, but most keep hunched over their work. My eyes drift up the lone staircase at the back of the room, leading to a door marked with gilded lettering.

The secretary to my right seems to catch my intention before I step forward. She clears her throat, but offers no welcoming comment.

I try a shy smile. "I'm looking for Mr. Elmhurst."

She looks me up and down. "Has something happened with his children?"

I tilt my head, and bite my tongue. "Mr. Elmhurst is expecting *me*. My name is Stella Sedgwick."

I catch movement in the corner of my eye. A young man lifts his head from his work and examines me with an unsubtle look of confusion. He rises. "My name is Daniel Bratton, I assist Mr. Elmhurst. What's this about?"

I can't help the wash of resentment that comes over me. Yes, perhaps I should've waited for her to be able to accompany me, but Lady Tess should've told her father who I was, what I look like.

"Mr. Elmhurst is expecting me," I repeat. "I'm here on behalf of his daughter, Mrs. Tessa Sinclair. I have some letters to pick up."

This seems to placate Bratton. "I see. Well. Right this way."

I follow him up a beautiful set of shiny wood stairs. The heavy, lacquered door emblazoned with "Richard Elmhurst, Editor in Chief," is open, but Mr. Bratton knocks anyway.

Mr. Elmhurst is an older, heavyset man with a head full of dark hair and a thick goatee. "What is it?"

"I have a Miss Sedgwick here to see you."

He looks up briefly, then points to a small stack of letters sitting on the edge of his desk.

Mr. Bratton steps forward, but I hurry in to grab them. "It's an honor to meet you, Mr. Elmhurst."

He looks up once more, but says nothing. I swear, there's no discomfort like this—being watched with the confused sort of glare that says, *Why are you speaking to me?*

Lucky for me, I'm not deterred by such things. "I've been reading *State of London* since I was, well, since I could read. Was probably too young for it." I add a small laugh.

Behind me, Mr. Bratton clears his throat. "Miss—"

"I write myself, actually, and I thought that you might like to see my pieces, and if there was a position here, for me . . ."

My voice trails off as Mr. Elmhurst's bushy gray eyebrow

❖ 162 ❖

slowly rises. It's the only movement his face has made.

Mr. Bratton looks at me curiously. He tilts his head. "Huh. That's. *Huh.*"

I smile sweetly at him. "Let's be specific, Mr. Bratton. Is it my gender or my coloring that confuses you? Or is it the curious combination of the two that is difficult for you to comprehend?"

He chokes out a surprised cough.

Mr. Elmhurst raises his hand. "I know you."

I pause.

"The name Sedgwick might have slipped my mind, but . . ." He leans back, still staring hard, as if wanting to commit every feature of my face to memory. "I remember now. Your mother had just as wild a tongue, though unlike you, she knew when to toe the line and when to cross it."

My brow pulses upward. "I didn't think you knew my mother well."

"I only met her physically once or twice, but it wasn't a face you'd forget, or a sense of humor, at that." He pushes up his spectacles. "Stella, is it?"

"Yes."

He looks over me once more. "Did you bring a sample?"

I don't wait for him to ask me to sit. The seat across from him is open; I only have to take it. "I did. Two, actually."

He looks over my work with infuriating stillness. Neither good nor bad, which I think is worse than if he slammed the papers down and told me to put down the pen forever. At least that'd be a reaction. I don't want to be so boring that I don't even earn a response.

I look to Mr. Bratton, who's glancing over Elmhurst's shoulder between glances at me.

Mr. Elmhurst lowers the papers. "What is this?"

I try not to swallow—I don't want him to see any hesitation or nerves. "An opera review."

He gives me a look between amusement and annoyance. "I see that. But why did you write it?"

"Because I have opinions about the show that I want to be made known."

He laughs dryly—Oh, I *can't wait* to tell Lady Tess about that. "The society piece is not very good."

I try not to jolt from the bluntness of it. "Because you disagree?"

"No, because it's poorly written. The talent's there, but you've let yourself get caught up in your emotions."

I can't tell if this is useful advice on my craft or if he simply thinks all women's writing is too emotional.

Still. *The talent's there.* That I'll accept.

"And yes, I do disagree. But I can appreciate a good argument well done, no matter the view. Anyway, I have a society writer and a reviewer." He stretches the papers toward me. "What I don't have is a Fiona Flippant. I've been searching for a writer to take up the mantle, and here you are."

I bite the inside of my cheek, though I should be biting my tongue. "I loved my mother's work, but I'm no advice columnist."

"Then it's the perfect way to sharpen your skills." He thinks for a moment. "Fiona Flippant was a hit partly because she

❖ 164 ❖

exposed the underbellies of society that fine society people did not want exposed, and yet, they could not get enough of it. It carved out an interest that our competitors couldn't touch. You'll start at five issues, and we will see from there."

Five issues as Fiona Flippant! Well, it's not why I came here, but it's certainly something. A start, a foot in the door. I've always marveled at Mum's writing, and while I've always thought I'd be rubbish at doing what she did, I have no choice but to give it my all.

Under all the wariness, I let a bubble of excitement to the surface. My own column. Not under my name, and not exactly what I thought of, but nonetheless, my words in ink. My thoughts on the page. My mother's legacy. I can only hope I do her justice.

I might fail, and spectacularly so. But I must try.

I hold out my hand. "I thank you for the opportunity, Mr. Elmhurst. When shall I begin?"

PART TWO

My dearest readers,

Did you miss me?

I think a break from the bustling streets of London has done me some good, and I have returned now with fresh eyes—and a sharper tongue—than ever before.

Pens at the ready.

Let us make some trouble.

—"Letters to Fiona Flippant"

May 1868

18

June 1868

The Fitzroy house called Enderly is the type of lavish property that makes one feel undeserving just looking at it.

I wander off from Livvie, Tess, and the servants, and find myself in an elegant sitting room. It's quite unlike the one at Kendall, and I think done to suit the late Mrs. Fitzroy's sterile tastes. The sofa is pale green. A vase rests on each side table, each holding a single rose. There's a back table for playing cards, and the soft white curtains are pushed aside to give the room a rather heavenly glow. While I always pestered Aunt Eleanor about her gaudy furnishings, the lack of color and comfort here is much uglier.

There's a bookcase, but the volumes look so clean and meticulously placed that I'm afraid to touch them. I hear Lady Tess chatting jovially in the hallway, so I settle on the couch and pray they won't find me. I'd be poor company anyway; I've been on pins and needles all day. Mr. Elmhurst put out the call for more Fiona Flippant reader letters in last week's paper. I should be excited, but seeing the ad was a little daunting. Under the letter I wrote announcing Flippant's return, the paper touted me as "a brutally honest and cheeky confidant with an inimitable voice." That's quite a lot to live up to, and my mother is a tough act to follow.

I want to pull my mother's old letters from my reticule, but I think of Livvie's voice as she once teased me. *You carry those as if they're a life-saving tonic,* she said, making me feel like a child dragging around a favorite blanket. But now that I've started writing as Fiona Flippant myself, I consider them to be research.

"You're plotting."

The unexpected sound of Nate's voice makes me jump, which makes him laugh, and I shove him as he makes his way to sit with me. "I'm not plotting! Can a lady not enjoy a peaceful moment alone?"

"Hmm." He's not impressed. Nate sits on the floor beside me, the same way he used to after convincing me to read him one of my stories, the same way we gathered at Mum's feet as she read to us from a book. He looks up at me now, light glinting off his brown eyes.

"I know you too well. That face"—he waves a hand before me—"is your plotting face."

"Plotting face?"

"Very serious wrinkled brow, tight lips . . ." As he describes these features, he acts them out on his own face. "Narrowed eyes, stiff jaw."

"This is my *thinking* face. You, however, look constipated."

He sputters a beautiful laugh, his forehead nearly colliding with my knee. A servant passes by and gives us a curious glance.

He rubs his eyes. "Plotting face does not suit me as prettily as you, it seems."

I bat my lashes and lean back like I'm going to faint. "Oh, Nathaniel, please! Compliments from such a fine young man are enough to bring on the vapors!"

"You should be an actress," he says. "You have a flair for the dramatic. Now. Tell me your plans for how we're escaping the dinner tonight."

A slow smile creeps up my face. I can't help it.

The servant passes by again, this time definitely looking our way. I think about what we look like. I'm lying back comfortably on the couch, and he's sitting next to me on the floor, his head propped up by a lazy fist, an elbow tucked into the cushions.

Perhaps this looks . . . bad. But I can't be bothered to move.

"I'm not plotting." I lower my voice then. "But if I was, let's imagine I've been peppering all of my conversations with Olivia and Mrs. Sinclair that I'm feeling a bit ill. You know, a tickle of the throat, a bit of a pain in my head."

He raises his brow. "An illness? Really?"

"I've been considering how far I want to take it. Do we have any plums?"

"You're allergic to plums."

+ 171 +

"Exactly! I think a good splash of vomit on Lady Tess's shoes might do."

He laughs. "That's the silliest thing I ever heard!"

"Well, you'll have to make up your own excuse. We can't both be sick."

"I just thought you'd have come up with something a little cleverer—like when I released Mrs. Ennis's chickens to get you and my sisters out of piano practice."

I narrow my eyes. "That was you?"

He opens his mouth, but only makes a little choking sound. "Did . . . Did I never admit that?"

"You had Gwen and me cleaning up feathers for days! They just kept showing up, under the cushions, in the food—"

"In Grandmother's wigs."

I laugh, and he joins in. Could it really be this easy? After years of silence and weeks of awkwardness, speaking to him is a skill I still possess. We fall into each other's presence with ease. I pull a pillow over my head. My words are muffled, so I only yell louder. "They were furious, and of course they blamed *us.* Your grandparents would never believe their perfect grandson could have committed such mischief!"

"Perfect grandson?" he scoffs. "Not in the least!"

"Oh, please, you're just as bad as stodgy Jane!"

I expect a quick retort—a mix of teasing and self-deprecation, but he's silent. I can't imagine I've actually cut him deep, but I pull the pillow from my face, worried he'll be upset with me. We've just started speaking again, and I hope I haven't ruined it.

But his face is turned toward the doors as he rises to his feet.

"Sweet Stella has returned," Jane Danvers says bluntly. She grins. "And where is Gwen to complete our troublemaking trio?"

Nathaniel answers her with a sweet hug. Over his shoulder, Jane winks at me. "Come on now, Stell. No love for stodgy Jane?"

I pull myself to my feet and take her spare hand. "It's not my fault you're so stodgy."

Thank God, she chuckles. Nate releases her, and she shakes her curls. Her entire outfit is crisp and elegant, from the delicate gold chain around her neck to her shimmering green satin dress. I wonder what she'll wear to dinner if she's been traveling in such finery.

She holds me at arm's length and inspects me up and down in a way that seems suitable for Lady Tess and Aunt Eleanor. She raises her brow a tick and merely lets out a soft *hmm*. "Well, you haven't changed a bit."

Her tone is familiar. It reminds me of how her grandmother used to compliment me in ways that I later realized were veiled insults. I was never as close to her as I was to her siblings.

She clasps my hand. "I'm going to freshen up. I'm excited for you all to meet my fiancé. He has such unique views on the world—I think even you'll be impressed, Stella. He's quite open to the changes of women in society, and even colored folks, too."

"A modern man!" I manage a thin smile. "I look forward to it."

She looks me over once more. "Are you wearing this?"

My mouth pops open. I close it quickly so as not to look like a hungry gull, as Aunt Eleanor would put it. I quite like my simple purple dress with the little frills at the hem. Sure, it's not as flashy as whatever Jane will be wearing, but I thought it was good enough.

Jane giggles. "Come, I have something you can wear. Nathaniel, entertain our guests while we get ready."

He nods, and leaves me without even an attempt at rescue! So I am pulled upstairs, under the careful eye of Jane Danvers.

"I look absurd!" I squeal.

Jane laughs as she adjusts my sleeves. "Stella, you are a *vision.*"

I blink, and the reflection in the mirror that is somehow *me* looks perturbed. She is wearing an elegant, soft pink dress of silk that is so delicate, I'm afraid to move in it. The bodice sits a touch lower than I've worn before, and though it's still *tasteful,* I feel foolish. I can't deny, my, well, my neck and collarbones have never quite looked so, er, nice?

Jane steps back to admire her work. The gloves are hers as well, as are the expensive shoes and pearl earrings. The only thing she did not change is my hair—I suspect she has no clue what to do with my coils—though she slipped on a silky headdress that even I have to admit adds a nice touch.

"I don't think I've ever worn such a nice dress," I say, smoothing my gloved hands over the fabric.

She slips on her own gloves. I am comforted at least by the fact that she is also so overdressed and made up. "I suppose I'll tell you now. I've invited a few more guests. It never hurts to make a fine first impression."

There's a knock at the door, but Gwen peeks inside before

either of us can answer. "What are you two getting up to—oh! Stella?"

I scoff. "Don't look at me like that!"

She turns into the hallway. I can hear Gwen's and Olivia's laughter, so keenly recognizable. "Gwendolyn, come and see!" Jane beckons.

Olivia squeals with delight and takes my hand. "You look like a princess, Stella!"

"Jane's hands can work miracles, apparently. We should get her to cure the sick posthaste."

Jane laughs. "Nonsense, the beauty was already there." She looks to Livvie. "You must be Miss Olivia Witherson, yes? I'm Jane Danvers."

"Pleasure to meet you, Miss Danvers!" Livvie is just thrilled. "I think tonight will be tremendous fun."

"Grandfather's opening a Bordeaux from his cellar, so I think it will be," Gwen quips as she adjusts her own hair.

Jane sighs impatiently, but hardly gets a moment to chide her. There's another knock on the door. "Jane?" says Nate, his voice unsure. "Have you captured all of our guests?"

"Come in!"

Slowly, he pushes the door open. "We're about ready. . . ."

He looks at us, but his voice trails off as he settles on me. I sigh. "*Don't.* I've already been thoroughly gaped at."

He blinks a few times, then catches himself. "Erm—"

"Shall we go?" Jane says quickly. She shoots Nate a curious look. "We can all continue admiring my handiwork later, yes?"

We file out one by one, Nathaniel stepping aside for us. As I follow the girls down the stairs, he settles behind me. "You look lovely. Truly, Stella."

I reach for the bannister—damn these shoes—but he offers his arm instead.

I grin. I felt foolish looking at myself before, but perhaps I judged too quickly. "Thank you, Nate." I take his arm.

His eyes glow at my casual use of his name. He dips his lips toward my ear. "So, no plums, then?"

I stifle a wheeze. "The night is young, so we'll see."

Over her shoulder, Jane looks back at us.

She smiles, but it doesn't quite reach her eyes. And she turns away.

19

As the guests file in, I understand that Lady Tess completely misunderstood what this dinner would be. Well, it's not a *large* party, but there are certainly more guests than I'd imagined. At least Jane warned me.

I spend about an hour's time curtsying to fine men and women whose names and titles I don't think I'll remember in a minute, much less during dinner. But for the first time since I've started attending such gatherings, I feel a little less out of place. These friends and colleagues of Mr. Fitzroy know my name and circumstances before meeting me, and my presence feels like less of a shock. That's not to say that Olivia and I are spared all mystified glances, but I imagine our treatment is more like Nathaniel's. We are all tolerated, at least.

"How do you keep all of the guests straight?" I mutter to Gwen.

She picks a skewered tomato from a server's tray. "I've known some of these families since I was a child. Or I bug Jane if I forget."

Growing up at Kendall Manor, I spent dinners in the servants' quarters with Mum, and so I never needed refined manners for entertaining this sort of crowd.

Olivia seems to be faring better. She's not a bit shy, and floats about the room with a soft sort of confidence that is attractive, rather than annoying. Mrs. Smith's lessons have done her well. I don't regret standing up for myself, but perhaps I should've paid more attention. "I'm starting to wonder if we're actually related," I say.

"She has many talents, but I see mingling is where her strength lies. But you have your talents, too."

I wait.

"Your wit!"

I roll my eyes playfully. "Say, what happened with those awful cousins of yours? The yellow-haired, snobbish ones?" I haven't seen them yet, but I have my guard up.

"Well, I think their hopes were dashed after my Aunt Etta could not convince Grandfather to give Kendall Manor to her side of the family. *Also*—" She drops her voice. "Apparently, my cousin Allison was caught consorting with some rake at a party. Aunt Etta had a fit and packed up for home."

I consider this for a moment. Allison was the girl who came in with that boy at Grantchester's ball in Duberney. I wonder how they were found out. Only Lord Grantchester and I had seen them, and he doesn't seem like the type to get involved in such gossip, and I said nothing about it to anyone. I'm relieved, either way.

Olivia strides toward us with Katherine Chen, who must have just arrived. Her hair is windswept, and she raises her hand to fix it.

"Let me," Gwen says, delicately tending to her strays.

Kitty lets her fumble for a minute, her head bowed patiently before Gwen. "Good evening, Stella."

"How are you, Kitty?"

"I'd be better if we weren't just caught in a swell!"

"Poor Kitty, caught in a swell," Gwen teases.

"I could have been injured!"

"At least you'd have an excuse to stay over." She eyes the room, unimpressed. "I'll need proper gossip time after this night is over." She shares a conspiratorial look with Kitty who smiles before turning away.

"I think the night has been quite enjoyable so far," Livvie says jovially.

A butler enters the sitting room to make an announcement. "Presenting Mr. Samuel Désir, and Mrs. Solange Désir."

Livvie's head snaps to the entranceway. "Oh, *hell.*"

Mr. Désir is impeccably dressed, as expected, though he's so handsome and stately that I imagine he'd look good in a pauper's rags. There's an older woman at his side. He's taller than she is, though the resemblance is clear. Her silky gold dress works magnificently against her dark brown skin.

The Désirs pull attention quickly. I poke Livvie in her side. "Are you just going to stand there?"

She sputters. "He's occupied!"

"I'm sure he's begging to be saved from all these opportunists wanting his father's favor with business in France. Who better to do the rescuing than the gorgeous girl he can't stop thinking of?"

I poke her again, and she jolts forward. "Quit it, Stell!"

She protests, but I pull her by the arm until we're on the fringes of the bubble surrounding Mr. Désir.

I clear my throat, not at all subtly.

Livvie raises a brow. "Are you okay?"

"I'm fine." I clear my throat again.

"You sound like you've swallowed one of Cheswick's fur balls."

I hack once more, now attracting the attention of Jane, who's been standing by the window with an older man. She waves me over, so I will have to obey. "Stay here. And drop your handkerchief or something!"

Livvie says something suspiciously close to a curse before elbowing me toward Jane.

The eldest Fitzroy heir holds her hand out to me, and I take it. "Stella, meet my fiancé, Adam Wright, the Viscount Amberlough."

I should be offered a great reward for managing to keep from gaping. I didn't think anything when I first saw them together, but now I can't stop seeing how *old* he is, at least in relation to Jane. He must be around Aunt Eleanor's age, and though I can't imagine pledging myself to anyone twice my age, I cannot deny that he is handsome. His silvery hair is coiffed neatly—sleek, like Jane's—and his face, seemingly carved by the skilled hands of a sculptor, wears its maturity well.

"Miss Sedgwick. Pleasure." He looks me up and down. "Aren't you a marvel?"

He says it like a compliment, but I feel discomfited by his eager gaze. I bow my head. "Is this your first time at Enderly, Lord Amberlough?"

"Yes, and I find it quite darling. I wonder how Jane survived such a small estate."

I laugh, and he chuckles, but I have the peculiar feeling that he is not jesting.

"Oh, finally!" Jane waves overhead. "Stella, there's someone I want you to meet."

Nate steps into the room, and I feel a little at ease. I lost him at some point, but here he is now with a familiar young man at his side.

Lord Grantchester's eyes widen at the sight of me. I try not to fidget, but it's hard when he looks so pleased to see me. His lips curl into a shy smile, and I'm happy to return it with one of my own.

He says, "Miss Sedgwick, how lovely to see you again."

"You've met?" Jane's voice is squeaky and high in a way I've never heard from her before.

I nod. "Yes, a few times."

Jane seems utterly thrilled, her shining eyes bouncing between us. "Well, how lovely! Where?"

"At the opera. We saw *Aurora*."

"Is that the one where the heroine poisons a small town

because they disapproved of her affair with the vicar?" Lord Wright asks.

Jane shakes her head. "What sort of drivel were you subjecting yourselves to?"

Somewhere behind me, the dinner bell is rung, and a server directs us to the dining room.

"Is your grandfather well?" I whisper to Nate. "I haven't seen him since we arrived."

He nods. "I was just tending to him."

"So that's where you'd gone!"

"As it turns out, a sick grandfather is a fantastic way to excuse oneself. No plotting necessary." He taps my hand. "He'll be here. You know how he loves an entrance. . . ." His voice trails off. "I hope you enjoy the meal."

On my other side, Grantchester presents his arm. I loop mine in his without thinking about it. How funny; something this simple would've felt foreign to me just a few weeks ago, and now it's the most natural thing in the world. This is good, I think. The more comfortable I become in rooms like this, the more authentic I'll sound playing at Fiona Flippant. He escorts me to the grand dining table where my name placard is placed between him and Olivia. Nate and Gwen are across from me, with Kitty on his side, and Mr. Désir on hers.

Lord Grantchester pulls out my chair. "I hope I didn't miss too much before I arrived."

"No, no, but Mr. Kingsley did show us all a rather interesting illustration of the train station being built up north. How exciting!"

❖ 182 ❖

"Exciting, indeed. But truthfully . . ." He takes his seat beside me, his arm just slightly brushing against mine. "I feel just as thrilled sitting here next to you."

The silliest, most *embarrassing* smile grows on my lips. Good lord, what am I, some blushing schoolgirl? I have to turn away from him, if only to keep myself from feeling more foolish, and he laughs, pleased by this reaction. "How kind of you to say so," I manage, still wearing a grin.

As the woman on Grantchester's right introduces herself to him, I glance across the far side of the table. My blood freezes. There's a man a few seats down from Olivia that I recognize, and my smile drops completely.

Under the table, I grasp Olivia's hand. "Livvie, is that not—"

She follows my gaze and gasps. "That horrible Mr. Royce?"

Next to her, Lady Tess gives me a nod of acknowledgment and a resigned sigh, as if to say, *You cannot make a scene.*

I lean back in my chair, biting back a groan. Across from me, Nate raises his brow, but Kitty says something that pulls his attention.

A part of me doesn't want to speak and potentially draw the attention of Royce, who is in the middle of his own conversation with several guests. It's a terrible feeling, and I mustn't give in. I look to Mr. Désir, who has finally broken from a conversation with a man attempting to goad him into investing in horse spurs. "And how do you find Enderly so far, Mr. Désir?"

Livvie jumps in her seat next to me, her ears likely burning with interest.

❖ 183 ❖

He seems grateful for the question. "I only wish I had more time to take in the country. I hear the rains of Enderly have a peaceful, restorative quality to them."

"Miss Sedgwick and Miss Witherson live in the country," Lady Tess interrupts, causing Olivia to make a sound like a cat whose tail's been tugged.

"Our home is not so grand as Enderly, though we have our comforts," I add. "Olivia here is quite the musician, and entertains us all day with the sweet sounds of the pianoforte. Does that not sound like a most agreeable time?"

I can almost feel the heat radiating from Livvie's face. Well, now she knows how I felt when Lady Tess pulled the same thing at the opera, inviting Lord Grantchester to Addyshire without a care!

Mr. Désir smiles sweetly. Finally, he looks to Olivia, and she raises her eyes to his. "It does indeed."

A servant arrives and announces the presence of Thomas Fitzroy.

We stand to greet him. An entrance indeed; Mr. Fitzroy slowly makes his way into the room. He seems to stand so stately and tall, even while leaning on a black lacquered cane for support.

Gwen, ignoring decorum, runs for him. It's sweet, but Mr. Fitzroy only brushes her cheek and waves her away. "Gwendolyn, always ready to pick up her grandpa should he fall on his face."

There's laughter, and we take to our seats. Finally, the room fills up with the smells of roasted birds and baked vegetables.

Not my favorite, though my mother taught me to never complain about having food in front of me. What I'd really like is a heaping plate of my mum's roasted goat stew, seasoned with pungent spices she used to haggle for at the market in Addyshire.

As I take delicate spoonfuls of soup, I get that distinct, unsettling feeling of being watched. There's a couple at the end of the table eyeing me. I think Gwen said they were friends of Jane's fiancé. The woman's neck is adorned with jewels. They sparkle in the candlelight as she leans toward her husband and whispers in his ear. I'm not sure what she's saying, but I've been stared at like *that* enough times to know that it's, at best, confused or, at worst, utterly insulting.

"Shall we go into the drawing room?" Jane says after the last dishes are pulled away, more of a proclamation than a question. "Before we leave the men to their cigars and brandy, I know my grandfather would love to hear a bit of music."

I laugh along with a few others, those that have spent enough time with Mr. Fitzroy to know that he despises music.

"Would I?" he grumbles, just loud enough for us to hear.

"Are you going to play, Jane?" Nathaniel asks playfully.

"Actually, I was hoping that Stella would."

I nearly choke. "Oh, no, I couldn't, not unless you all wanted to leave with sore ears."

There are a few chuckles, but Jane insists. "Come now, it's not a party without dancing."

I nod toward Olivia. "My cousin is the talent, not I—"

"Don't be ridiculous! You were taught with me at Kendall,

and Mrs. Marstock was a great teacher. Go on."

I don't know why she won't leave it, but seeing as I already crossed into rudeness by refusing the first time, I don't really have a choice here. As the dinner party makes its way into the sitting room, I consider my options.

I could make myself vomit, though I don't want turtle soup ruined for me for eternity. Or I could claim a hand cramp; actually, I think I might just make a run for it out into the night—

Bah. Reluctantly, I go to the pianoforte and place my fingers on the keys. I begin a poor impression of an English worship song that Mrs. Smith taught us. It's too slow, and I have to correct a few notes, but at least it's a semblance of music?

Thankfully, Nathaniel asks Gwen to dance, and the party's attention drifts into little pockets of conversation.

Slowly, Olivia slides onto the bench next to me. She puts her fingers to the keys, and I drop mine into my lap. She's skillful at taking the song to its proper tempo, its proper notes. "Imagine my mother's face if she saw this!" she teases.

I groan. "She'd be well and smug—*do you see why a lady must attend her lessons!* How embarrassing. You mustn't tell her a thing."

"Where's the fun in that?"

I flick her fingers, and she laughs briefly, the moment interrupted by the presence of Mr. Royce.

He clears his throat. "Good evening, then."

Olivia nods. "Good evening, sir."

He looks her over. "Miss Sedgwick. I wanted to offer an apology for our . . . misunderstanding last month—"

"I think you mean to be addressing me, sir," I interject, my blood growing hot. Olivia and I look nothing alike, this is just absurd!

He looks to me, then to Olivia, and makes a waving motion with his hand, already bored with this.

I can feel Jane hovering, her back to us in a circle of chatting guests, but her head tilted ever so slightly in our direction.

I smile pleasantly. "You may keep your apology, Mr. Royce, for I was not hurt by your words. After all, is a wolf wounded when a lamb bleats in her direction?"

He jolts as if I've slapped him. "Be *civil*—"

"Civil? I imagine you hold a very different meaning of civil behavior than I do. Truthfully, I'd like to see you thrown out of two parties. Mr. Fitzroy would—"

"No. I don't think he would."

I pause. It's well struck because, truly, he's right. Mr. Fitzroy might have done right by my mother and myself, but it would be too much to claim him as any sort of ally. He did invite Mr. Royce, after all. The two of them are friends, and that says enough.

I concede a shrug. We are quiet enough under the sound of the conversations around the room, and I keep my voice level despite my growing agitation. "Well, I only mean to say that you are not forgiven, because you have not hurt me, because you never could hurt me. I don't find myself offended by the views of a man who means nothing to me. Enjoy your evening."

I rise from the piano, and Olivia rises with me. We leave him in search of kinder company.

"Was that too much?" I whisper to Olivia.

She shakes her head, but I catch the nervous flicker of her eyes, which confirms that it indeed was.

I find Gwen, Kitty, Nate, and Mr. Désir milling by the fire, but I feel a gentle touch at my elbow first.

It's Jane. "Stella, could I steal a moment? Out here." She leads me away from the party and into the foyer. "It can get so warm and loud in there. I needed a breath. Have you been enjoying yourself?"

I force a smile. "I have, thank you Jane."

"I'm thrilled to hear it. Well, I just wanted to remind you of how happy I am to see that Kendall Manor will be going into the hands of someone my family knows and loves."

She's sweet enough, but I keep silent. Something tells me that this conversation won't be so simple or so pleasant.

She smooths back a loose strand of hair. "I'm impressed with how well you've adjusted to society—only, might I offer some advice?"

She steps closer, and pushes back my own loose curl. It doesn't obey like hers does.

"I couldn't help but hear your conversation with Mr. Royce," she says, as if she wasn't craning her neck to hear us. "You shouldn't be so unpleasant to guests, even if you aren't fond of them. Dare I say, you were awfully rude to Mr. Royce just now. I wish you'd be more agreeable tonight."

✤ 188 ✤

I swallow hard. "*I* was rude?"

"As I understand it, he was only offering an apology for what had transpired in London."

"No, he began by apologizing to Livvie, because apparently telling us apart would be too much effort for the man. And what, pray tell, had transpired in London? Because he said something similarly vague about a *misunderstanding*. No mention of the ugly words he said to me, no regret for insulting me specifically."

"I only mean to say that you could stand to be a bit kinder. It's a party, Stella, likely my grandfather's last." I bite back a retort. She takes my hesitation as understanding, and places a gloved hand on mine. "And you'll never catch a man like Lord Grantchester with such a temper."

I pull my hand away. "I've no desire to."

Her birdlike little face furrows with concern. "Oh? Then how will you keep Kendall?"

I part my lips, but can't think of a damned thing to say that doesn't make me sound foolish.

"Stella, it will be . . . difficult to keep Kendall under your name, no matter what Grandfather has in his will."

"I know, yes, Mr. Adams explained it to me."

"Oh, good, because it belongs to Nathaniel, really. Well, I'm sure he wouldn't be opposed to your living there, but . . ."

She doesn't have to complete her sentence. Jane Danvers knows that my pride is my eternal vice. That I'd be no more than a burden to Nathaniel's kindness makes my stomach turn. In the end, I'd have nothing, really.

Speak of the devil; Nathaniel appears, peeking into the foyer. "There you two are. Conspiring, of course."

His words fall to silence. Jane turns to smile at him. I'm reminded of her face earlier as she watched Nate and me come down the stars, or when Nathaniel appeared with Grantchester at his side. It's a well-practiced smile, but hints at displeasure.

Watching her now, it's like a lock has clicked into place.

"Just a moment longer, Nathaniel," she says. "If you don't mind."

His brow rises when he glances at me, but he leaves us.

Jane sighs. "I know society living is difficult when you're new to it, but do you understand now? Marry before Grandfather passes, or your claim to Kendall will be even weaker than it is now."

I sigh myself, a bit exaggeratedly. "Well, I suppose I could always marry your brother."

There.

Jane's jaw sets, which is as much a passionate emotion as you'll ever get from her. "Nathaniel is as good as engaged."

I laugh again, and touch her hand. "Oh, but I'm only joking! Silly, indeed—could you imagine such a thing? And we both know that Fitzroy has no such love for me, and I'm hardly looking to marry anyone at all."

We fall into a brief but tense silence. When Jane smiles once more, I know I've hit the mark; Jane is worried that I'm after Nathaniel! A ludicrous assumption, and yet it stings a little bit that she does not see me as good enough for him, as much as I wish it didn't.

✦ 190 ✦

"I've kept you for too long," she says finally. "The party will be missing us."

Jane doesn't wait for me to walk with her, so I'm left to follow, feeling a little like a child in school who'd been taken to task for misbehaving. She returns to her fiancé's side, not sparing a look for Nate, who's leaning against the doorframe.

"Stodgy Jane," he whispers.

I look up at him. "No fun at all."

He only half smiles. His mind seems far away, but he keeps his eyes locked on mine. "Stella, I wanted to ask you something. When you're in Paris with your cousin—"

"*A toast!*"

We turn to the center of the room, where Jane's geriatric fiancé is lifting his glass. "A toast to Thomas Fitzroy, and many blessings on him. And to the Fitzroy family for letting us into their lovely home and me into their lovely hearts." He looks to Jane, eyes yearning.

Delicately, she touches her reddening cheeks. "And to our ever-growing family." She turns to me . . . just before extending a hand to Kitty.

I lean toward Nate. "What were you saying? About Paris?"

He swallows, parts his lips to speak, but there's Jane, waving him over to stand with her and with Gwen. He clears his throat. "I hope you'll have a lovely time, that's all."

He leaves me. Olivia stands with the Désirs, beaming and laughing sweetly. Lady Tess and Grantchester are chattering with friends, and though I could join them, I feel so alone in this moment. After Royce's cruel insult at the party, I'd felt a sense of resolve and determination. But now I only feel cut down.

Nathaniel and Gwen are already in this life. Olivia has one foot in it. And I am so far from the starting line, I'm beginning to wonder if it's worth the effort.

20

I wish I were in Addyshire.

My conversation with Jane at last night's dinner has shaken my ground. I woke feeling homesick, missing sounds of the farm in the morning—Chapman and Townsend chatting in thick country accents as they tend to the animals, chickens squawking, Aunt Eleanor's whistling while kneading dough for fresh bread. I even miss that rascal Cheswick! Meanwhile, Olivia is *prancing* around Lady Tess's sitting room. Though she woke the moment the slimmest stream of sunlight hit her eyes, she's got more energy than Cheswick in one of his excitable fits. It's Lady Tess's fault; she's just told us that the trip to Paris has been settled with the Désirs.

"Paris!" Olivia says once more. "Oh, I can't wait!"

Lady Tess shoots me a pleased look from the armchair in the

corner. Olivia twirls toward her, narrowly missing her teacup. "Easy, my dear!"

"*Ah!*" She plops next to me.

"Now look what you've done!" I exclaim. "My stitches are ruined."

She inspects my embroidery circle. "Stella, those stitches have looked like that for the past hour."

"Well, sure, but all your trouncing about isn't helping. Look at my poor rose. It's wilting now."

"Rose?" She furrows her brow. "S'that what that is? I thought it was a dying red ferret."

Lady Tess laughs, and I drop the circle into my lap. "Will you tell her she's being much too excited about a man she hardly knows?"

"Let her have her fun," Lady Tess replies. "And, Stella, are you going to read my father's notes, or not?"

She gestures to the envelope waiting on the coffee table before me. Just the sight of it makes my palms sweat.

"I'm working on my stitches," I reply.

"Did I hear that correctly?" Lady Tess says, looking up from her own needlework. "You're ignoring correspondence from my father, whom you begged me for an introduction to, in favor of needlepoint?"

She's right, and I know I'm being ridiculous. However, the concept of writing for *State of London* is a little less exciting when met with the prospect of *editorial feedback*. Mr. Elmhurst thought it might be a good idea to have me answer some old letters as practice while we wait for new submissions. It was more fun than I'd expected, actually. I can see why mother enjoyed it so. But self-doubt insists on rearing its ugly head, and now I wonder if I was wrong to tell the arrogant Green-Eyed Gallant that he was, in fact, an arse for poaching his neighbor's best footman—and his daughter for a bride.

Olivia picks up the letter and waves it in front of me. "Come now, he hired you, didn't he?"

"Yes, but out of love for my mother's work, not mine."

"I don't think a man as busy as Mr. Elmhurst would waste any time with you if he didn't see something he liked in your samples."

"Very true," Lady Tess adds. "My father may look intimidating, but he does enjoy fostering new talent. If you're serious about writing, you'll need to get accustomed to feedback, no matter how critical."

"All right, all right." I take the letter from Olivia and rip it open quickly, before I have a chance to lose my nerve. It's the same responses I wrote, but covered in strikethroughs and corrections. Hell, the whole thing is marked up in red ink! "He hates it!"

Olivia leans over my shoulder to see. "Please—Stella, he's just made some suggestions."

"'Too harsh . . . more of a disapproving governess than a loyal confidant.'" My frown falls into an ugly grimace. "Mr. Elmhurst's suggestions take all of the bite out of my answers. It doesn't even feel like my voice anymore—"

"Isn't it meant to be Fiona Flippant's voice?" she replies gently.

I groan. Well, she does have a point. Looking over his notes

❖   195   ❖

once more, I suppose I can see how my advice comes out as judgmental. Mr. Elmhurst thinks my *severe tone undercuts the wittiness*, and these columns always used humor to charm readers. I brace myself against the self-doubt and read the notes again, this time trying to keep from reacting with despair at every red mark. He doesn't say what he likes about my writing, but seeing as there's no mention of my immediate termination, I suppose I'm safe for now.

I slap the papers against my knees. "Well, I should get to revising. I'd like to show Mr. Elmhurst that I can handle a little criticism."

Olivia grasps my shoulder suddenly. Her arm is outstretched with a finger pointing to the window behind Lady Tess. "Was that not Lord Grantchester walking across the street?"

He's gone before I can see him through the window, but when the doorbell sounds, well . . . My heart *stutters*.

Lady Tess straightens her hat, and even I cannot resist smoothing out my dress and my hair.

Lord Grantchester appears beside a footman. He greets me with a grin and removes his hat as he bows his head. "Good afternoon, ladies. Mrs. Sinclair. I hope I'm not interrupting."

I curtsy, hands clasped nicely, the way Olivia does it. "Lord Grantchester, to what do we owe the pleasure?"

"I was hoping you might accompany me for a walk, Miss Sedgwick, if you aren't already preoccupied."

"She isn't!" Lady Tess answers quickly.

I'm a little flustered, but manage to nod. "Yes, that would be lovely."

❖ 196 ❖

Lady Tess's and Olivia's faces are plastered to the window as Lord Grantchester escorts me down the steps of the town house, my hand in his.

The city is busy, but the feel of Lord Grantchester's arm in mine keeps me grounded in his presence as he chats about the sights. He seems to know the history of every building and street in the city. I like the way he turns to me every few moments, as if checking that I'm still by his side. Two servants—a man and a woman—trail after us with enough space that I don't feel hovered over, but close enough to keep an eye on us both.

"I wish we'd done this earlier, I've nearly gotten lost a hundred times," I say.

He laughs. It's a lovely sound, and widens the smile on my own lips.

In the park, he directs me to a bench overlooking the river. "I used to visit this park all the time as a child when my father came into the city on business. I drove my governess mad chasing pigeons all around the park."

"Oh, I wish I had such adorable childhood hobbies. Instead, I was writing nosy little stories about every person who passed."

He points to a trio of refined ladies chattering excitedly. "What would you say of them?"

"I assume a law has just been passed to make wearing crinolines illegal. Why else would they look happy?"

It's a joke that toes the line of impropriety, but one that amuses Grantchester greatly. I don't remember us sitting so closely, but we're practically in each other's lap with laughter.

Grantchester composes himself and points out a man. "And what about this fellow—"

He cuts his sentence short, finger still lifted.

The man nods at us. He eyes Lord Grantchester with a strange expression. It doesn't seem friendly at all.

The sight of this man changes Grantchester's mood. He gives me an apologetic look. "I must ask for your forgiveness, Miss Sedgwick."

"Whatever for?"

"That man was an acquaintance of my father's, but did wrong by him time and time again. I've ignored his correspondence thus far, but I should stop avoiding him and be done with it." He sighs deeply. "I'll only be a moment, I swear."

"Take all the time you need! Really, it's no problem at all. I'll enjoy the weather in the meantime."

He gestures toward his female servant. "Mrs. Crowe will watch over you while I'm gone."

Mrs. Crowe looks like she'd rather do anything but, actually. I nod in thanks.

He leaves me then. I people-watch for a few minutes before I notice an older woman with a friendly face and neat brown hair. I know her, no need for a double take. She hasn't changed much since I saw her last, though her clothes are nicer, and her pale face further lined. It's poor manners, but I can't resist standing and calling out, "Mrs. Marstock?"

The woman turns. It takes her a moment to recognize me after all this time, but I know instantly that I'm not mistaken.

"Miss Sedgwick?" She looks me up and down as she walks

toward me. "Oh, Stella!" She hugs me gently, then catches herself as if this was a mistake, though I'm not uncomfortable with it in the least. "Dearie, you're all grown up! What are you doing in London?"

I sputter a laugh, because I hardly even know anymore. "I was actually at Kendall a few weeks ago, and was surprised to not see you there."

"Yes, well, I've moved into a fine household just south of here. I'm here visiting my daughter, that's all—she's just had a baby." She lifts the packages she's carrying. "I'm spoiling the child already."

My heart warms. "Many congratulations!"

We chat for a while, and it's oddly comforting to speak with someone from my past life who isn't a Fitzroy or Danvers. I enjoy the stories she tells of Mother and me, and how she cared for me while we lived together in a home that wasn't ours.

Mrs. Marstock takes my hand. "I'm thrilled to see you doing so well. You've really grown into a fine young lady."

That's certainly the first time I've heard *that*. "Thank you, it's been lovely to see you as well. And, really, the new staff can't hold a candle to you."

She pats my hand twice. "You know, I did stand behind your mother when I could. It was a difficult time for all of us, and I hope you bear me no ill will."

My shoulders tighten. "My mother? What do you mean? And why would I ever think poorly of you?"

She hesitates. "Did she not tell you why she left Kendall Manor?"

❖ 199 ❖

The image of Mr. Fitzroy stuttering about my mother in his bed returns to me. I'd forgotten it, brushed it off as a dying man's ramblings. Perhaps I was wrong. "I . . . No, well, she simply said my aunt Eleanor needed some company, and help with my cousin. . . . Mrs. Marstock, what are you saying?"

She wrings her hands. "If your mother didn't tell you, I don't know if it's my place, lass."

"My mother is dead now. She can't tell me what happened, but you can."

Mrs. Marstock tries to look away from me once more, but I step into her line of vision so she doesn't have a choice.

"Please, Mrs. Marstock. If you're going to ask for my forgiveness, at least let me know what the slight was."

She lowers her voice, though Mrs. Crowe is hardly paying us any attention. "Between you and me, I don't think she was the one to take the ring. Ginny wasn't the sort to go round nicking things. I should've tried harder to convince the missus of that."

My face heats up. "What ring?"

"It was a beautiful emerald, and so precious to the lady, an heirloom passed down from her forefathers. Anyway, one day it went missing from her jewelry chest, and somehow she had it in her mind that it was Ginny who'd taken it." She squeezes my hand. "I swear I told Mrs. Fitzroy that it couldn't be Ginny. Your mother was nothing but good to all of us, even the staff treated her poorly out of their own prejudice. But Mrs. Fitzroy wouldn't hear it, and the other servants turned on her lest they be suspected in her stead. It was horrible, Stella, and if you don't mind me saying it, I'm very happy that you do not remember it."

✦ 200 ✦

I shake my head. "No, I don't." My eyes are heavy. The very thought of my mother being so mistreated makes me want to weep.

"The missus found the ring lodged between two couch cushions a month or two after you both left. Of course, she made no effort to apologize. Simply slipped it back onto her finger as if nothing had happened."

I take a deep breath to ground myself. How is it that neither Lady Tess nor Aunt Eleanor have told me about this? This ring—heavens, is *that* the reason I'm here in London? A lost ring and a false accusation stoked Mr. Fitzroy's guilt so fully that he's chosen to bestow a fortune on me? He'd called her Ginny. Said he should've protected her. Since he cannot do that, he's decided to rectify his guilt with me?

Mrs. Marstock tries to smile, but it comes off as a little sad. "It's nothing to fret over now." She glances over my head. "I think your companion is getting impatient."

I look over my shoulder, and there's Lord Grantchester walking toward us.

"Well, he's awfully handsome," she says, impressed.

I grin. "He is, isn't he?"

He looks at Mrs. Marstock warmly. "Good afternoon."

"Lord Grantchester, this is Mrs. Annie Marstock" I say. "She used to work in Kendall Manor."

I can see that Mrs. Marstock is stuck on his name. "My pleasure," she manages. "I must take my leave, but, Stella—" She clasps my hands. "Do take care. And give Nathaniel and the girls a good tug on the ear when you see them next."

❖ 201 ❖

I laugh. "Yes, absolutely."

She nods shyly at Lord Grantchester before leaving us.

"Are you used to that?" I ask plainly.

He lifts a brow.

"The shock when someone recognizes your name. You must notice it!" I add that last part quickly, because he seemed about ready to deny it.

With a small smirk, he shakes his head. "Miss Sedgwick, you always speak so openly. I wonder if that wicked tongue has landed you in trouble."

I flash him a smirk of my own. "Only a few times."

We set back for Lady Tess's town house.

While my mind is still trying to process my conversation with Mrs. Marstock, I must not be rude to Lord Grantchester. He still looks taken aback by the sight of his father's associate in the park. "I hope that conversation wasn't too hard for you," I say gently.

He chuckles, but there's little humor in it. "It's a boring tale. My uncle has some gambling debts, and my father attempted to pay them all off before passing. But with every account settled, another debtor appeared out of thin air. There was a day my mother and sister were accosted by a man in Liverpool. It was an ugly affair. We had to call on a solicitor."

It's nice to know that Lord Grantchester does have some worries in what looks like such a polished life, and I do sympathize, but these are awfully . . . *genteel-people problems*. Then again, perhaps this conversation might be good knowledge to have for a future Flippant column.

It takes a flicker of sunlight on his bare, smooth face to remind me that he's really just a young man, and one who's just lost his father, at that. "If you get run out of Grantchester, you can always visit us in Addyshire."

He chuckles, truly now. "I might have to take you up on that."

When we arrive at the town house, Lady Tess and Olivia are no longer waiting by the windows, thank heavens. "It was very good to see you, Lord Grantchester. I appreciate you for thinking of me."

This pleases him. Grantchester touches his fingers to my wrist. "I actually have another reason for calling upon you. Erm, I was hoping . . ."

He goes on, but I'm distracted by Lord Grantchester's footman. He's watching us from a respectable distance, but I can't help but notice how his scowl deepened at the touch. How he looks at me, dark eyes under a dark brow, white skin flushed in what I think could be shame. Or anger? Am I making this up? I'm so sick of the *stares*—

". . . if you'd find that agreeable—Miss Sedgwick?"

I refocus. "Hmm?"

"Grantchester. Would you like to visit Eastwick Abbey? My estate is but three hours' carriage ride from here."

"Oh!" I can't hide my shock. "That's . . . Well, I wouldn't want to put you out—"

"You would never, Miss Sedgwick. It would be my honor to host you."

Lord Grantchester is certainly fond of that small, sweet, dimply smile. In spite of myself, I am growing fond of it as well.

"I would love to," I say. "Will Gwen and Nathaniel join?"

His brow twitches. "Oh, er—yes! I shall extend the invitation to our dear Fitzroys—though Jane is likely occupied, as I imagine. Please do invite Miss Witherson, and I'm sure Mrs. Sinclair will want to chaperone."

"I'm sure she will be just as thrilled as I am with the invita—"

My voice cuts off, for he's taken my bare hand in his and brought it to his lips. It's nothing. A kiss on the hand; he's done it before. But it feels awfully intimate, so much so that I feel my face going warm.

"Good day, Miss Sedgwick."

"Good day, Lord Grantchester."

My hand still feels warm from his touch as I push through Lady Tess's flat and find myself nearly barreling into her and Olivia.

They're both attempting casualness, but I can picture them with their ears pressed against the door. "Have some dignity, ladies!" I reprimand them on my way to the sitting room.

Lady Tess is bubbling with excitement, and thus begins a barrage of questions and excited babbles that I have to shout over. "Listen, I ran into Mrs. Marstock. She used to work with Mum at Kendall Manor."

Livvie says something about how that must have been nice, but I'm paying much more attention to Lady Tess's reaction. Silently, she drops her gaze, sits back in the sofa across from us, and immediately straightens the tea cozy on the side table next to her.

"Mrs. Sinclair, you told me that Mum left the Fitzroys to

be with Aunt Eleanor, but Mrs. Marstock mentioned something about a ring that belonged to Mrs. Fitzroy. She said my mother was accused of stealing it. And when I saw Mr. Fitzroy last month, he'd started rambling on about *making things up to Ginny.*"

"Is that why he's put you in his will?" Olivia asks curiously, her gaze flitting between Lady Tess and me.

I shrug. "It must be. Honestly, at the time I thought he was just having a lapse, so I didn't think to ask him about it further—"

"And you must keep it that way," Lady Tess says curtly. "Best not to go dredging up old trouble."

"But—"

"And I don't want to hear of this again," she warns. "It's not your place."

My retort dies in my throat. Lady Tess generally doesn't get so firm with us. Perhaps she has a point. Whatever happened, my mother and Mrs. Fitzroy have both passed on. Old trouble, as Lady Tess called it, can't do any good. But forgetting it is easier said than done. I struggle to push back the nagging curiosity. I could send a letter to Aunt Eleanor, but I have a feeling she'd react similarly. The two of them think I'm old enough to look for a husband, but they still try to coddle me. The only others who might know anything about this are Fitzroys; I could ask Nate and Gwen. Oh, and that reminds me—

"There is one last thing." I brace myself for the surely oncoming squeals. "Lord Grantchester's invited us to his estate!" I can barely say it without laughing.

Olivia grins. "Well, what's so funny?"

"Not funny, just . . . strange." I touch my face, still warm.

Heavens, I can no longer deny the little voice that has been growing and growing since he asked me to dance at Trinity Hall.

Lord Grantchester is courting me.

Eastwick Abbey

Though I have always considered the Withersons to be comfortable and the Fitzroys to be wealthy, I realize with one look at Eastwick Abbey that there is a division of wealth that I have never even imagined.

"It's a *castle*," I blurt out. I'm so dazed by the estate that I nearly miss the earl himself holding out his hand as I step out of the carriage.

He's quick and slips his hand under my elbow. "Is it too much?"

I don't know what to say. I count four stories of stucco, capped at the top by a lovely balcony. The garden terrace leading to the front doors is a marvel of its own, brimming with delicate rosebushes and pale trees, not to mention the acres and acres of rolling hills in the distance. I wonder if Lord Grantchester ever wakes up unsettled, or angry, or even just slightly annoyed—how could you ever find a thing wrong with life when waking up to *this*? Admittedly, my fascination isn't all admiration. It's no secret that a family who has acquired such wealth has done so by partaking in *trade*. Shipping. Importing and exporting goods. Labor done by enslaved hands. A man like Lord Grantchester can likely trace his ancestors back generations. I cannot. I do not even know my great-grandfather's name. I'm trying to remember how lucky I am, but all I can think of is how unfair the world is for me and for mine.

Does Fitzroy ever consider this, I wonder? What it means to have his inheritance? I'm sure the Fitzroy line made their generations of wealth in the same way. I hardly know how I feel about Kendall myself—is it shameful to reap the benefits of money made from the backs of our tortured ancestors, or satisfying to have broken the lily-white line of inheritors? The thought leaves a sour taste in my mouth.

I see the castle before me, and I wonder if there are ghosts.

I still can't think of a proper response. I sputter, "What do you do with—with, oh, *all the rooms*? Like that one—" I point to the uppermost corner of the castle, where there's a window dressed in yellow curtains.

"That's the reading room. Well, one of them."

I blink. "And that one?"

"Ah, my mother's rooms, empty now as she's on holiday with my aunts and my sister, but really—" He gestures vaguely toward the east side of the castle. "All that's hers. That bit's my sister's, and then there's mine—"

"Of course, you have your own wing. You'd get so bored

lounging in the sitting room all day."

He scrubs the back of his neck. "It's a bit much."

"It's lovely, really," I manage. "But it must be lonely when your family's not in."

"Much of the time we're entertaining visitors, and when we're not—well, there's a reason I spend so much time in London chasing after Fitzroy and criticizing his poor decisions."

"Oh?" I turn to find Nathaniel descending from the carriage he shared with Gwen, shaking out his perfect brown curls. "There's a story I'd like to hear."

Lord Grantchester leads us through the front doors, held open by two finely dressed footmen. The estate holds even more riches than I'd imagined. The rooms are one thing, but the furnishings, the statues, the fine art! He practically lives in a museum, and Lady Tess and Olivia are consummate tourists, nudging him with questions as we go. By the time we enter the third sitting room, I'm nearly out of breath.

"It gets old eventually," Nathaniel jokes, giving Lord Grantchester's shoulders a little shake.

"I doubt that," Gwen quips, eyeing the crystalline chandelier above us.

Grantchester's blushing. "Lunch will be served shortly. Then I was hoping you'd all be up for a tour of the gardens. I'll have the stableman ready the horses." He turns to me. "Would you enjoy that?"

I manage a wry smile. "Yes, that sounds lovely."

Olivia lifts a brow because she knows what I'm thinking.

Oh, blasted *horses*.

* * *

"What magnificent creatures!" I say between a tight smile of clenched teeth. "They're just so . . . *enormous!*"

Next to me, Livvie chuckles. She knows as well as anyone how I despise the beasts.

"He won't bite," she sings, taking the reins from the stable hand.

The horse shakes its head suddenly, and I jolt out of the way, holding my hat as I go.

"I think he can smell fear," Gwen teases.

As I inspect the remaining steeds, Nathaniel and Lord Grantchester are already atop theirs, trotting around in circles.

As lovely as a ride through the gorgeous Eastwick grounds sounds, I do not *do* horses. But today has been quite lovely so far. Lord Grantchester seems determined to ensure that I'm enjoying myself and has remained rather close to my side. He really is charming, and I never feel like he's just waiting for his turn to speak when we're in conversation. In fact, he's such a good listener that he had his cooks prepare an unconventional snack of maple-cured bacon with our tea. I'll have to thank them for the trouble. I didn't think Lord Grantchester would've remembered that conversation we had near the end of the dinner party at Enderly, where'd I'd lamented over my aunt's home cooking.

Fitzroy approaches, Lord Grantchester in tow. Nathaniel's wearing a twin smile to Gwen's. "Come now, Stella, you used to love horse riding at Kendall."

I lift a finger. "Yes, well, that was when I was young and fearless."

He laughs. "All right, I suppose you can ride with me."

Lord Grantchester gives him a pointed look. "Or perhaps Miss Sedgwick can accompany me."

I look at Nate, my eyes moving on their own. His smile has gone tight. "Yes, but which of us has been riding since we were just a boy? I think Stella would be more comfortable with a rider who's more experienced."

I look back to Grantchester, Gwen's and Livvie's eyes following. Thank goodness Lady Tess is suffering from a sinus headache—the country pollen does not agree with her—for she would've dropped me into Grantchester's arms herself.

"Well, aren't you both fine gentlemen!" With an unsteady hand, I reach for the reins from the stable hand. "But I think I can manage it on my own."

"Well done," Gwen whispers. "Up you go."

Lord Grantchester trots toward me on his own steed. "Morris, lead the others," he says to the stable hand. "I'll stay back with Miss Sedgwick."

I exhale. "That is very kind of you, but you needn't trouble yourself."

He must see right through my attempt at a cool facade; admittedly, it's hard to even keep my voice steady when I'm bracing to be bucked from this horse at any moment. "It's not a problem, I can go riding at any time. I wouldn't want you to feel uncomfortable. Anyway, this is Berry; she's the sweetest of the pack."

I think Berry smells like a barn, but it's hard to not feel at least a little comforted by Lord Grantchester's dimply smile as he rides alongside me, close enough so that he could take Berry's reins if needed. He's like a prince out of the storybooks

Mum used to read for us. The swooping blond hair, the perfect politeness, the easy handsomeness—not too striking, though certainly admirable. As he shoots me a reassuring smile, I wonder how I've found myself being courted by an earl. Well, yes, I am wickedly funny. I do think I hold a conversation well, and perhaps I'm rotten with a needle and thread, but I'm witty. And though this country and its genteel society are trying their very best to convince me and others that there is no beauty in dark skin, *I don't believe them.*

Still. Still. I know a family like Grantchester's would never think to bind their wealthy heir to a dark-skinned girl who spent the whole of last year learning to be a servant to his kind. There are plenty of wealthy, high-society girls in London. So what could it be?

I know what Olivia would say, what Lady Tess would say, what Gwen would say. *Maybe he just fancies you.* Could it be that simple? I shall try to be less pessimistic, and more accepting of his attention.

We ride on a path up to a hill overlooking the grounds. From here, the massive castle looks even more elegant, and imposing.

"This view is gorgeous," Gwen says before dismounting. "And here I was pitying you for the seclusion, dear Grantchester. Think I'd miss the bustle of the city, though—there's no fun to be had here all alone."

"Oh, it's just all right," Fitzroy says over his shoulder. He's standing at the top of the hill, looking out at the perfect view. His tone is playful. "I might argue that the view of the lake across Enderly is a much prettier sight."

Grantchester claps a hand on Nate's shoulders. "Now, now, as if Enderly could compare to an entire apple orchard."

"But you haven't seen Enderly in the winter. Snowfall makes it look like a scene out of a painting. Tell him, Stella."

I exhale a laugh. I look to Olivia, who's too genuinely enamored by the view to be of any help. "It really is lovely, Lord Grantchester. So tranquil."

Together, the five of us set the quilt. Grantchester's attendants are fussy, but he shoos them away to do his own arrangement of the food and drink, even taking the time to pour us all a bit of watered wine.

We're well through our cups when Gwen clears her throat in a way that I already know means trouble.

"I want to play a game," she says with all the brash confidence she possesses without the added spirits. "We shall go around the circle, and everyone will say two fibs and one truth about themselves, and it'll be up to one of us to guess what is true."

Gwen and her games. "Can't we just play whist?" I ask.

She ignores me. "I'll begin. One—I am terrified of birds—"

"That's true," Nathaniel interrupts, to Gwen's displeasure.

"But you're supposed to let me finish! And you can't answer, you know me too well. Let it be Miss Witherson who guesses."

"Everyone knows about the day you were attacked by seagulls in Brighton, Gwen."

I sputter a laugh. "Oh yes, you'd gotten the damned thing's feet caught in your hair!"

She shakes her head. "Never mind. Olivia, you go, I'll guess, and, Stella, please don't spoil it."

Livvie's wearing a barely noticeable blush—I can't tell if it's from the drink or because she knows this is a game her mother would find unladylike to participate in. "Well, let me think. . . . Okay. One, I cannot whistle, even if my life depended on it. Two, I love eating figs, and three . . . I have never been outside of England."

Oh, bless Olivia. She's so *sweet*. I do believe that Gwen wanted a little more scandal in this game.

I think Olivia senses this—she shakes her head, hiccups. "No, I take that back. My third—I have kissed Samuel Désir of France."

My mouth pops open. See, I know that Olivia could whistle an entire concerto if she had an audience for it, and I also know that figs give her bright pustules all over her mouth.

I squeal. "Olivia! You didn't!"

The others are laughing, and I can barely hear her under the drunken jeers. "Well, technically, he kissed me."

My mind is buzzing. *Olivia's kissed a boy before me?* And, no, that peck with the butcher's boy down in Addyshire when I was fourteen doesn't count!

I can't suppress my shocked smile, but before I can press on further, Gwen's shouting, "You next!" And waving to get my attention.

My tongue feels thick. "Well, there's nothing I have that's so scandalous as that!"

"Somehow, I doubt that," Nathaniel says into his cup.

I turn to Lord Grantchester. "I suppose this one is for you to guess, since you don't know me as well."

He pumps his brows upward. "A pity, that, and something I hope to rectify. Go on."

My face warms. "Three things: I like a rainy day more than a sunny one. The pinky finger on my right hand is slightly shorter than that on my left. And finally, I once shoved a boy to the ground for insulting me. What is the truth?"

"The second," he says, at the same time that Nathaniel says, "*The first.*"

Olivia shakes her head. "They're all true."

"Well, that's not fair!" Nathaniel laughs, then starts to reach for my hand before thinking better of it. "Let us see."

I hold my hands up next to each other, pinkies pressed together. "Hence, my lack of skill with the pianoforte."

"I never noticed!" he exclaims.

"You were never forced to do piano!"

Grantchester laughs. "Well, whoever you shoved, I'm sure he deserved it."

"Oh, he did. Believe me." I nod toward him. "And your secrets, Lord Grantchester?"

He's fully turned to me, now. He rests his chin against his knee and inhales. "I bloody hate horses."

I can't help but laugh. "And what else?"

"I once stole a prized gold ring on display at school—and returned it the next day, of course. And three. You were right. I am awfully lonely in Eastwick Abbey."

He's staring deep into my eyes here, and for a moment, I forget where I am, that there are others, that this seems unreal. "Are you lonely, Lord Grantchester?"

Even under the haze of the wine, I sense the tender desperation in his words. "I am."

"Then I wouldn't call you a thief."

Slowly, he grins. "Well, I *did* return it." His voice is low, a whisper just for me.

There's a vicious thunderclap in the distance. It breaks the reverie.

Gwen chuckles. "By the gods, Lord Grantchester, are you drunk?"

He laughs. There's that funny feeling in my stomach again. "Perhaps. Don't tell my mother."

"Your father wouldn't have liked it either," says Nathaniel. He's smiling still, but the playful edge to his voice is certainly, well, an edge.

"Now, I think we've all had too much to drink." Grinning, Lord Grantchester rubs his glass against his lip. "Where's Kitty, by the way? She wasn't able to accept my invitation."

Nathaniel runs his hands through his curls, his telltale sign of discomfort. "On holiday with her mother and father, I believe—Italy."

"Ah. Shame, she always knows how to liven up the mood."

"I think it's the perils of being an only child," Gwen says with a laugh.

"If that were true, Olivia'd be much more energetic." I laugh.

I mime a tug on her hair, but she doesn't seem so amused. In fact, she gives me an annoyed glance.

"We should probably get back," Nate says. I turn to him and find him angled away from me, gazing off to the rain clouds in the distance.

"But you haven't had your turn," I reply.

"Oh, you all know enough about me," he mutters, then pops up to his feet.

"He's right, and you never know when one of these Grantchester storms will sweep you away." Lord Grantchester seems close to me—have we always been sitting this closely? I must've leaned in to hear that low whisper of his. Dare I say it? I'm a touch disappointed to leave his side.

"Easy," he says, helping me to my feet.

Was I swaying? I hadn't noticed. I know it's not proper to be a little drunk, and even less so to admit it, but alas. "Had a cup too many." I giggle.

Nathaniel's already mounted his steed. "I'm sorry, have you noticed the rolling clouds racing towards us? No? Just me, then?"

I roll my eyes. "Fitzroy, it's fine." It comes out sharper than I intended, but he's being such a spoil-sport. With Grantchester's help, I rise up to the saddle, just as a nearby boom splits the air—

It's awful timing. Grantchester loosens his grip on the reins, and my bloody horse throws a fit, lifting onto her hind legs, and suddenly I'm lopsided, shrieking as I'm flung from the horse. I can't right myself quickly enough, and in foolishly reaching my hand toward the ground, I land hard on it.

"Ah!"

Immediately, pain shoots up my wrist. I make a sound I don't recognize somewhere between a grunt and a scream—*hell*, I have never felt such a pain before.

There are a few shouts of my name that I can't quite focus on. Fitzroy kneels next to me.

❖ 217 ❖

"I'm fine," I spit out of habit, even though my heart's pounding and my wrist is searing with pain.

Livvie's behind me, having a fit like she's the one that's just been *thrown off a bloody horse.* "Oh, heavens, a doctor—we need a doctor!"

"Can you stand?" Grantchester asks from my other side.

"Really, I'm fine!" Well, it'd be easier if I hadn't just had three cups of wine.

Nate, again. "We do need a doctor, send for a carriage, Grantchester."

Lord Grantchester sounds furious. "Nonsense, she must stay here!"

"It's nearly dark! No doctor will visit, and London's only three hours from here, call a carriage—"

"You'd rather her travel in pain than rest comfortably for the night?"

"I'd rather she had ridden under my care, as I'd offered!"

"Are you both quite done?" My voice is like a siren's death shriek. My head is throbbing, my face is numb, and these two shouting over me is making me want to vomit—oh, no, that's the drink. "Get me out of the mud and away from these horrible stinking horses, now!"

22

"I'm fine," I say for what must be the hundredth time since we returned to the house. "I swear it. It's only a little sore. I'm no physician, but I really can't imagine it's serious."

Lord Grantchester can hardly stand to look at me, even though his fingers are resting delicately on my wrist. "I feel horrible, Miss Sedgwick. Fitzroy's right. I should not have gotten distracted."

Nathaniel has been sulking in the corner by the fireplace since dinner ended. Though Gwen's thrown three biscuits at him, he's barely given her a glance. I keep catching him in the corner of my eyes—elbow rested against the mantel, sleeves rolled up, brown skin glistening in the firelight. He's thinking hard, and he keeps rubbing his knuckles against his lips and running his fingers through his hair.

Olivia's trying to give Grantchester and me our space, but I can see that her ears are perked up like a pup's.

Lady Tess returns to the sitting room, doing her best impression of a woman who is not furious, and poorly so. "Stella, we will take a coach tomorrow to the town doctor—"

"I'm fine, don't you hear me? Look, if I were badly hurt, could I do this?" I perform a series of ridiculous waves and twirls with my hands that only hurt a little.

"What *exactly* are you doing?" Gwen asks, either perturbed or amused.

I drop my hands into my lap. "It's possible that I'm still a bit drunk."

Olivia exhales sharply. Lady Tess purses her lips into a thin line. "I think it's time that you retire for the evening."

Finally, Grantchester moves away from me. "Good night, Miss Sedgwick."

I nod. "And to you, Lord Grantchester." I rise from my seat and turn toward Nate. "Good night, Fitzroy."

He spares me a small glance. "Night, then."

Lady Tess waits until the attendant is gone and the door is closed before letting her cool demeanor slip. "If you were going to fall off of a horse, you could have at least let Lord Grantchester catch you!"

The sheer ridiculousness of the statement sends me falling back onto my bed with laughter.

"I'm pleased you find this funny, but I'm being quite serious! And who told you to drink so much wine? I am tied up with knots just thinking of what you might have said at lunch, Stella!"

"I behaved perfectly, didn't I, Livvie?"

From the other side of the room, Olivia shrugs. She's finger-combing her curls, smoothing them with an aloe and oil concoction that Aunt Eleanor makes.

Lady Tess is serious. "How is your wrist, truly?"

I sigh. "It's only a little sore, I mean it. I wouldn't be so blasé about the hand with which I will write my masterpiece."

Finally, a smile, albeit a hopeless one. Lady Tess kisses my forehead, bids good night to Olivia, and leaves us.

"Want me to do your plaits?" I ask.

Livvie shrugs again.

"Or not?"

"I've got it, Stella." She's avoiding my gaze in the mirror. "And I wouldn't want to irritate your glorious writing hand."

I furrow my brow. Olivia doesn't get *angry*. She merely makes little quips and avoids eye contact until she's finally had enough and comes out with what's bothering her. I'd much rather cut to the chase. "What is it?"

"What?"

"Out with whatever you're upset about."

"Why do you think that I'm upset?"

"Either you tell me right now, or I'll—I'll—" I look around the room. "I'll throw one of these nice pillows at you! With my good hand!"

Predictably, she doesn't smile. "I'm only tired. Good night, Stella."

Oh, forget it. I don't feel like entertaining her. My mind is still reeling from everything that happened this afternoon, and

I don't even mean the fall. I mean the way Lord Grantchester spoke with me, sat with me, *looked* at me.

Silently, I prepare for bed. Livvie's asleep before I can prod her further.

I'm on the cusp of sleep when a shuffling outside the door rouses me. I think I hear a knock, but it's so faint that I can't quite tell if I dreamed it.

I throw on my bed jacket before plodding to the door.

I expect no one, but it's Nathaniel, turned away like he's had second thoughts. I squint at the lantern light, and he lowers it. "Sorry," he mumbles.

Quietly, I close the door behind me. "What are you doing here?"

He opens his mouth, closes it, opens it again. "I don't know."

I look down the hall. "Well, you must've had a reason for knocking." I don't say what we both know, that being caught like this without a good reason would be enough to start a scandal.

"Your wrist." He leans in. The lantern is down by his side, and so I can only see the side of his face by moonlight. His voice is deep and unsteady. "I wouldn't have let it happen. You know that, don't you? I would have been paying attention—"

"It was an accident! We'd had too much to drink, and the thunder—"

"No." He steps closer. "I would've caught you, Stella. Hell. It would have been my honor to do so."

Heat spreads across my face. For a moment, I think I forget to breathe.

"It's unfair," he whispers. He shakes his head; a curl lands in front of his face. "The way he talks to you. The way you look at him. I don't want to see it—"

I pull away. The mood has changed, now heavy with a dangerous, alluring electricity that threatens to unravel me. "You don't know what you're saying. Fitzroy, go to bed."

"Come with me," he says, breathless.

My own breath catches in my throat.

I know what I should say.

No.

That's ridiculous.

How dare you.

But.

But.

I find myself pressed against the door, and he is close, dangerously so. His eyes are shut like he's lost in prayer. Everything feels fuzzy, dizzying. I can't think straight. I lift onto my toes. He tucks his hand behind my neck, his thumb stroking my cheek. The intimacy of this moment makes me tremble.

"If someone sees us . . . ," I start, but the warning dies as Nathaniel dips his head down to press his lips against my collarbone.

I'd very much like to stay in this moment, savoring the way his lips feel against my skin as he traces my neck with kisses, how hungry his breath sounds as I wrap my arms tighter around him, my hand in his hair, the two of us holding each other desperately.

I could . . . could let him lead me back to his rooms—wait,

❖ 223 ❖

heavens, *what am I saying?* We could never speak of it. We can't even speak of *this*. A man's reputation could not be ruined by a singular night of lust the way a woman's could. And worse—*Kitty*. This is wrong. He has Kitty, he will marry Kitty.

And you would be left a fool, Stella. I won't let a man abandon me the way my father left my mother.

I disentangle myself from him. "Bloody hell, Fitzroy," I say in a searing, tense whisper. "Are you mad? Are *we* mad?"

And suddenly, it's like he's been *punched*. He looks at me, a return to the unamused Fitzroy who has done nothing but scowl at me. He is unkempt. His curls are a mess, my doing, his hands shaky, his amber skin blooming with a blush.

"I have no desire to be one of your conquests—" I want to shake him, I want to kiss him. "*You* get to do that and come away unscathed. Me? I'd be *shamed*, you know that, don't you? I may not be a proper genteel lady in the eyes of society, but I do know the rules."

He adjusts his shirt. "This was a mistake—"

"Oh, finally, some sense out of you."

He releases an exasperated sigh. "Must you be so *dramatic*, Stella?"

I gape at him. "What?"

"You've always got such overblown reactions! Throwing quips and jabs!"

I scoff. "Better that than letting people walk all over me and groveling for their approval."

He quiets for a moment. "I beg your pardon?"

It's like a flood, the way all of my built-up annoyances come pouring out. "That night at Mr. Désir's ball, you hardly even

❖ 224 ❖

stood up for me, you know. And I saw you afterward, running after Royce's carriage to get his attention, to make nice."

"What the devil are you talking about? I was there, I admonished him."

"Sure, after he'd had his say, after I threw the drink in his face!"

He's having a hard time keeping his voice level. "Mr. Royce is a miserable man, but—"

"*But?* Do you hear yourself? You would take his side—"

"I'm doing no such thing! What did you want me to do? Get into a brawl with the man in the middle of the ball? Challenge him to a duel?"

"It would have been something! Anything! But too much to ask, I see. It would ruin your perfect life. Tra-la-la, tea and parties and operas and insulting girls with your best mates, how fun!"

"This again?" He looks down at me, and I've never seen him so *furious*. "You have *no idea* what my life is like, or what I've been through. Mr. Royce is my grandfather's good friend, and has been trying to convince grandfather that he's gone mad to include you in his will, and your reaction didn't help! I had to go clean up that mess, Stella, I swallowed my pride *for you*. I begged him to forget it, *for you*. And when Lord Grantchester had mentioned seeing my cousin Allison in the arms of some boy, I knew what challenge they might bring to your fortune, so I used that to have them sent home. For. *You*."

"That was you?"

His eyes are shiny with hopelessness. "Of course it was me! Who else?"

✦ 225 ✦

I cross my arms stubbornly. "I didn't ask you to do any of those things."

"And yet I did!"

"Why, if it was so much trouble for you to go through?"

He takes a step back, voice still shaky with barely restrained frustration. "Because I care for you, Stella, *obviously*! And I would like to see my grandfather's wishes come true. But you're so damn selfish and unseeing, you never think twice, and you tend to your grudges, and—" He pauses for breath. "Honestly, ever since you came back to Kendall, I've been nothing but miserable!"

My heart is pounding. My eyes fill up instantly, the hot tears sliding fast down my face. He said he cared for me, and I felt my heart flip. He said I've made him miserable, and now, I only want to cry. How can one person unravel me so completely with just a few words?

He breathes deeply, and closes his eyes.

I wring my hands. I'm struggling to string a sentence together. "I understand."

"No." He squeezes his eyes before opening them. "I apologize."

"Don't apologize if you don't mean it." I offer a sad, hopeless smile. "Yes, I can be shortsighted and impulsive. Can you blame me? I know what place this world would like to see me in. I know what roles they would permit me to exist in. So yes, maybe I am selfish and brash. But I can think of no other way to keep from being insulted, or exploited, or mocked. It's made me tough. Skeptical. Untrusting. I've hardened my heart. The

❖ 226 ❖

world wants to take my joy from me, and I'm trying my best to hold on to it. But I do know my faults, Fitzroy. You'd do well to learn yours."

He's stricken speechless with what, shame? Disbelief? Whatever it is, he takes a step back from me. Though we're still fairly close, it feels as though a chasm has formed between us.

"I did not come here to . . . I only wanted to say . . ." He looks up at me, a sad smile on his lips. "Well, it doesn't matter now. I apologize for waking you, Miss Sedgwick."

The chasm grows by the second. There are so many things I could say to repair it, but I only nod. "Until tomorrow, Fitzroy."

23

In the morning, I find myself grateful for three things: that my wrist feels less tender, that the apples are sweet, and that Nathaniel Fitzroy has clearly decided that last night did not happen.

He's sitting on the other end of the breakfast table, at Gwen's side. Fitzroy's never been so charming. He's all smiles, cheerily telling a story of how he and Lord Grantchester once got lost in the Scottish Highlands, their gamesman having left them to fend for themselves.

". . . Honestly, I thought we were about to suffer a rather cannibalistic consequence," he says with a laugh, breaking half of his bread to share with Gwen.

Grantchester replies with a warm smile. "When the gamesman returned—after stopping in a pub for a few rounds, mind you—he said we looked like feral beasts! Then kindly reminded us that it had only been four hours."

"Not quite woodsmen, are we?"

"No, I think not."

I don't bother forcing a laugh to join the others. All I want to do is disappear. Fitzroy's words last night were so well struck, I'm unable to muster up the energy to pretend to be enjoying the discussion. I can still feel the weight of his furious eyes on me. I can still feel the imprint of his lips against my neck.

"I quite like a brutish man," Gwen adds with a smirk. "I find that society men are so . . . *proper*, wouldn't you say, Stell?"

I look up from my cinnamon spiced porridge. I shoot a quick glance at Lady Tess, who'd surely admonish Gwen if she were her own child. But she's distracted in conversation with Mr. Rosin, the keeper of the house. And Olivia's silently stirring her own porridge, obviously uninterested in saving me from this conversation. She's still upset about *something*; I want to shake her out of her mood, but she seems intent on fostering it.

"Would I?" I start, diplomatically. "I think all society folk would do well to be a little less buttoned-up."

"So you'd rather them unbuttoned?" Gwen laughs.

What would usually be cause for a quick retort instead makes my face hot. Nathaniel is laughing into his tea. I force an eye roll, a chuckle.

Olivia perks up, finally. "It's so lovely out. Shame the sun arrived on our last day."

"We shall make the most of it," Grantchester replies.

"I assume no horse riding, though," Nate interjects.

❖ 229 ❖

"Well, don't temper your enjoyment on my behalf," I say. "I'd be more than happy to sit and watch you all go by on your steeds. It might give me some time to write, actually."

Lord Grantchester smiles to me. "And how's that coming along?"

"Oh, I've just been—" I wave my hands vaguely. "Honing my craft." It's a nothing response, but I can't very well tell him that I'm running an anonymous advice column. And that all of our exchanges might make good fodder for it.

"Well, I'm looking forward to it, whenever you're published."

"It will be cause for celebration," Nate says, with genuine pride.

It's *aggravating*.

As a servant herds us into the sitting room, Grantchester pulls me aside. "I was hoping I might be afforded a moment of your time. A walk, perhaps?"

I smile, the first genuine one all morning. It would be good, actually, to get away from the others for a bit. "That sounds splendid."

I don't think much of it—I know Grantchester enjoys speaking intimately rather than in large groups, but as we go, Olivia has a soft smile and curious expression that I can't place. But it's Fitzroy's gaze on us that nearly gives me pause. I meet his eyes briefly, but once we connect, he turns away.

Lord Grantchester holds out his arm, and I take it.

"We should cherish this sunny day," he says once we're outside. "I imagine the rain will return, as it always does."

"I don't mind the rain so much. I quite like the country after

❖ 230 ❖

a storm. The air always smells fresh and new. Besides, my aunt says that I was born during a horrible rainstorm, and that my comfort in the rain comes from being held by my mother as the thunder roared."

The earl smiles. He seems genuinely moved by this admission, and the effect is a pang of endearment in my heart. "You miss her dearly."

I nod. "I can only try my best to make her proud. In some ways, I feel she's still with me."

"I think she'd be happy to see that you are well taken care of." He slows, and we stop beneath a leafy oak tree overseeing the hills of Grantchester. "This is a lovely view, is it not?"

I laugh. It's perhaps the prettiest thing I've ever seen. "Yes, Lord Grantchester."

"As a child, I always wished for snow so thick that I could slide down the hills on a toboggan without abandon. My parents ended those dreams quickly. They claimed I might crash and die."

"Well, now you'll be able to do with the hills as you see fit."

"Indeed, but I have more important wishes now." He pauses and sets his mouth with determination. "The one I wish for most ardently is your hand, Miss Sedgwick."

I giggle and squeeze his arm. "Luckily, you have it already."

He cocks his head at me and gives a healthy laugh. "How I cherish your clever amusements. Only you could turn a proposal of marriage into a moment of laughter. Is it a yes, then, or shall I do it properly?"

He drops onto one knee.

I freeze.

Marriage? What in heaven's name is he going on about? When were we ever discussing marriage—?

Oh!

My *hand*!

Stella, you fool!

My face must wear a hundred different shades of confusion, because Lord Grantchester's cheeks are steadily turning red. I'd consider this vulnerability sweet if he hadn't just proposed! To me! Have you ever heard of something so silly? Well, yes, I did gather that he felt some fondness for me, but *this*?

"Lord Grantchester," I start, my mouth moving faster than my brain. I scramble for what to say next, and make odd noises of shock in the meantime.

"Stella. I believe I've made my love for you known—"

"Love?" I sputter. "Why, you hardly know me!"

Now his face is the one painted with confusion. "I know you have . . . unique sensibilities regarding society, but I think the time we've spent together has been enjoyable, no? I feel you know my heart and that I know yours."

I bite the inside of my lip. Do I really have a choice? This marriage would settle Kendall and secure the entirety of my financial future. I wouldn't have to rely on the Withersons to support me, and I wouldn't have to work to earn money. More than that, I could continue to pursue writing without worrying about how I might feed myself.

Slowly, he rises to his feet and stands next to me, the two of us facing Eastwick Abbey now. "I would treat you well," he says. "You would deny *this*? For what?"

✦ 232 ✦

I think of my mother, and her mother, and hers. Would they have expected this? Their own descendant living like a princess in a castle, wanting for nothing? Owned by no one?

Though I know that this isn't what I want, how can I decline when this proposal would change my life in every single way, and largely for the better? Every day, daughters are made to marry men for money, for connections, for titles and land. Older men, cruel men, husbands that care more for their possessions than their wives. I may not know Grantchester well, but I know that there are far worse matches to be made.

I turn away from the castle and look into his eyes. They are kind and expectant. I can only hope that I will not regret this.

"Yes, Lord Grantchester," I whisper, hardly believing the words as they pass from my own lips. "I accept."

He smiles, his eyes crinkling at the corners. "Splendid! Simply splendid."

In one elegant movement, he swoops me into his arms and kisses me gently. It's a tender moment, and not at all unpleasant, but overshadowed by my own frantic thoughts. And while he kisses me, I think of how little it compares to the mere memory of Nathaniel's mouth on mine.

Still, I smile when we part, I laugh when he kisses my hand, and I hold on to his arm tightly as we walk back to Eastwick.

I brace myself for the congratulations and the excitement and Lady Tess fainting with joy. But as we walk up the path to Eastwick, it's clear that something is wrong. The doors are open, and a few servants are milling about the entrance speaking to each other with expressive gestures.

Lord Grantchester—hell, should I be calling him Bernard now?—slips his arm away from mine. "Sanders! What the devil is this?"

The footman Sanders hurries to Lord Grantchester. "My lord, we've had a visit from a Mr. Lewiston and a Mr. Graves. They demanded—"

Grantchester cuts him off. "I'll deal with Graves and Lewiston later. I'll not let them sour such a lovely day." He squeezes my hand and uses the other to wave the servant away.

The servant glances at me. "Understood, but sir, they're still here."

At this, Lord Grantchester stops abruptly. "What?"

"They said they would not leave until they spoke with you. Your guest, Mrs. Sinclair, offered her assistance. They're all in the drawing room now."

I look between them, feeling unsure of what I should say or do, if anything. What is appropriate now as this young man's future wife?

Grantchester decides for me. Fitting, I guess. "My dear, go in and join the others," he says. "I'll settle this . . ."

His voice trails off at the sight of Nathaniel, Gwen, and Olivia at the top of the steps. They all have a discomfited look about them, but Nathaniel looks particularly furious.

Grantchester's fingers stiffen in mine.

Nathaniel glances at our clasped hands. "So you proposed."

Grantchester grins. "Yes, I'm happy to say that Stella and I are to be married."

I smile sheepishly. It's a bit awkward, considering neither Olivia nor Gwen rushes to hug me as I would've expected. The three of them just stand there wearing strange expressions of unease. It's Livvie that concerns me most of all; she looks pale from shock.

"I cannot congratulate you, my friend," Nathaniel continues. "Not when this engagement is based on lies."

"Lies?" I look to Grantchester.

With his cheeks and forehead reddening, Grantchester says, "I've long wondered when you would make the extent of your jealousy known."

My heart stutters. Jealousy? Lies? What in the world happened in the thirty minutes that Grantchester and I were walking?

Nathaniel looks about ready to march down the steps, but Gwen steps in front of him, her face severe. She says, "I should be quite glad to see such dear friends joining in marriage, but your associates had much to say to Mrs. Sinclair about your family's debts, and I wonder if you've told Stella."

My skin goes hot with embarrassment. "Your uncle's debts?" I ask softly, looking to him for some understanding.

"And if you intend to marry my cousin, you'll do so honestly," Olivia adds. She meets my eye. "Let her decide after she knows the full truth of the matter."

Lord Grantchester shakes his head as he turns to me. "Stella, my love, this is simply a misunderstanding."

"Is it?" Nathaniel's voice is rough with skepticism. "Tell us then. What is Eastwick Abbey worth? Anything at all? You know I'd consider you a friend whether you were the richest man in the world or utterly penniless, but I won't see you use Stella in such a way."

Nathaniel's gaze on me is searing. Fury, yes, but sadness too.

And jealousy, perhaps? Grantchester might have just been trying to discredit Nathaniel, but I cannot deny the little thrill I feel at such an admission.

"I think that's enough," I say. I pull my hand from Grantchester's grasp, my heart racing. "Lord Grantchester, I have not heard what these men have to say, but I can only assume that your uncle's debts are what compelled you to ask for my lowly hand, is that right? Is one of these men the same that stopped you in Hyde Park?"

My gaze is focused on Grantchester, but I notice that Olivia and Gwen seem content to give us privacy. Nathaniel stands there, disgruntled, arms crossed over his chest, until Gwen taps him on the shoulder. He gives us one last look before turning away with them.

Lord Grantchester folds his hands together, suddenly becoming poised once more. "Nothing I've said was a lie. I do enjoy your company, and I truly believe we would be happy."

"You might not have lied, but what did you keep from me?"

He exhales sharply. "It's true, yes, that the money my family once had has mostly been squandered. Eastwick is becoming more and more difficult to maintain, but my mother refuses to sell it, and honestly, no one who could afford this property would sink so much money into a castle that is falling apart. But despite our friends' dramatic concerns, I believe this would be a mutually advantageous situation. We'd sell Kendall Manor, settle the debts, and have more than enough to live off of here in comfort." He takes both of my hands. "Stella, I am not a cruel man."

There's a patronizing lilt to his voice that unnerves me. It

＊ 236 ＊

reminds me of Mrs. Smith, the way she used to smugly explain things to me as if I were no more than a child. My stomach flips, but not in the sweetly satisfying way it has during our past conversations.

He continues, "Let me speak with Lewiston and Graves, and then we can properly celebrate, yes?"

Under all of my discomfort in this conversation, there is a seed of relief in the pit of my stomach. As ridiculous as it is to be engaged for a whole half hour—and I do hope I'll find this amusing someday—I am thankful that this drama has happened now.

I slip my hands out of his grasp. "Forgive me, Lord Grantchester. I no longer believe that this is the path for me. But I do enjoy your companionship, and . . . well I hope that we can remain friends."

He looks at me with a brow raised as if unsure if he'd heard me correctly. "Surely, you cannot be serious."

"I am, actually. Quite serious." I wring my hands together. "Truthfully, I should not have accepted in the first place. If we were to marry, you would still be in want of a doting wife, and would find yourself attached to a woman who has no interest in keeping a house—or bearing children. My companionship would bore you, and my quick tongue would irritate you."

He shakes his head. "I would not be asking if I didn't think you agreeable. Do you not find me agreeable as well?"

"I won't marry a man who only sees me as a means to settling his financial affairs."

"You are new to this, so perhaps you don't understand.

Marriage is not always done for love. And if it were for love, I say this truthfully—I could love you well enough. Couldn't you love me?"

"Perhaps," I whisper.

"Who has stolen your heart, then, to make me so unsuitable?"

"No one has my heart. It belongs firmly to me. And for that, I must decline."

Lord Grantchester gives me a hard look that I can't decipher as fury or embarrassment. Finally, he seems to accept that there will be no convincing me.

Because he is a gentleman, Lord Grantchester offers his arm once more. We walk up the castle steps in a silence so complete, I think he might hear my heart beating. If it weren't for society, I'd feel completely at ease with my decision. But people talk, and I know there will be much to say about the young woman who denied the Earl of Grantchester.

24

"*H*mm." Mr. Elmhurst has a peculiar talent for fitting amusement, disdain, or indifference into one perfect *hmm*. Only thing is, I can't quite tell which he's conveying at the moment.

I fidget in the chair across from him—which he actually offered me this time, I might add. Progress! "I could edit down the bit about the—"

He doesn't look up at me from the papers, only lifts a finger to silence me. Rather rude, but I've seen him do the same to Mr. Bratton, so I suppose I can't be all that offended. "This is much better, though I think we can omit your condemnation of the writer as a *lovesick fool with pigeon feed for brains.*"

I hold in a chuckle. "Yes, I figured as much. And the one about the woman whose prized horse was snatched out from under her nose by her rival? Acceptable, yes?"

"More Like Hate-Thy-Neighbor." He flips through the papers. "Ah, yes, but let's cut a hundred words or so. Brevity is key to keeping the reader engaged in a column like this. Well done, Miss Sedgwick. We'll publish these next."

I exhale in relief. After the disastrous end to the trip in Grantchester, I needed this.

"And after that, I'd like to run something different." He laces his fingers together in front of him, and I tense up. I haven't known Mr. Elmhurst long, but he's wearing the same expression that Lady Tess wears when she's about to tell me something very serious—or to admonish me for leaving her couch cushions scattered about after a nap. "Perhaps you should take a break from answering questions and pen your own column."

I perk up, my eyes widening, but he continues—

"Something a little salacious. I hear you've been in and out of London, attending high-society events."

He winks, and I know that he's heard the news. Of course he's heard. Even if it wasn't his own daughter that told him, all throughout London, I am known as the one who dared reject the Earl of Grantchester.

Two weeks have passed since we returned from Eastwick Abbey, and Lady Tess is still trying her hardest to make me change my mind. While she agrees that his behavior was certainly unsavory, she thinks I should have at least discussed matters with her or with Aunt Eleanor before outright rejecting him. Even if she could convince me, I doubt Lord Grantchester would stoop so low as to take me now that the whole city knows

❖ 240 ❖

I turned him down. Heavens, it's still so odd to think about. My hand. He asked for *my hand*. And I agreed and denied him all in the same day—in the same hour.

News traveled so quickly that we received a letter from Aunt Eleanor before Lady Tess even managed to send one. Mercifully, she was much more understanding than Tess, but she warned me against making any other decisions that might have me suffering the rest of my years in *misery and destitution* without consulting her first.

I'm a little tired of traveling, but I'm grateful that we'll be in Paris for the next week. A few days out of the city—out of the country!—sounds perfect right now.

I fold my hands together politely. "Mr. Elmhurst, I did not take on this column to make it my journal. Besides, Fiona Flippant only works if her identity is kept anonymous."

He parts his hands in a gesture of compromise. "No, but Fiona Flippant could simply report on some gossip she's heard?" He says it like a question, but I know he isn't asking from the way he taps the stack of papers in front of me, signaling that this conversation is ending. "Let's try a new approach, Miss Sedgwick. A personal one. You may find it much easier than responding to the whims of your readers."

I don't know what's worse. The fact that my name has become even more known through the social season, or that Mr. Elmhurst would now like me to *dwell* on the one thing I'd like most to forget.

The whole thing makes me uneasy. "Letters to Fiona Flippant" might not be the most important writing in history, but my mother took her role as an advisor seriously. To turn it into any old gossip sheet—what had Kitty called it, *salacious drivel*—diminishes my mother's vision. But Mr. Elmhurst dismisses me with a nod, and I hold my tongue. If I want to eventually convince him to let me write more serious pieces, I need to present myself as a willing and agreeable employee.

The secretary on the first floor is the only one who pays me any mind as I leave. The men here aren't like the genteel folk, after all. They have occupations, unlike Grantchester, Royce, or Fitzroy. But the secretary must've heard *something*, for she smirked at me when I walked in, and is smirking now.

"Good day, Miss Sedgwick," she says, seemingly holding in laughter.

I shoot her a strained smile before opening my umbrella and heading out the door.

I'm grateful for the rain. The last time I came into town, I was actually stared at, and not for the usual reasons. There was *whispering*. I thought I heard the word *heartless* in front of the cobbler's, but that might've been my own imagination.

Olivia is there for me, holding the door to Lady Tess's townhome open. "Saw you from the window. How'd it go?"

I shrug off my coat and put my umbrella in the corner. The air smells like apples and sugar. "Not well. Is that pie?"

"Warm cider," says Livvie. "Sit, I'll make you a mug."

My eyes flick upward—

Olivia sighs. "Our Lady Tess is napping, for the rain gives her migraines."

I head into the sitting room and plop onto her velour sofa—

and regret it. I keep forgetting that Lady Tess's sofa is much too firm for plopping. Oh, I miss home. "Well, then we have a few moments of quiet, don't we?"

Olivia heads into the kitchen, and returns with two piping warm mugs. The sweet, tart spice hits my tongue, and I am immediately at ease. "Brandy, Livvie?"

She chuckles. "Don't tell Lady Tess."

I wink. "Obviously."

The storm roils outside. Lightning and thunder, the wind whipping around the building.

"Have you finished packing?" I say at the same time Olivia quietly asks, "Do you regret it?"

My brow twitches. "Finally, then." She's been dancing around the subject since we got back from Grantchester. She's still been in that foul mood, but it seems to have passed. I suppose being invited to a rich man's estate in Paris will do that to a young lady.

"I thought I'd let you share when you wanted to," she replies.

I take a moment to gather my thoughts. I don't know how to articulate how I feel right now—the uneasy tummy, the unsteady heartbeat. And yet, relief, still. "I don't know. I keep trying to picture myself as Grantchester's bride, and it doesn't look so bad. It's the afterward that escapes me—as mistress of his house, an eternity at his side. *That*, I cannot envision so handily. I just feel so young. I want so many things that do not easily fit into the life he could've given me. At nearly one and twenty, he would've tired of me easily, I think, and wanted a family."

"You don't see yourself having children?"

❖ 243 ❖

"I feel like a child myself! Honestly, between you and me . . . I initially accepted the proposal because I felt like I had to. And even though the whole business was uncomfortable, I'm grateful for those men, Lewiston and Graves. Grateful even that Lord Grantchester lied to me. It gave me a way out."

She chuckles softly. "I thought so. You didn't seem too out of sorts about your broken engagement."

I lean back, slipping my hands behind my head. "Who would've thought I'd get engaged before you, Olivia!"

She rolls her eyes and laughs. "A ten-minute engagement. That must be some type of record. Oh, before I forget, Jane Danvers's wedding invitations came in!" She gathers the envelopes from the side table. Aside from a short letter from Gwen about a ball we missed, I haven't heard from the Fitzroys at all.

I turn the lush invitation over, finding myself grateful once again. Imagining the invitation announcing the wedding of Lord Bernard Grantchester and Miss Stella Sedgwick sends a nervous chill through me.

"And I have finished packing, by the way," Olivia says with a sigh. "In fact, I actually began to arrange your things."

"I suppose my wardrobe will consist solely of tangerine-colored dresses, then?"

"Yes, and you're welcome."

"*Thank you.*" I click my tongue. "I need to write."

"Didn't you just turn in your latest?"

"Not exactly." I hop to my feet, and, mug in hand, retire to the study. Livvie brings me the paper and pencil, heavens bless her, and I . . . Well, I stare out into the distance for quite some time. I let my thoughts turn. I try to stay with my feelings instead of pushing them away, as uncomfortable as it is to do so.

I do not usually do this, my dear reader, but a few choice pieces of gossip have conveniently fallen onto my ears, and it would be cruel of me to keep them from you. Now, a lady never reveals her sources, but suppose a little bird told me and for the good of society, I must make a few things known. I only ask that you keep these secrets between us.

On the matter of the doomed engagement between the season's oddest participant, a baseborn girl with a mouth that never stops moving—we'll call her Queen Sass— and a handsome young man who has just ascended into royalty, let it be known that Lord Perfect Hair himself was the cause of the conflict. Seems Lord Perfect's books are far from it, on account of his family's massive debts. A strange match, indeed. One can only wonder how much longer Queen Sass will last among the London elite. I am not a betting woman myself, but I expect we'll be free of the troublemaking girl within a fortnight.

She is not the only new young woman to watch, however. The prize of the season—heiress Prim & Proper, may have her own scandal on her hands, by way of her father's duplicitous nature. If you attended the showy performance of Aurora early in the summer, perhaps you saw what I did—Prim's own father, locked in an eye-opening embrace with a woman who looked little like his

✦ 245 ✦

precious wife. What is it with men and their wandering eyes, and wandering hands?

Autumn is upon us, lords, ladies, and jesters. What engagements—and entanglements—will we see next? I know who I have an eye on, and I do wonder if the Frenchman is as perfect a match for Delicate Rose as he seems.

Yours, earnestly,
Fiona Flippant

I look it over, and despite the aliases, I wonder if Gwen, Nathaniel, or even Lord Grantchester could suss out my identity. While I don't think anyone would assume a young Black woman to be behind Fiona Flippant's voice, I have been vocal about wanting to write, and hell—I've been going around London with Elmhurst's own daughter as my chaperone.

I need to supplement the column, but with whose stories? I haven't paid much attention to the scandals of the social season. What was the name of that girl Gwen and Kitty mentioned once? Hattie Dover? Her mother introduced her into society early. But she was only fourteen or so, and gossiping about a child feels so low. And see? This is why I prefer fiction! There's so much less guilt involved when writing about characters who don't exist.

I sit up in my chair, the movement nearly knocking one of Lady Tess's porcelain birds from the desk. There's a way I can bolster this column without dragging anyone else into it—I'll just make it all up! Aliases with no one behind them, stories that sound true enough without an ounce of truth.

I write about Shining Knight and Princess Pauper, two star-crossed lovers sharing the same house on a hill—one upstairs, the other downstairs. I warn London's well-bred ladies about the Rosy Rake, an orange-haired rascal with a habit of falling in and out of love with the tides, and the Dastardly Duo, a pair of clever sisters looking to marry their way out of trouble with the law.

Honestly, this is the most fun I've had with Elmhurst's assignments. The readers only want a good story, and I know how to give them just that.

25

Paris

It is odd . . . watching Olivia fall so absolutely in love.

It isn't just fluttering eyelashes and giggles at unfunny jokes, but the way she reaches toward Mr. Samuel Désir in hopes that he might accidentally brush his knuckles against her hand. How she smiles sweetly, brown eyes beaming when he turns to her first among us to teach us all about the history of Paris as we walk down the Rue Royale. She's always first. He wants her attention, wants her to know that he's thinking of her, with every word. It's so sweet that I can hardly find the energy to be skeptical of it.

I don't understand how they could barely know each other and yet seem to navigate each other's space and presence as if they've been in love for years. They have swiftly become the center of each other's worlds—and Lady Tess's too, thankfully.

Just this morning, the woman was *still* mourning my refusal of Grantchester's hand like she'd been rejected herself. Fortunately, with Livvie and Samuel to push together like little dolls, she has no time to dwell on my supposedly fatal mistake.

It is not just *odd*. It is quite delightful as well. I want to hate that Samuel has all of my cousin's attention, but he is too kind to hate. And I like that he understands the unsavory parts of our lives—France has its own prejudices and distastes for people like us—in a way that Lord Grantchester could have never related to.

It is hard to hate Paris as well. As Samuel's ostentatious carriage swiftly glides through the streets, the air feels different. Or maybe I'm just happy to get away from London society for a bit.

After a day of sightseeing and my pretending not to notice the lovebirds doting on each other, we return to the Désirs' lavish apartments for dinner.

Samuel leads us into the dining room. "You remember my mother, Mrs. Solange Désir."

"Miss Witherson," she says with a smile. Only I seem to notice how thin the lady's smile seems. "It's a pleasure to see you again. I do apologize for missing the most of your trip." She has a round, dark brown face, and her gray hair is done up in neat curls. She is wearing a simple and elegant purple dress and a string of gaudy pearls.

Olivia curtsies, the sweetest smile on her face. She seems so nervous, poor thing.

Samuel gestures toward Lady Tess and me. "Miss Stella Sedgwick and Mrs. Tessa Sinclair."

"Lovely," Mrs. Désir says, hardly sparing us a glance. "Dinner, then?"

Dinner comes and goes with little consequence. The conversation is polite and boring. Samuel's mother is certainly fluent in English, but she insists on quipping to her son in French every so often, even while looking right at us. It's like having someone gossip about you to your face, but so quietly that you can't hear it, and you can't really be sure.

Damn it. I should've been practicing my French all these years.

After dessert, tea, and a few more pleasantries, Lady Tess suggests that we retire for the evening.

It seems like Mrs. Désir has been waiting for this, like she did not want to be the one to call the night first. But she agrees, and quickly rises from her seat.

Samuel and Olivia haven't had a moment alone together, were not even allowed to sit next to each other the whole evening, but the fondness between them is palpable as he kisses her hand and bids her good night.

"I think that went well," Lady Tess says as we're led to our rooms, though, dare I say, her heart isn't in it.

"Yes," Olivia says. She's smiling, but she's not as good at hiding her anxiousness as Lady Tess.

Our three rooms are connected by one suite. The suite itself is bigger than Lady Tess's sitting room and kitchen combined, and is full of all sorts of wealth—the gilded mirror, the furniture, the plush rug lining the floor.

Lady Tess gives us both a small peck on the forehead before

retiring for the night. Once she's gone, I stop Livvie from undressing. "They're probably downstairs talking about you, you know."

She looks up at me and drops her hands from the sash across her waist. For once, we are entirely on the same mischievous page.

Sneaking back down to the sitting room is easy, and to our wide-eyed dismay, we don't even have to get too close to the entrance. Samuel and his mother are both speaking in raised voices as one servant fills their wine glasses and another cleans up their plates. Their presence must be why Samuel and his mother speak in English—I've already learned how quickly gossip can spread from the mouths of house staff.

"*Mon dieu*," Samuel says. "You are being so unfair!"

Mrs. Désir scoffs. "She is a lowly country girl. Her manners have been well polished, that is clear, but you have more promising options before you. When I sent you to London, I thought you might've known better than to set your sights on a no-name upstart! How eager she is, and her chaperone—that Sinclair woman would not have been able to hide her shameless, hungry eye for matchmaking if it could fit in a thimble! I'll not have my son tied to such a conniving sort. When your father returns, he'll convince you if I can't."

I feel Olivia chill beside me.

I turn to her. "Don't listen to—"

She shushes me, her eyes intent on the light coming from the sitting room.

Samuel lowers his voice a smidge, out of pure resignation.

"You said I could choose, Maman."

"I did. That was a mistake. And now I must correct it."

"And if I say no?"

The air out here is as tense as it must be in there.

Mrs. Désir sighs. "Sam, marry well, it is your duty. But if your heart is still tricking your mind into believing that this is love, then take the girl as a mistress if you must. That's all a girl like her is good for."

I slap my hand against my mouth.

What?

How dare she?

When I turn to Olivia, she's already halfway up the stairs.

Well . . . this is a first. Yes, there are many people who would judge Olivia purely by her tawny brown skin, but she's never been downright disliked by those that have met her, or cared to know her. I want to go in and defend Olivia myself, but I don't think my cousin would like that at all. Regrettably, I'm forced to remember what Fitzroy said to me about jabs and quips, my penchant for dramatics. This seems a perfectly reasonable time to act out on those supposedly undesirable traits, but I force myself back to the bedroom.

I manage to wait before the door is closed in our rooms before letting out an angry grunt. "Listen to me, don't you dare consider a single word she's said as truth. . . ."

My words trail off as Olivia breaks into something between a laugh and a sob. She's smiling, she's *crying*. "He loves me."

I sit next to her on the ridiculous puff of a bed. "He does, he truly does."

"But I cannot have him."

"You don't know that."

"You heard his mother. He's the son of a wealthy and connected lawyer, and should be after a well-bred woman, not, not a country girl."

I lift a finger. "Don't you dare. Olivia, you are the kindest, most polite, gentlest, sweetest person I know. And almost the wittiest girl of our age if I didn't exist."

I get a small hiccup instead of the laugh I was aiming for.

"Fine, fine. The wittiest too." I take her hand. I don't know what else to say. I'm so used to Olivia being *loved*, even more proof that Lady Désir's head is full of worms.

"What will I do?" she asks. "I haven't made any connections with other young men. I should have been more open—"

"Heaven's sake, you won't immediately crumble into ash if you don't have a marriage proposal by eight and ten years of age! I mean, just look at me, eighteen and, you know, doing well enough for myself—"

She does look at me, and she frowns.

"Never mind, don't do that."

A giggle, finally. "Stella, you needn't put yourself down to make me feel better. It doesn't work, because there's no one that thinks more highly of you than I do."

Oh, bless her. Comforting me even when she's upset.

"And you managed a nice catch, lest we forget it."

"No, let's definitely forget it. And as silly as I think marriage is, Mr. Désir is not the be-all and end-all. You will find yourself at the center of a young man's affection, I know it."

To my horror, she only begins to cry some more. "But they won't be him," she mutters, before laying her head down on my shoulder.

There's a small knock at the door that makes us both jump. It comes from the door to the hallway and not the door from the suite, so it can't be Lady Tess.

Livvie and I look at one another.

"I can get it," I say, more of a question than an offer.

She shakes her head, wipes her eyes, and stands. "No, it should be me."

I go into the suite and settle into the window seat. For a moment I feel like I'm back in Addyshire, cuddled up with a cup of sipping chocolate, Cheswick pawing at the ends of my day dress—

"Stella! Wake up!"

I groan. "Huh? Wha—" I hadn't meant to fall asleep, but here I am, head against the window, a rather unbecoming bit of drool on my face. I wipe it away and look at Livvie. "What happened? Was that Mr. Désir?"

Olivia swallows hard. She's . . . nervous? Or trying very hard not to seem like it, like she's building up the courage to do something. "Compose yourself, quickly! We're going out. *We're sneaking out.*"

She whispers *sneaking*, and it's so adorable that I nearly laugh. "Livvie, you look like you've just stolen a queen's prized pearls right out from under her nose! You. Sneaking out?"

"Samuel—"

I widen my eyes.

✦ 254 ✦

"Mr. Désir is taking us to a dance hall."

"Now, in the middle of the night?" I frown. "You know, I'm all for ditching Lady Tess, but it doesn't seem very gentlemanly of him to suggest we follow him without our chaperone."

She sits at the corner of my bed. "It's a place for us, Stella. For people who look like you, who look like me. Lady Tess would likely feel a little . . . out of sorts."

This intrigues me. I raise a brow.

"A few dances, and then we'll come back." She grins conspiratorially. "Mr. Désir's awfully humble, but you've seen the types of balls that he throws. He says we should dress casually, but I wonder what riches we'll be treated to."

Olivia squeals in disgust. "What is this, a hovel for highwaymen?"

Samuel—he's become adamant that he does not want us to refer to him so properly anymore—laughs. "No, no, it's just a dance hall, as nice as any other." It's freer than I've heard from him before, and so young that I do a double take. He's a different man here, especially with his simple linen shirt and black trousers. I'm grateful that he warned us to dress casually; I feel comfortable in my simple blue linen dress and flat shoes. Across the room, a few men are either celebrating or arguing, and smashing their glasses on the floor to do so. "Well. It's nice on most nights," he adds. "This way."

The dance hall, I didn't catch the name, is in a rather unsavory part of Paris. Then again, unsavory is likely what the pale bourgeoisie would call it, for no other reason than it's

✦ 255 ✦

primarily populated by colored people. It's comforting to see all the shades of brown, the loose curls, the tight curls, the plaits. The dance hall is three stories tall, simple brick and wood. Music and people spill out into the street, full of joy—well, aside from the man spewing over the railing.

Olivia looks green herself, and I have to hold in my laughter.

Sam is undeterred. He beckons us forward, just as cheers break out. The band has started up with a boisterous, intoxicating music that I've never heard before. It's heavy on the drums and fiddle, and less so on the piano, though the man slams on the keys with passionate glee. I find myself nodding along even as Sam weaves us through the hot crush of bodies. I'm hypnotized by the man and woman dancing in the center of the room, the rest of the people clapping and stomping on the beat for them. The dance is quick, but nothing like the constrained and neat line dances of the English ballroom. People here actually dance *together*, bodies hugging each other before pulling away.

"How fun!" I blurt out excitedly.

Olivia blushes. Then she sputters a laugh and grins. "It's not what I expected, but you're right."

"That's the spirit!"

Finally, Sam brings us to two empty tables in a corner of the room. Judging by the way the young serving girl greets him—full smile, braids bobbing behind her—I think he's at home here.

The girl can't be more than fourteen, but she holds herself with all the confidence of an old barmaid. One fist rests on her hip, and the other hand carries a tray of mugs. "C'est bien, the lonely prince returns!"

He grins. "Bonjour, Nathalie. These are my guests from London."

She looks us over. "Would you like some wine? It's not the best, but it's French, so likely better than what you're used to."

I laugh. "I think you're probably right. That sounds lovely, thank you."

A rather raucous pair of men at the next table over are playing cards, and one of them leaps up in glee, nearly crashing into Nathalie. Expertly, she weaves out of the way.

Sam's friends, a boy and a girl, emerge from the dance floor to join us. I think they may be twins. They have the same golden skin and big hazel eyes, though the girl's head is covered in brown curls while the boy's is shorn to his scalp.

The girl's eyes are wide as she greets him. "Samuel, look at you, all dressed down like you're one of us!"

She sees Olivia and me, then does an odd thing with her face. It's not a frown, but not a smile. It's quizzical and confused. "Why did you bring these nice girls here? They look stricken!"

Her brother, presumably, furrows his brow. "Eh, pardon. Which one of you is Olivia?"

And for the first time, Samuel Désir is caught totally off guard. His eyes widen, and he grabs his friend by the shoulder, which makes the boy burst into hearty laughter. It's sweet, the type of jest for brothers. I'm not the only one warmed by the sight. Olivia is wearing the most satisfied grin.

"That laugh of yours, like a hyena's, you'll frighten the young

❖ 257 ❖

ladies," she says, elbowing her brother playfully. "My name is Monique Ziani, this is my brother, François."

Livvie nods. "I'm Olivia Witherson, and this is my cousin, Stella Sedgwick."

Monique raises a brow. François sputters a last laugh, but then stills. They're looking at me, though it's Livvie that should be garnering their attention, no?

Monique shoots me a wicked smile before turning to her brother. "This is the girl that insulted that fussy earl!"

My heart falls into my stomach, no, into my feet!

"The earl—" François holds his hand up, pinky out, and straightens his spine in a display of pompousness. "Has decided to drown his sorrows in French wine and French girls."

"He's here?" I ask, heart pounding.

"No, went off to Italy a few days ago. Our father is keeper of a hotel a neighborhood over. Nice place, but you'd think a man of his standing would stay somewhere much fancier." He laughs. "You really broke his heart!"

I shake my head. "Don't be mistaken. He only wanted me for . . . Well, it doesn't matter now."

François runs his hand over his shorn head. "Wealthy men like him are all the same. Told no for the first time in his life, and can't bear it."

The music rises. The floorboards jump, the drumbeat running through all of our veins.

Sam peels off his sporting coat. "Miss Witherson?"

He does not have to say anything else. She rises, takes his hand, and lets him lead her to the dance floor.

❖ 258 ❖

"Bah!" exclaims François. "He's gone now, totally gone."

Monique looks to me. "Sweet girl, she is. So pretty."

"The prettiest," I agree.

"I'm sure she's lovely," François cuts in with a little edge. "But I'm not too happy that she's stolen away my friend—I was supposed to run him out of his riches over six games of coucou tonight, not see him off dancing around."

I laugh. "Well, if you teach me to play, I'd be happy to join, but I'm also not worth much, so—*so . . .*"

My voice trails off. If my heart had fallen into my feet before, it has just leapt up into my throat.

"Sorry," I choke out, rising from my seat. "I have to—"

I point vaguely toward the other end of the dance hall before going in that direction myself, narrowly missing swipes from the dancing couples. My heart is pounding with the quick and mighty drumbeat. Honestly, I think it might burst out of my chest.

By the bar, there's a small table of dark-skinned men laughing over cards.

And one brown-skinned boy.

I knew him from his curls.

I'd know him anywhere.

"Fitzroy," I say, a whisper of disbelief.

Even with all the music and noise, he turns.

His shoulders go up, and he releases a soft breath of relief. His eyes are big and wide. There's a touch of a smile. Joy and disbelief.

For one blissful moment, everything is okay. We've both

forgotten the tension of our last conversation. He is happy to see me, and I am happy to see him, and we're both grinning like fools.

But then—it's like we catch ourselves. I fix my face into indifference, and he steps back from me.

"What are you doing here?" he asks quietly.

"What are *you* doing here?" I ask, matching his disbelief. "Mr. Désir brought us—We're visiting, I don't know." I expel a stunned chuckle. My face is warm, but before I can reach my hand up to touch my forehead, Fitzroy gently wraps his fingers around my wrist.

"This is perfect," he says.

I don't pull away. "Perfect?"

Oh, he's *beaming*. Okay, maybe a little drunk, but it's bright, it's beautiful. "I was trying to tell you back at the party at Enderly. I want you to meet someone."

He steps aside so we're next to each other, and a man comes into view. He's at the head of the table, grinning at a companion I assume he's just bested in the game. He's a little worse for wear—bald, thin, and the grin reveals a few missing teeth. But there's a youthfulness in his eyes that radiates from within.

I can't help but stare, because I was wrong about where Nathaniel got his sculpted cheekbones and square jaw.

Nathaniel squeezes my wrist affectionately. "Stella, this is my father."

26

All I know about André Laurens is that he got tangled up with a woman he shouldn't have, according to the rules of genteel society. I didn't realize he was even alive, though I hadn't heard the contrary. I guess I'd just assumed.

Nathaniel's pure, unadulterated happiness is like drinking honey. He smiles down at his father and steps back, as if presenting me to him.

He gets his smile from his father, too.

The man stands, offers his hand. "Stella, oui? Enchanté."

I take it. "Je suis désolée, my French—" I make a gesture, waving my hand back and forth. "It's not great."

"No problem," he says in English, his accent thick. He turns to his son. "Mon fils, you can't bring a beautiful girl to meet me and not give me some time to prepare!" Dramatically, he dusts off his shirt.

Nate's grin grows sheepish. "My fault, Papa."

We've just met, but I really like this man.

"I would offer you my chair, mademoiselle, but I think you young kids should be dancing, not sitting around." He sucks his teeth and shoos Fitzroy. "Besides, I think Paul here would like a chance to win his watch back." The man next to him mutters a curse before wiping sweat from his brow. They argue for a bit in French before Nathaniel's father turns to me and says, "I feel like I know you. My boy speaks of his sisters often, but with you, it's like he can never tell me enough—"

"Okay, dancing!" Nathaniel interjects, shooting his father a warning look.

I shake my head immediately. "I don't know how to dance like this! I can barely do the line dances in Addyshire!"

"You'll get it, come here!"

"No, no, no—"

He places his palm against my waist, and my body stills, obeying his touch.

He is close. As close as he was that dangerous night at Lord Grantchester's estate.

But this time, his expression is more joyous than brooding. I like him this way much better, though the touch of his hand on my waist is just as intoxicating.

"Just follow my lead," he whispers.

"You'll step on my toes," I whisper back.

He throws his head back and laughs—oh, I just want to bottle up happiness and keep it forever.

I hardly feel it, the way he sweeps me into the fray of the

❖ 262 ❖

dance floor. Couples swirl around us. He starts to bring his body close to me. "This okay?"

I nod.

His hands are gentle on my waist. "You should, um, hold me, Stella."

"*Right*, of course." I think I sound nonchalant enough, though I feel the gooseflesh start on my arms as I wrap them around his neck. "Don't laugh!"

He attempts to wrench the smile from his face, but his grin only widens. "I'm not." He starts to sway his hips, and I follow, trying to focus on the music and not the way his eyes have gone soft.

He adds the steps, swinging me, dipping me, putting distance between us and then closing it quickly. I feel dizzy, not from the spins, but from the feel of his body so pressed against mine. We don't speak, but his eyes never leave me, and with the way he holds me, I don't think we need words at all.

He slips behind me, his fingers lingering on my waist. We move against each other to the music, our hips rolling to the intoxicating beat.

He dips his head down, his lips against my ear.

"Stella."

"Yes, Nate?"

"I missed you."

His breath kisses my neck, and I'm reminded of his lips on my skin and my fingers tangled up in his hair as we both desperately tried to understand the attraction between us.

Suddenly, I'm pulled away, Livvie's hand in mine. There's

a large circle of us, running around the room hand in hand as the last bits of sound crash out from the band. The song rumbles the floorboards and bursts into my chest. I'm happy here, tucked between Nathaniel and Olivia, their hands in mine, running the length of this tavern in a frantic circle.

I am *breathless* with joy.

Needing to catch my breath, I return to Samuel's table. Fitzroy follows wordlessly; I can feel him close behind, the two of us careful not to lose each other in the crowd. Livvie and Samuel remain dancing, utterly drowning in each other's gaze, and Monique and François are occupied with cheering on the card players at the table over.

I lean close so that I don't have to shout at Nate over the music. "Sorry to steal you away from your father."

He smiles, so genuinely happy. "Nonsense, we get the month together. Better than last year, when it rained the whole time and I nearly caught pneumonia. Still painted the cathedral, though," he finishes with a grin.

"Last year? How did these visits start? I didn't even realize your father was in your life."

"Oh, it was just after you left. There was a letter that came in for Grandfather, you see. I used to bring him his mail, slip the notes behind my back, and ask him to guess how many pieces he had delivered that day. If he guessed incorrectly, I got a sweet." He pauses to gesture to the serving girl for a drink. "One day, there was a letter that made his face pale. He looked like he'd seen an apparition. He forbade me from touching his mail after that, which, of course, only made me want to know what he'd read. A month later, there was a letter that came in with the same handwriting as the one that had worried him. Naturally, I read it. As it turns out, the father I thought had abandoned me was frequently checking in on my wellbeing."

He sighs. "Of course, I was furious that Grandfather didn't tell me. But he claimed it was my father's own idea to keep his distance. He cared for me, but knew that there was no place for him in London society. The scandal, the gossip."

"I can't blame him," I offer.

Nathaniel nods. "But he also wanted to see me, his only child." He says this with such tenderness that my heart aches for him. I place my hand on his. He strokes my pinky with his thumb. "So, here I am. Sometimes I wonder if my grandfather would've told me if I hadn't opened the letter. Or maybe I would've visited Paris one day, and we would've found each other the same way you found me."

I smile. "It's nice to see you so happy."

He looks down at my hand still on his. I wait for him to draw away, but he doesn't. It's so natural, and I don't feel the least bit awkward about it. "I am happy," he says. "This is a perfect night."

I'm the one that pulls my hand away. The moment's tenderness remains, but I can feel myself slipping into melancholy just thinking about how unfair it is that this night can't last forever.

"Stella?" Nate asks softly. "Where have you gone?"

I attempt a small smile. "I'm trying to savor this before I have to go back to the real world."

His brow twitches. "This is real."

"No, this is a holiday! Soon I'll be back in England, trying to stave off my aunt's watchful eye. I need to figure out what I'm going to do next."

He wrings his hands. "Our trip to Grantchester ended so abruptly. I never got the chance to ask how you were faring with all the . . . excitement."

I laugh. "Excitement, yes. That's one way to put it." I shrug. "That business with Grantchester isn't what's troubling me. I think I'm just . . . I don't know. Tired."

"Oh. I can escort you back—"

"Not in *that* manner. Just." I roll my shoulders. "Oh, you don't want to hear it."

He says nothing, but looks at me in that softhearted way that I can't help but adore.

I take a long draw of my wine, the sour sweetness coating my teeth and loosening my tongue. "Is it so wrong that I want more than what the world intends to offer me? That I want to make a life and name for myself, and be independent, and content in my own company? I look into the mirror, and I like what I see, and I bloody well should—it's not up to me to change, and it's not my fault that the world I've been born into is as narrow-minded as it is cruel! I'm tired of wanting. And I'm tired of being tired of all of the things I cannot change." I look at him. His eyes are focused, his brow furrowed slightly in concentration. "You're lucky—well, compared to me. And you have no idea."

"I know I'm lucky."

I laugh, anger rising so abruptly that I could not tamp it down if I wanted to. "Do you? Nathaniel Fitzroy, you love your art and can practice it as you please. The art *I* love cannot be practiced because its gatekeepers will not have me. Not the way I'd like them to, with my name signed, my opinions known, my values appreciated, my presence seen without shame."

"And you think I could do that? Have my art hanging in some nice museum?" He gives me a pointed look. "There are so very few colored artists that reach that type of success. And I may live in a nice house. I do not doubt that my family loves me. I have never wanted for food or comfort. But have you ever been asked to not attend a dinner in your own home?"

I can only stare at him.

He wipes his palms on his knees. "There were times. My grandfather wanted to entertain a guest who would not be seated at the same table as I was. You know, Gwen's always been envious that I got to be tutored in sciences and maths, but the only reason I had a private tutor is because the finest schools wouldn't take me." He laughs, but it sounds sad. "I've always been jealous of you."

"Of *me*?"

"Do you know how lucky *you* are? To have lived in Addy-shire with your aunt, who looks like you?" His voice is raw. "I am lucky. I am. But as pretty as my life looks, you have not seen every cut of society's blade against me."

My face grows hotter by the second. "I'm sorry. I know that this world isn't easy for you either. I do not hate you, Fitzroy—I never could, because you were the first person who ever really understood me, I think. Since we were kids." I nudge him with my shoulder. "Even if I do make you miserable."

"*Agh.*" He squeezes his eyes closed. "You don't make me miserable. You don't. What I would give to snatch back those words." He drops his head into his hands with a hopeless sigh. "It will give you no comfort, but I'd gladly hear you speak or read your words for hours on end, if you'd grant them. Come." He rises. "Let's take a walk, I'm dying for a bit of fresh air."

I follow him out of the dance hall and into the cool night. It's dark, the moon only just peeking out from behind the clouds. At first, I think we're just walking aimlessly. But he takes me to a small bridge overlooking the Seine, and I realize he meant to bring me here all along.

He rolls up his sleeves and rests his elbow on the railing. "Have you had a chance to visit any museums?"

"Oh." I wave my hands. "Loads of them."

"I'd like to open my own gallery one day, even if Grandfather thinks painting is a waste of time."

"How will you have an exhibit when you won't let anyone look at your work?"

"I let people look at my work."

"Not me, not ever."

He drops his head toward his feet, though I catch the slight edge of a smile on his lips. "They're just portraits."

"Portraits? Since when do you do portraits? I thought you liked flowers and vases and other boring things."

He shakes his head, the smile growing. "Since I was little!"

"When an art director comes calling for your best piece, which will you offer? You've done some of Gwen and Jane, I imagine?"

"Jane, yes. Gwen can't sit still." He lifts his head. "Though, neither would be my favorite."

"If you say your favorite is a self-portrait, I'm leaving."

He chuckles. "*Ah.* Remind me when I return for Jane's wedding. I'll show you."

"You promise?"

His smile softens with genuine sweetness. "I promise."

After a bit of comfortable silence, we make back for the dance hall. Olivia and Samuel are waiting on the steps, though the party is obviously still raging on inside, but Livvie sees us first and bolts for me. "Oh, there you are!" She catches herself, gives a small curtsy to Nate. "Fitzroy, hello, what a lovely surprise."

"My fault," he says, pressing his hand against his chest. "I apologize for keeping you both waiting."

Sam nods at him. "Not a worry, seeing as you are both well. I was thinking that we should return home."

"Of course," I say quickly.

"Good, I'll call the carriage."

Olivia looks at Nate and me once more, and then accompanies Samuel.

I turn to Nate. I know what I should say—that we cannot go on like this, that our affections for each other cannot be romantic. The trouble is saying it while he's looking at me, silently pleading, because I think he knows too.

"Stella," he says, my name sounding as lovely as ever in his mouth. "I just want you to know that everything I said tonight was from my heart. You are so dear and so important to me. Whether we are together or apart, friendly or fighting, I know that you're the only person who understands me to my core. For that, I will always cherish you."

I nod. "And I you," I offer softly. "You are my best friend, Nathaniel Fitzroy."

Our friendship is enough. It *has* to be. Friends are all that we can be. He has been claimed, and I am not the one he will offer his hand to . . . not that that's something I want, of course. And while I have the excruciating thought of lifting my mouth to his perfect full lips, I tamp it down. It's too easy, the way he makes my nerves flutter. I can't let myself be enraptured by him, but my heart doesn't seem to understand.

He smiles, though his eyes are shining with tears.

He waits with me in silence until the carriage comes around. Our parting is simple. A curt good night. No last look, no secret touch of the hand, no last flit of longing. I step into the carriage, he steps back into the dance hall.

And it is *agonizing.*

27

The summer's nearly over. Here in London, the leaves have not yet turned, but a distinct breeze runs through the city, signaling the end of the season. The sun is out, the air is cool, and it is a perfect day for a wedding.

I'm miserable. Miserable for spending the weeks since Paris ruminating on my friendship with Nathaniel. I brace myself every time I pick up the newspaper, expecting to see an announcement of his engagement to Katherine Chen.

"Perk up," Lady Tess chides as we rumble on in the carriage. "You can't frown your way through a wedding."

"Want to bet?" I mutter.

She sighs before turning to Olivia in hopes of easier conversation. I don't blame her. I've never been great at carrying on while in a foul mood, but today is particularly difficult to plaster on a smile.

The carriage slows. Our first stop is the market for the costly set of plates that Lady Tess has commissioned for Jane and the viscount. We step into the square, which is full of people tottering about, as always, but it feels . . . louder? Everyone's very chatty, and a man nearly bumps into me. His head was down as he scanned some important paper.

"Stella!" Livvie turns to me, picking up a discarded sheet from the steps of the jeweler's. "It's Fiona Flippant."

"*What?*" I take the half sheet. I didn't realize Mr. Elmhurst was going to give the column its own separate printing.

At first, I feel the sharp, acidic pain of terror rising in my throat.

But then comes an odd sort of pride. I look up at the ladies gossiping amongst themselves on their strolls, the dwindling stacks of newsletters that the boys are selling.

I did that.

Lady Tess's face has gone a pale shade reserved for apparitions and corpses. She scans the words quickly. "Stella, this is—"

"*Brilliant.*" I laugh. "I've always liked your father, have I mentioned that?"

"You once said he was so stodgy that he must've been raised by statues."

"A genius, he is!"

"Wait!" Olivia's still examining the sheet in my hand. "Is that *me*? Delicate Rose?" I can't tell if she's flattered or furious. "Why did you write about me?"

"And Kitty?" Lady Tess adds through clenched teeth. "What happened to the anonymous questions? Fiona Flippant is an advice column, not a scandal sheet!"

"Your father—who, as I mentioned, is a genius—thought the column needed a bit of spice!"

"Much more than a bit," Olivia mutters. "Wait, who are these—Rosy Rake, Keeper-of-Coins . . . ?"

I shrug. "Had to lead people off the scent, so I made them up."

Lady Tess frowns deeply.

"What? If they're fake, how is anyone's reputation hurt?"

"Because gossip, dear Stella, demands investigation," she says. "I bet every well-to-do family on a hill will be shocked when their friends begin interrogating them about their son's dalliances with his maid."

Oh. I suppose I didn't think of it that way.

Olivia lifts her brows in disbelief. "Heavens. I am happy for you, Stella. Your name may not be on the page, but who else could say they've stopped London in its tracks with a sheet of paper?"

I run my fingers over the inked name.

"One day it *will* be my name," I whisper. "And with something even more jaw-dropping."

"I wonder if the Chens will still come to the wedding," Livvie says nonchalantly.

My stomach drops a bit, but I perk up at the sight of the scandal sheets flying in the wind.

We travel about an hour out of London to a town so small that it almost feels like the entirety of it has been outfitted for Jane's wedding. Gloomy clouds hang in the distance, and the air is heavy with the promise of rain. Hopefully there'll at least be some warm brandy to keep us comfortable.

We join the line of spectators entering the church. Lady Tess adjusts her hat. She seems calmer now that we're out of the city, but I wonder if she'll be speaking to her father about the newest Fiona Flippant. I told no lies, nor was I particularly mean. It's just a bit of gossip, that's all, and it wasn't even my idea in the first place.

As we make our way into the small, lovely chapel, Gwendolyn heads me off. *"Finally."* She's out of breath. "Argh, all the attendants in the world, and Jane has *me* triple-checking the seating." She exhales. "Hi, Olivia, Mrs. Sinclair. You're in the third row."

Lady Tess and Olivia go on, but Gwen keeps me back. "Have you seen this?" Under her list of names, she's got one of the Flippant sheets. "Fiona Flippant is back, and . . . Stella, she's written about you."

I am no actress, but I think I play surprised quite well. "Oh, yes, we heard about it in the city."

"Well, it's kind to you, at least. Less so to Lord Grantchester, though he deserves it after trying to pull the wool over your eyes." She flips the page over, and her lips go tight and grim. "I just wish she'd kept this nonsense about Kitty out of it."

I peek over her shoulder as if I need reminding. "Oh, yes. Something about her father's indecency—"

"How *horrible*. Would it have hurt the writer to have considered the embarrassment of his wife and children before publishing such a thing?" She shakes her head, genuinely perturbed. "Kitty doesn't deserve this."

My face prickles with heat. "Perhaps *he* was the one doing the embarrassing, no? Flaunting his mistress at some public event—if what is written is true—is shameful in its own right."

◆ 274 ◆

"Well, of course! But to brandish it for the whole city to see isn't right either. Who is hurt more? Him, or his family?"

"I—" My voice catches. "Well, I don't know."

Gwen sighs. "Anyway, we'll talk later. I want to hear all about Paris!"

As I walk to my seat, I feel an awful pang of nervousness in the pit of my stomach.

"What was that about?" Olivia asks quietly.

"Nothing," I whisper back. "She just wanted to chat about Paris." I crane my neck—the woman in front of us is wearing an *ungodly* creation atop her head, one to rival the dead bird atop Lady Tess's. "Switch with me," I mutter to Livvie.

"What? No."

"But I can't see—"

"But then *I* won't be able to see!"

The air shifts. It's like there's a collective gasp, and for a second, I think that this has all begun very quickly if Jane's already gliding down the aisle.

I turn, but it's not Jane. Kitty Chen has arrived.

On Nathaniel's arm.

Her head is up, but quirky, cheery Kitty looks a little worse for wear. She's holding on to Nathaniel tightly, as if she'll fall without him there. I don't envy her. No one's making an effort to hide their gawks and whispers as Nathaniel leads her to the front row in the opposite aisle.

There's a moment where I think he's going to look to me. He shifts a little, turning his head slightly to his left. I turn away before I can know for sure.

❖ 275 ❖

It is better this way. Easier, I think, to not speak of friendship, of late-night dances, of strolls down the Seine. I have only a few days left in London. He will become the heir his grandfather wanted and a husband for Kitty.

I feel a tap on my shoulder. I turn. It's an attendant, dressed better that I am on most days. "Miss Sedgwick? Jane Danvers is requesting your presence."

"Oh?" I glance at Lady Tess. She gives me an exaggerated shooing gesture; I think she likes that everyone has heard the lady of the day has requested my company before she weds. She seems to think this is a good thing. An honor. But dread grows in my chest.

In a back room of the church, Jane's attendants are performing last touches. Her veil is being adjusted, her hair smoothed.

From underneath a white cloud of mesh, she smiles at me. "There you are."

"You look beautiful, Jane."

The smile grows. "I should hope so." She snaps at her attendants to leave us.

I'd expected Gwen here, at least. Or maybe one of Jane's friends. But now it's just us.

She gestures for me to sit in the chair across from her.

"You know," she starts. "I've always adored you, Stella. Well, when I wasn't mad with jealousy."

"Jealous?"

"You had such a free nature about you. Hardly a care for what you looked like, sounded like, or who might see you and judge."

I'm sure that was an insult, just doled out in sweet tones. "I'd prefer to be born rich. *That* is true freedom."

❖ 276 ❖

Her smile thins. "Then why did you reject Lord Grantchester?"

I feel an odd sense of relief. Is that what this is about? "Freedom tied to a man is hardly freedom at all."

Silence stretches between us, nearing an uncomfortable amount of time before she says, coolly, "No. No, I don't think that's it." She flicks her eyes downward in a contemplative pause. "A marriage between my half brother and Katherine Chen seems unlikely now. As it turns out, the young woman with whom her father was having an affair is the daughter of some German merchant." She waves her hand, like this is unimportant. "Apparently, a deal between them has fallen through, and Mr. Chen is suddenly not as wealthy as he once was. I can't have my Nathaniel in such a badly done pair. His match reflects on all of us, after all."

"I—" I pause, trying to think of how to respond. My mouth always did move faster than my mind. "I'm sorry to hear it." And I am. Despite my own resistance to seeing Nathaniel and Katherine married, I did not mean for all of this to happen.

She regards me with certain interest. "Are you?"

I say nothing. I can't read her at all.

"I've come to make you a deal. See, Grandfather is adamant that you should have Kendall Manor. I do not entirely understand why, but as it is my papa's wish . . ." She leans forward, places her snow-pale hand atop mine. "My soon-to-be husband has some connections at the barrister's office, and he may be able to pull some strings so that when Grandfather dies, Kendall Manor will be yours, Stella, whether you marry or not."

I blink a few times, still stunned by her admission that she is none too pleased to see me inherit Kendall. "Oh."

❖ 277 ❖

"You don't look very happy."

"Well, truthfully, it's always been difficult to imagine what exactly was going to happen after Mr. Fitzroy passed."

"Well, consider it done." Her blue eyes flash with glee. "I only ask one thing."

The underlying dread in my stomach tightens, a gut feeling saying, *I told you so.*

"I ask that you leave Nathaniel alone. Dare I say, I'm a little embarrassed for you, at this point."

I draw my hand back. My veins are running with ice. "You are mistaken—"

"Mistaken?" She chuckles, dripping in condescension. "No, I know you too well. You can't lie to me."

My face is burning. I want to stand and leave, but Jane's gaze has me rooted in my seat.

She sucks in a breath. "Thing is, my fiancé doesn't understand why I wouldn't prefer the two of you betrothed. *It makes sense,* he says, in that bumbling way of empty-headed men, because it would keep Kendall firmly in the Fitzroy lineage. Yes, *perfect sense,* he says. Only—you bring nothing to the table. You are poor, stubborn, selfish, and too chatty for your own good. To think, you, a *Fitzroy?*" She laughs as if she never heard such a ridiculous thing. "My mother did her part to bring shame upon my family name. Ironic, that her son has a chance to restore it with a proper, good match. I think, a few generations of good matches down the line, we can root out my mother's mistake entirely."

I swallow hard. My thoughts are reeling with the insults,

the sheer pride, the way she looks at me like I'm nothing but a speck of dirt under her shoe.

"So I would give up Kendall Manor easily if it meant that you wouldn't fumble Nate's prospects."

I pause. "What role do I have in hurting his prospects?"

Jane's entire demeanor changes. What was once snide with a bit of amusement is now just plainly annoyed. "Oh heavens, Stella. You can't be serious? It's quite a talent you have, being so clever and so utterly clueless at the same time." She waits, brow raised. "Do you really not know? He'd throw everything away to marry you."

I'm too baffled to speak for a moment. "You're wrong."

"Am I?" Her grin is viperous.

Well, now . . . now I don't know. I hate the way my nerves pulse all at once, the way I feel nausea and anxiety in the pit of my belly. My tone is acidic, like fire on my tongue. All that I want right here and now is to go home to safe, familiar surroundings. "You needn't worry, Jane. Keep Kendall, I don't want it."

She sighs deeply. "Come now, Stella, don't be so stubborn—"

"And I have no desire to speak to you about this again. I'd like to go home."

"I see." She leans back in her seat and considers me for a moment. Then, she nods, as if expecting—no, *wanting*—this. "I'll have my own valet take you. You should be in London in an hour."

"No, I want to go to Addyshire. Olivia and Mrs. Sinclair can stay, yes? No reason to cause a scene." And, honestly, I'd prefer to take this ride alone.

✦ 279 ✦

Jane tilts her head, as if gauging my seriousness. "Of course." She stands, her beautiful white dress billowing out from her. All this horrible talk, I forgot that she was a bride.

Unceremoniously, I leave without another word. My stomach twists with shame. It's all I can do to keep from angry-crying. Shoulders back, chin up, I stride toward the front staircase. My own hurried steps are so silent under the roar of thunder that it's no wonder I don't hear the steps behind mine.

"*Stella, wait!*"

Nathaniel's voice stops me at the edge of the covered steps, just before the blanket of rain tunneling over the side of the awning.

This is the *last* thing I want. I know that seeing him will only make this harder. And yet I can't leave without saying goodbye.

Gently, Nathaniel reaches out and touches my hand. His deep voice is rattled like I've never heard it before. "I went to check on Jane, and I saw you—Stella, she said you're leaving for Addyshire." He huffs, attempts to catch his breath. "What's happened?"

"Nothing's happened. I . . . I'm just not meant to be here."

His brow flinches. "Jane—"

"This isn't about Jane," I say, and it's mostly true. "This is about me, how I've never been meant for this life. I will refuse your grandfather's offer."

He hasn't stopped shaking his head.

"We are on different paths. You are to marry a well-connected, wealthy, proper lady—"

"Oh, bollocks," he chokes out. "Has it come to this, finally, is this the moment?"

❖ 280 ❖

Heat rushes into my face. I can hardly stand to look at the despair he's levying at me in those brown eyes, the worry lines in his furrowed brow.

"You once told me that I should learn my faults, so here I am. I've decided to stop lying to myself, and to be honest with you." He exhales, still trying to catch his breath. "I love you, Stella, and I should've told you long ago."

I look away from him, pain lancing my heart. "And when did you decide this? In between all of your insults and jabs at me? Before Lord Grantchester's interests or after? I arrived in London, and you treated me like a stranger, and now you want me to believe it was love?"

"I knew I loved you when you left Kendall all those years ago."

I swallow hard, trying to keep my emotions at bay. "You were a boy. We were children!"

"And yet I still feel it all." He dips his head down and runs both hands through his hair. "My coldness toward you was not born of hatred. It was fear. I was to marry Katherine, and you—just your presence at Kendall, at the balls—you made it so *difficult*. Do you understand?" He shakes his head slowly, as if I'm the one who's missing something. His face is tense, serious, and painfully lovely. "Suddenly, doing something as easy as falling into my set match became impossible. It was *easier* when you were in Addyshire, Stella. I could ignore everything I felt for you. But you returned, and I *was* miserable. Miserable because I could not stop thinking about you."

"I don't believe you," I whisper shakily.

He steps closer, his fingers resting on my knuckles. "Stella, hear me. You must know that I love you now as I have always loved you—with a complete lack of restraint. And, well, I don't think my heart can bear keeping it a secret any longer."

"Please," I whisper through the tears. "Speak no more of this." I spin, and keep walking, but he's in line with me step by step. "I have nothing to give you, Nathaniel."

"That has never mattered to me—"

"Marriages aren't done for love!" I'm taken back to Eastwick Abbey with these words that Grantchester had once thrown at me. Here I am again, a rejection on my tongue. But this one is infinitely more painful. "And it does matter, Nathaniel, even if you are too naive to see it! I'm going home."

The carriage is here now. The wedding bells are chiming.

"Well, then I'll come with you!" Nate's arms are open, and he gestures to himself as if he'd come just like this, no possessions on him but a jeweled ring and the damp clothes on his own back. "Ask me to, Stella, and I will."

I can't look at him. The words are on my lips, but I have to force them out. I know that if I do this, I will lose him forever. But I don't think I have a choice. How could I, with Jane's views made known? Could I do what Nathaniel does—choke back my anger at the hatred we face? Attend dinners and parties with the likes of people like Royce? I couldn't live like that, not even for Nathaniel. "I think my greatest regret is letting you believe I loved you as you love me."

I hear a sharp intake of breath, and then he is silent. I should go now, before he can convince me otherwise, but my feet are frozen in the spot.

✦ 282 ✦

He wraps his hand around my wrist. "The least you could do is look at me as you break my heart."

I turn up to him.

His eyes search my face for regret, the seconds passing in agony. When he does not find it, he drops his hand. "I understand," he says, so softly that I would not hear him under the rain if he wasn't so close to me. He steps away. "Safe travels, then."

He pulls my hand upward and kisses my knuckles.

I hold my breath, and I do not release it until I'm settled in the carriage.

PART THREE

Troubled sister, I am sorry that I do not have more words of wisdom on your predicament. I often wonder what this world would be like if we were encouraged to stand at our partners' sides rather than behind them. And—dearest readers—if we valued a man's ability to thrill and comfort with an embrace rather than with his purse.

—"Letters to Fiona Flippant," Issue 8

December 1863

28

Addyshire

Aunt Eleanor takes one look at me and laughs. "Don't tell me, you've refused yet another proposal of marriage."

Promptly, I begin to sob.

"*Stella!*" Aunt Eleanor wraps her arms around me, never mind my soaking clothes, and brings me inside. The house is warm, smells like honey and cumin, and between the feeling of familiarity and my aunt's arms around me, I just can't stop crying.

Aunt Eleanor asks no questions. She simply peels off my damp coat, leads me to the sitting room, lets me have her nice armchair with the blanket I'm forbidden to touch, and leaves to fetch dry clothes and tea. And when I've changed and settled with my cup, she waits, humming to herself on the sofa as she finishes folding laundry. No questions, because she knows me like I'm her own daughter.

"I missed you," I manage, another cup later.

She only nods, but I see the hint of a smile on her lips.

I put the teacup to the side. "You haven't asked about Olivia and Mrs. Sinclair."

"To be honest, I expected you to run away from London much earlier than this."

A chuckle bursts from my lips. "Understandable."

Finally, she puts down the laundry and gives me a good, hard look. "My dear. Tell me who hurt you, and I will take a carriage down to London myself."

The humor vanishes, and I can feel the tears once more. "As much as I'd like to see you chastise someone who isn't me, that isn't necessary. Oh, Aunt Eleanor. I've messed it all up."

She gives me a sympathetic glance. "The Fitzroy boy, yes? Mrs. Sinclair had mentioned . . ." she trails off, sparing me any further hurt.

My throat tightens. "I had him. He was mine. And he offered me a love that I didn't think really existed. But I couldn't give it back."

"You can't force yourself to love someone, Stella. It's why we very rarely are given the chance to marry *for love*."

"And that's the problem." My voice breaks. "See, I do love him."

She exhales softly. "I see."

"And I didn't tell him."

"I wonder if he might know anyway."

I shake my head. "No, I said rather plainly that I did not." I'm so exhausted, I have no energy to spare but to dab at my eyes with the heel of my hand. "And I turned down his grandfather's offer. Well, I'll have to write Mr. Fitzroy, I suppose. I just don't want a thing from them. No favors, nothing to owe."

Aunt Eleanor swallows hard, but nods once more. "It was always going to be difficult, I think."

I leave off that Jane had offered it to me. There's no point in disappointing Aunt Eleanor further. I just want to forget about it.

She comes over and strokes the intricate braids I'd done for the wedding. "Go rest, my child. You've had a long journey, and I know you'll feel better with some sleep."

She kisses my forehead, and I think, *How lucky am I to be loved like this?*

Falling back into Addyshire is easy. It's like I never left.

The garden is coming along nicely. Clearly, Mattie and Annabeth missed me, judging by their moos. My second day back, I pull on my boots and wade through the muck to greet them. I've felt so drained since I returned. Not just mentally, but physically. Sluggish, even. Aunt Eleanor is certain that I'm coming down with a cold and constantly tells me to rest, but I'd rather keep active. It helps to have tasks. I'll do anything I can to take my mind off things I'd rather not be thinking about, and that includes milking the cows, collecting the eggs, and . . . watching supportively from a distance as Mr. Chapman brushes the horses. *Blasted horses.*

It's only Cheswick who sneers and hisses at me, and I hiss back like I've always done, a force of habit.

✦ 289 ✦

"Absence is meant to make the heart grow *fonder*," Aunt Eleanor chides me, taking the fat orange cat into her arms.

I grimace as I pull off my light coat. "He started it. Bolted across the hallways to trip me, he did. You should have seen it."

She rolls her eyes. "Let Chapman and Townsend do their jobs. If you need something to do, we can always work on your stitches."

"Ah. Stitches."

"Mm-hm."

"You see, I would, but I have to write."

Aunt Eleanor raises a brow. "You don't mean to continue playing at Fiona Flippant? Even on this side of the Thames, I'd heard some chatter about gossip, scandal, and ruin. Sounds like trouble."

"Sounds like a successful column." I bite back an unwanted pang of guilt. "I'll be in the study."

"Before you weasel out of my sight, I heard from Mrs. Sinclair."

I fidget.

"She's . . ." Aunt Eleanor sighs. "I think she feels badly about all this, like it was her fault."

"Nonsense! Lady Tess helped me immeasurably. I may have been pushed out of London society, but I do have my column, don't I?"

As it turns out, my column is a rather stubborn fiend today.

Hours pass, and all I have to show for it is a heap of discarded pages. Mr. Elmhurst had wanted a bit of spice. Fat lot of good that did.

I don't remember falling asleep, but the sun's about to fall when I jolt awake.

There's shouting downstairs. My head throbs from the sound of it.

"This is awful, just awful!"

That's my cousin's voice. I rush to the stairs and look over the railing. "Olivia?"

She pops her head out of the sitting room. "Oh, apologies, I saw you were sleeping and didn't want to wake you . . ." She sniffles, and as I walk down to meet her, I see that her eyes are rimmed red with tears.

Livvie can be a little dramatic, but there's a horrible pang in my stomach that tells me she's not throwing a tantrum over something trivial.

Sure enough, Olivia starts crying harder, her shoulders bouncing up and down as Lady Tess tries to still them. I clasp my hands around hers. "Goodness, what's happened?"

It's like I've just announced Cheswick's untimely death. Livvie pulls away from us and sinks onto the sofa. She's trying to hold in her sobs, but her efforts are futile. "I'm ruined, Stella!"

"Ruined how?" I look to Lady Tess, who is fumbling with her gloved hands. She's still wearing her jacket. Whatever happened here, it happened quickly.

Olivia hiccups. "There's a . . . a column."

"A column?"

Lady Tess straightens her back and puts on a most refined lilt to her voice. "'A Lord's Guide to Ladies.' Absolute drivel, and dare I say, a poor impression of our Fiona Flippant."

❖ 291 ❖

My heart swings into anxious beating.

Olivia finally lifts her head. Her cheeks are streaked with tears, and her wide brown eyes are puffy. "It speaks of our trip to Paris. There's a claim that I was seen in an unsavory embrace with some rake."

"What nonsense! Who are they claiming you were seen with?"

"I don't know; I'm the only one named!"

Lady Tess hands me a copy of the paper, and I scan it quickly. "How can someone write such horrible and untrue things about innocent people and publish them?" Lady Tess exhales sharply, but I spin to her before she can speak. "Come now, this is nothing like Fiona Flippant. This was done specifically to ruin Olivia's reputation. God knows why!" I turn the pamphlet over. "Whoever's behind this must have the connections to get such slander printed."

"And money," Lady Tess adds. "Perhaps some wealthy family with an eye on Mr. Désir."

"Or perhaps someone simply doesn't want me in London," Olivia says quietly. "And now they'll get their wish."

My heart shatters. I've never heard her sound so resigned. I kneel at her feet and take her hands in mine once more. "Dear cousin, you can't think Mr. Désir would believe this, even if he heard all the way in France!" I lean in. "And wasn't he with you the whole time?"

"It won't matter what he believes. I can't imagine his family will want his name attached to a girl tied to such vicious gossip. His mother already hates me! He will certainly find a girl richer and prettier than I!"

✦ 292 ✦

"Oh, stop! Your beauty stands so high above any other lady that Mr. Désir can hardly see them in your presence. Olivia, you know me to be an immovable cynic about love, but I've seen how he looks at you, and I swear, it melts even my cold heart."

She smiles a little. "Even if that were true, a man like him has no business socializing with anyone in such drama."

"Then I must clear your name. I promise, I'm going to find the person who did this to you."

Aunt Eleanor rushes in from the kitchen, two cups of tea in hand.

She sits next to Olivia and fusses over her. Livvie sinks her head onto her mother's shoulder and takes steady, measured breaths.

Lady Tess looks at me, and nods toward the hallway.

I follow her out, and she slides the doors of the sitting room closed. "Stella, what happened in Paris?"

Nervously, I lean against the checkered blue wall. "Nothing! Well, nothing like this!" I wave the pamphlet at her. "You were there!"

She plants her fists at her sides. "And yet, I have a sinking feeling in my stomach that there's something I don't know."

I cringe. "Well. Did we get into any trouble? No, we didn't. Did we sneak out after midnight to dance? Erm. Maybe?"

Her eyes widen. "*I beg your pardon?*"

"But did we get murdered or robbed or drunk? Of course not! Okay, maybe I was a little bit drunk—"

"Oh, Stella—"

❖ 293 ❖

"But I guarantee you that Livvie was *never* in the passionate embrace of some rake! Sure, we all danced, but nothing like this! She was with Mr. Désir the whole time, and he treated her very well."

She drops her voice. "I know that Olivia would never, but she can be impressionable. . . . I feel I must ask to be sure. There's no possibility that she'd been charmed by some devious man and found herself in his embrace in front of the Seine?"

"No, there's no possibility . . . I'm sorry—" I pause. "The Seine?"

I look at the pamphlet once more.

There's some talk about men's fashion and the newest wares from the hottest shops, but the "Local Scandals" section is obviously where the eye is meant to be drawn to.

As with every season, a fine gentleman must navigate society with an eye toward the best young woman to run his house. She must be agreeable indeed, with talents as well as beauty, for the match to be a suitable one. There is always competition, after all, especially if one would stand next to one of the wealthiest men in Paris. And who would be lovelier to have but the season's sweetest new face, one Olivia Witherson—only, she was seen tenderly held in the arms of a suitor far paler than the worthy Frenchman, and kissed just as sweetly on the banks of the Seine, her lovely suitor nowhere in sight.

I thank the heavens that my cheeks are not prone to blushing, for I'd look like a proper tomato if not.

Oh no.

It's *me.* Me and Nate. But there was no embrace! No scandalous kiss! Oh hell. I don't know how this happened. I don't understand. And why did they think it was Olivia? We look *nothing* alike, though I guess they never bothered telling us apart anyway.

My stomach turns. "I must write a response, I must—"

Lady Tess purses her lips then. "Stella, I think you should leave it alone."

"We can't let this writer get away with this."

"Don't you see? This column is a direct answer to Fiona Flippant. You've upset the wrong person."

"You think it was Grantchester, or the Chens? They couldn't have known it was me that wrote it."

"No, but if you wanted to get some heat of your own scandal off of your back, what would you do? You'd target the two girls that people could be united against. The outsiders." She sighs apologetically. "I want you to leave this alone, my dear."

I don't like it, but I don't know what else to say. I feel a headache coming on. And I do not think I can write my way out of this.

29

Under Lady Tess's instruction, Olivia has sent one short letter to the house of Désir. Livvie deserves the chance to redeem herself. It might be a while until we hear back—according to Gwen's letters, the Désirs have not come to London since we saw them last. Gwen's cross with me for leaving so abruptly but also says that she misses me dearly and would like to visit as soon she can. She makes little mention of Nathaniel, only to say that he is well. Unfortunately, the same cannot be said of their grandfather, who is watched all hours of the day. She doesn't put it so bluntly, but it seems they are preparing to say goodbye. When she asks how Olivia is faring, I lie.

Truthfully, Olivia is a shell of herself.

While I've been attempting to drown out my anxious mind by keeping busy, all my cousin does is mope around. She sits in the chair by the window, feet curled under her, staring out as if willing Mr. Désir to come to her on a white horse at dawn. She does her stitches, and for once, I can claim that mine look better. She picks at her food, leaving more to Cheswick than she took for herself.

She weeps. *A lot.* I can hardly stand to hear it. My head has been throbbing since I arrived back in Addyshire, and today's been the worst of all.

"Olivia, let's go for a walk," I suggest. "We've got fresh eggs, and I would really love to see Mrs. Smith's face when they hit her windows."

Livvie doesn't turn to me. She manages a small smile, and says, "I'm not feeling up to it."

Truthfully, neither am I. I think Aunt Eleanor was right about me coming down with some illness. My body is achy, and I feel cold despite the summery weather. But I can't bear to see Livvie like this all day. "Okay, forget the eggs. We should go to the garden, get some air, water the daisies."

"No, I—I don't want to miss a letter if it comes."

Sighing, I sit next to her. The room spins, and I close my eyes for relief. Between my pounding headache and Livvie's sour mood, I feel my patience growing thin. "Even if he did call for you, you wouldn't seriously consider him still?"

She shrugs. "He loves me. I know he loves me."

"Not this again," I mutter, eyes half-closed.

There's silence for a moment. "What was that, Stell?"

"His mother disapproves, and he's already discarded you once. Isn't it time to stop being so foolish about the man?"

❖ 297 ❖

I open my eyes and find Livvie staring at me. "You cannot lecture me on foolishness over a young man. Anyone but you, Stella."

"Oh?" I reply sharply. "Have you decided to finally stand up for yourself for once? It's odd, I'm so used to doing the defense. I hope you'll be there for yourself when the Désirs inevitably send you home crying once more."

She exhales sharply. "You're right. I have grown a spine. And I hope, one day, you'll join me in acting like a young adult rather than a petulant child! And you think highly of yourself, don't you? *My savior*, as if you weren't the one sending sharp cuts my way anytime you wanted to feel good about yourself—"

"*What*—"

"Because you're better than me, aren't you, Stell? You're better than all of us. Stella Sedgwick, the writer, the eternal single woman, the independent thinker. I'm only daft, naive, *boring*, as you were always so quick to say to everyone." She stands suddenly. My mind flashes to this same expression she wore, moping during our trip in Grantchester. "If I was a burden to you, then it's only fair that you know how you were one to me. Could I enjoy myself, knowing you were always sulking in the corners, ready to fight anyone who looked at you the wrong way? You were chained to me, Stella. Every embarrassment you made of yourself reflected on me. And now this? What is my crime, pray tell? Wanting a better life for my mother, and *for you*? Playing by society's rules?"

"*Stop*—" I plead. My mind is rushing, my head is spinning.

But Olivia only leans in, planting her hands on either armrest

❖ 298 ❖

to lock me in. "I'm not a fool. I know it was you and Nathaniel Fitzroy at the bridge. Who else could it have been?" Her voice is full of angry tears. "You did this! You and your letters! You got me into this trouble, but I know better than to let you attempt to see me out of it. Because you've never been my savior, Stella. You've only ever been a hindrance to me saving myself."

I don't know what comes over me, but I scream. *"Be quiet!"*

She jolts back. Her expression is hard to decipher. It's angry, regretful, *tired*. She looks me up and down. "You're ill, Stella."

"Stop, enough already—"

"No, I mean . . ." She backs away. "I'm fetching mother."

She leaves, and it's all like a dream. I feel myself get to my feet, and I hurry up the stairs as fast as my sluggish legs will take me to my room.

You and your letters.

She's right. She's *right.*

I never should have thought I could do this. I never should have gone to London, or to Paris, or to Mr. Elmhurst's office. Being Fiona Flippant has brought me nothing but pain.

My dreams are the root of all of my problems. My writing, my poor attempt at playing Fiona, my damned imagination— they've ruined everything.

Ignoring Aunt Eleanor's call, I go to the chest and rip the bottom drawer from its tracks. My writing spills out—old diary entries, scribbled short stories, discarded drafts. Notebooks and loose sheets of paper; my words, my useless words, my damned, horrible words. I take stacks of my mother's old drafts, too, for she shares the blame as well. I despise her for starting the column, for making me love writing, and most of all, I hate her for leaving me here to navigate life without her.

The heat grows thick as I toss them into the fire, the room spinning under the intensity of my own fever. I want to lean in and watch the ink and paper char black, but I stumble—

"Stella!"

My name sounds distant, even as Aunt Eleanor yanks me back. Olivia is there too, I think. I can hear her worried sobs.

"What are you doing?" Aunt Eleanor shouts angrily, but I hardly hear her. I'm tired, I'm so tired, my body is burning, my arm feels like I've taken a pot scrubber to it.

The next moments are a blur. My body hurts. I'm hot and cold at the same time. I feel hands push me into bed, the bitter taste of laudanum, the sweet relief of a heavy, slow sleep.

When I wake, I am alone in a dark room. The fire's out. I feel cold.

Downstairs, there is laughter.

Gingerly, I pull back the covers and step out of bed. The room spins a bit, so I have to clutch the railing as I go. The laughter grows louder and louder with each step.

Aunt Eleanor is having a dinner party.

I watch for a few moments, taking in the scene. Every single person is dressed in impeccable finery. Olivia is laughing with Mr. Désir, their arms linked together. She looks older, more mature, and radiant. Her silky gown moves sumptuously as she rushes over to Gwen's side to whisper something in her ear. Gwen throws her head back and laughs, blond curls bouncing, and though I can't hear it, I have the odd feeling that it was something said about me. Fitzroy and Grantchester are cool in the corner, speaking and judging as young men do, downing their cups and smoking cigars. Only when Kitty spins into view does Nathaniel turn from his friend. He cups her chin, brings her face toward him, and delicately kisses her.

There is music suddenly. It's too loud, and I feel like I'm drowning in the tense staccato of the violin and the crashing drums. I wince against it. When I bring my fingers up to my ears, I find my hands and arms clothed in lush gloves.

"Nice dress," a voice snickers behind me, words dripping with malice. I turn back up toward the stairs, but there's no one there. I look down and see that I'm dressed in my tattered old farming dress and mud-splattered boots. The gloves are the only pretty thing about me.

My hearts batters in my chest. Sweat runs down my back. I shake my head, and the world spins. I have to get back upstairs, I can't be seen like this, I have to change—

"There she is!" Aunt Eleanor exclaims. From the head of the table, she holds a hand out to me. She's dressed in a large mass of silks and lace, like a gilded queen, like I have never seen before.

I step into the light. A few chuckles scatter throughout the room. Aunt Eleanor wrinkles her nose. "My dear, must you always be so sloppy?"

Heat rises up my neck and face. I stammer out a response. "I didn't know you were having guests."

From next to her, Lady Tess waves my words away. "Stella,

❖ 301 ❖

you know we've been planning this dinner for months now. But you've never cared about impressing people, or anyone at all, isn't that right?"

I feel like the floor is being pulled from under me. "Months?"

There's a gasp from the other side of the room. "Are those my gloves?" I turn, and Kitty's making toward me. She grabs my hands roughly and inspects the silk adorning my arms. Before I can protest, she rips them from me. "I've been looking everywhere for these! You see!" She holds the gloves up over her head, showing them to everyone like an inspector with a clue.

My bare right arm is discolored, raw red skin snaking up the limb.

Livvie looks at me with sorrowful disappointment. "Oh, Stella. How cruel of you."

Without the gloves, I feel a wash of cold come over me. "I didn't take them, I was just—I was just wearing them—"

"It's so like her," Nathaniel quips, speaking of me as if I'm not even in the room. "To ruin a night simply because *she's* not having any fun."

"Hear! Hear!" Grantchester adds with a sharp chuckle. "And to think, I nearly married the girl." He turns to Fitzroy. "You were so right about her. *Tiresome.*"

The room breaks out into more laughter, higher, and higher, the music growing with it until I just can't take it, and I run from the room—

But the room doesn't end. Every step forward gets me nowhere, like I'm running in place. I hear the cruel jabs behind me, louder still.

I don't stop running until I am out of breath and, finally, collapse on the floor.

The impact wakes me with a start, my entire body drenched in sweat. I heave for air, though every intake brings about a prickly pain in my throat.

The world is fuzzy and dark, but I know Olivia's voice. "Go back to sleep," she coos.

"*Livvie* . . ." My tongue feels thick. "Sorry . . . I'm sorry . . ."

I feel a damp towel placed against my forehead. I'm trying to feel for my dress, my arms, *those gloves*, but I can't. I'm too weak. She pushes me gently back into the pillows.

"You need rest," Livvie says. She sounds like she's speaking to me from underwater. "There, there. Close your eyes, Stella."

30

My entire body is stiff. My limbs seem to have two-stone weights attached to them. The lightness in my head is bested only by the queasiness in my belly.

And yet my eyes are clear. It takes a moment to understand exactly where I am, but once I do, I'm relieved. *Home.* Here in my bed in Addyshire.

Aunt Eleanor sleeps in the armchair beside me. She's always been such a light sleeper, and I feel a little guilty that she's curled up uncomfortably instead of in her bed.

There's a bowl of thin soup on the side table. Gleefully, I devour it as quickly as I can, though my arms are so weak that I can't lift the spoon quickly enough. I'm lucky that it's still a little warm and that there's even a piece of crusty bread and fresh butter to go with it.

Aunt Eleanor startles awake. "Oh!"

"I tried to eat quietly, but I think soup's made for slurping."

She looks up at the ceiling and closes her eyes.

I manage a weak smile. "You can't already be fed up with me."

"I'm not praying for your silence. I'm praying in thanks."

I bite my lip. "Yes. Right. Thank you, God, for allowing me the time to pester my aunt further."

She smiles. "And now I know you're truly getting well."

I slump back into the pillows, tired again. "How long was I sick? I don't remember much of it. I feel like I've been dreaming for a year."

"A few days, in and out. The fever broke the first night, thankfully, but this is the first time you've really woken up."

Absently, I look down at my arm, which is tender. There are marks from where bandages must've been. I look over at the fireplace. There's a trail of ash, and I remember the smell of smoke.

And now it all comes back to me. I was so angry at myself, I wanted to burn away my drafts, stories, notes, every bit of writing that ever made me dream of becoming a writer, including my mother's old letters.

I'm slammed with grief, as if I've just run head on into a brick wall. "What have I done?"

"Stella," Aunt Eleanor says gently.

My eyes fill with tears. "I was angry at myself, but why did I have to burn *mother's* letters as well? What was I thinking?"

"They were paper. Paper and ink, that is all."

"*Her* papers, *her* ink." I choke on the words. "Her words, her memory. It's like I've lost her again."

❖ 305 ❖

Aunt Eleanor takes my hands, blinking away her own tears. "And your mother's memory lives beyond them. Don't punish yourself over it, I will not let you. Stella, you are greater proof of her brilliance than her column ever was. I see Ginny in you every day, and I know that she would be *unbearably* smug with pride if she were here now." She laughs sadly. "I mean, really, who else could say their daughter writes for one of the city's top papers by day and breaks the hearts of men by night?"

My chuckle comes out thick from all the tears, but it feels good despite all the grief. "I'll remember these kind words the next time you're cross with me."

She squeezes my hand, then wipes her eyes.

"Where's Olivia? I thought I saw her, thought I heard her."

Aunt Eleanor smiles. "She was by your side every day. Really, she wouldn't eat, wouldn't sleep, refused to take her eyes off of you. But Mr. Désir was here. He wanted to take her to Paris to meet his father."

The memory of our last conversation floods me in shame. "Please tell me she went. I will never forgive myself if she's denied him because of my horrible words."

Eleanor nods. "Tessa went along with her, and . . . well. They're engaged now. We just received word this morning."

"Oh!" Thank heavens I already devoured my soup, or else I would've flung it to the ceiling in shock. "What incredible news! I only wish I was there to witness it. She must've fainted!"

Aunt Eleanor exhales. She's trying to keep her own emotions in check, but I can see the pride brimming in her bright eyes.

"Wow . . ." I settle back into the pillows. "She really found her

❖ 306 ❖

match. And a rich man, at that. Olivia Witherson aims high."

"She really didn't want to leave you, Stella. I nearly had to pry her hand off of yours."

I clutch that very hand to my chest. "She's too good. I don't deserve such a loyal cousin."

"Don't say that."

"You didn't hear what I said to her, what I've *always* said to her."

"Hush now. She's forgiven you, just as you've forgiven her."

"Am I horrible?"

Her face drops. "Horrible? My girl, you are a bright star in my life."

I shake my head. I know she has to say these things to me, and I don't believe her. "I've driven everyone away. They can't stand to be near me, because all I do is snip and complain."

With a tender touch, she places her hand atop the satin scarf wrapped around my head. "Stop, you're getting yourself worked up for no reason."

I nearly choke on my words. "But I feel trapped. I always have. And maybe that makes me difficult, or disagreeable, but I can't change how I feel. The truth of the matter is this: when I think about the duties that are put upon me because I am a Black woman, I want to scream until my voice is raw. I want to pull my hair out for the utter unfairness of it! I don't want to be bound to anyone, or made gentle and unfeeling unless my husband likes me otherwise. And I simply wish that wanting to be alone or to be loved didn't have such societal attachments and judgments! Shall I be a passive wife or a homely spinster? How can I choose one cage or another?" I can feel my voice ready to crack and break, and I hate it. The shame wells up in me, making me feel worse. "How can you bear it?"

"I've found happiness where I would have it. Long walks with your mother, hearing all her plans for great plots and schemes. Or when I met Edward. And when Olivia was born, her big brown eyes finding me, and the relief of her heartbeat against mine. And you, Stella, my bright star. I found joy when your mother came around and said, 'Watch her, she's fussy,' and left you in my care so she could finish a letter to Mr. Elmhurst before she demanded you back because she couldn't stand to be away from you for long." She laughs, she's near weepy. "You *were* fussy, mind you, and you threw tantrums like a banshee, but I know how special it is to be able to come from where we do, to be where we are, and be treated to a healthy child's wail."

I lift my head. I let the hot tears fall. For once, they feel freeing rather than shameful. "I want my mother. I want her to tell me that I'm not mad for how I feel."

"Alas, you only have me. And I am telling you that you will have a life of joy. It may not come from a man, from a marriage, or from a child. But you have your words, your passions. I have no doubt that all of London will know the name Stella Sedgwick."

I hiccup. "All of England, I think."

She exhales. "There she is." She takes my empty bowl. "There's something I haven't mentioned. Miss Danvers is here."

"Gwen's here?" My heart lifts.

But Aunt Eleanor shakes her head. "No, it's the eldest. Jane. The Viscountess Amberlough now, I suppose."

Immediately, I ease back under the covers. "What? Send her away!"

"She's been waiting near two days."

My eyes pop open. "Why would she do such a thing?"

Eleanor lets out an exasperated laugh. "To talk to you!"

"No, no, tell her I'm retching something awful!"

She sits at the edge of the bed. "I've a mind to throw her out for what she did to you. But she seems determined to speak with you, and you and I both know your mother would not have stood down against a pretentious wretch like Jane Danvers."

Aunt Eleanor seems older here than when I saw her last. The wrinkles in her deep brown skin are a touch more defined. And her laugh, her posture, the way she moves her hand to touch mine . . . all are weighed down by fatigue.

I squeeze her hand. "Thank you for restoring my good health. I am very lucky to be under your care."

"Anyone could have done so," she says, looking away.

"No, no, Lady Tess would have fainted at the mere *suggestion* of vomit."

She laughs again, livelier this time. "Shall I send for the lady?"

"I don't know why you insist on ruining this perfectly nice moment."

"She's been waiting for *two days*!"

"What's one more?"

"*Stella.*"

✦ 309 ✦

"Fine." I wave, conceding. "But if you hear screaming, I've taken a scissor to her hair."

Aunt Eleanor leaves, and I curse myself for not asking how I looked. I can't imagine my complexion's glowing after a feverish week. The room is not so pleasant either. It's stuffy, and there's a discarded pile of towels on the floor. I touch the scarf around my head, and then—it's like magic—I suddenly decide that I do not care.

It's freeing.

Jane appears, every bit the perfect lady. Her casual muslin dress is nicer than my finest dresses, and her hair is done in a messy updo. She hasn't been sleeping well, and looks a little ghostly for it. Her eyes find me first, then the room, and then return to me.

"Pardon the mess," I say plainly.

"I could come back when you've had a chance to compose yourself." Her voice is very unlike her. Soft, and cloying.

"Now is fine. Besides, what would be the point in trying to impress a person who thinks so little of me?"

She sits across from me in Aunt Eleanor's rickety armchair. "I am quite fond of you. You know that, don't you, Stella?"

"You keep telling me this, but I don't think I do."

Jane has always been a master of composure, but here, she looks lost. "I told your aunt not to tell you, seeing as you were sick. My grandfather passed a few nights ago."

I stiffen. "Oh. Heavens."

"I'd sent a courier, but you were in no state to travel for the funeral."

❖ 310 ❖

"I'm sorry to hear it. My mother never had a bad thing to say about him, which made him honorable in my books."

"He was. He was a good man." She looks down at her nails. "I'll never claim to know what it's like to be in your position, and likewise, you'll never know mine. Believe it or not, there are unique burdens in being the eldest daughter in a good family."

I try to be civil. Compromising, even. "I don't doubt that."

"I have been burdened with making a fine match for myself, running a house, fighting off vultures circling my grandfather's deathbed, and making sure my half brother and sister are well placed in society should I fail or die. And when I have a moment for myself, I can't even take a deep breath lest someone think I'm doing so too loudly." Jane wrings her hands. "I think I have done well enough. Gwen's incorrigible, but she understands her place. And Nathaniel? I'm so proud of the young man he's become. It was set, Stella. *It was set.* But he couldn't get over his childhood love."

I swallow hard, my heart twisting with both pleasure and pain.

"Can you believe it? All I've done for him while tending to my own new marriage, and now he can't bear to look at me!" From her purse, she pulls a thin stack of envelopes tied together with twine. "But a new match will be set—there's always an heiress waiting in the wings for a man like Nathaniel—so I suppose there's no harm. *Here.* If only to clear my conscience."

She places a stack of letters next to me. Some are new and fresh, but some have turned yellow with age.

My heart races. The first envelope in the pile is marked

with my name written in a boy's hand. I thumb through them, watching as my name becomes more elegant with each passing note—each passing year.

All this time I'd felt abandoned by the Fitzroys once we left.

All this time, Nathaniel was trying to reach out to me.

The last thing I want to do is cry in front of Jane, but my eyes are refusing to cooperate. "Why—"

"I was doing him a favor. You as well. It could never be, Stella."

She continues speaking, but I hardly hear her. The last note is not in an envelope. It's simply a folded piece of paper, the first line written and scribbled over again and again in the handwriting of a secondary schoolchild, but I can just make out the opening lines, and my heart stops beating.

Dear Fiona Flippant, I am hopelessly in love with my best friend. And now she's gone.

"You say he loves me," I whisper. "Since we were little, it seems. And you were smart enough to know that the affection needed to be snuffed out before it grew into something else." I can't help but laugh as a few tears fall. "It was you. You sent my mother away from Kendall Manor."

Jane's eyes snap to me.

I cut in before she can claim otherwise. "My mother always told me that she left your grandfather's employment because Aunt Eleanor needed company after my uncle died, but that wasn't true. My mother was sent away for stealing a prized emerald ring."

Jane pales and stiffens. She curls her hand into a fist, the

❖ 312 ❖

enormous green jewel on her finger tightening around it. She has always been a master of perfect composure, and I am honored to be the one to see her crumble.

"Heavens, you are something else, Jane."

She catches the malice around my words and leans back into her chair. "The deed to Kendall Manor is yours. You did as asked."

I drop the letters into my lap. "I don't want the deed, nor do I want your company. You've said your piece, and I think you should leave."

She looks to her hands. "I know you think I'm—"

"What I'm thinking of is a night at a ball. You weren't there, but you know all about what Mr. Royce said to me."

"Mr. Royce is a pompous man. I've always thought that."

I chuckle. "I want you to know. You may think you're less hateful, but really, I feel the same way about you now as I did about him then. The only difference is, well, I wish I wasn't so surprised. I trust you can find your way out, yes? Great. Get out of my sight, Jane."

God, that felt good.

Jane's face goes blotchy and red. She opens her mouth in protest, but I hold my hand toward the door.

She leaves, finally. It takes a moment for the adrenaline to subside, but when it does, I ease back into the pillows with a satisfied grin.

31

"Pay attention, Aunt Eleanor. Don't you blink."

She's staring at Cheswick over her teacup, unamused. "What exactly am I looking at?"

"Prepare to be amazed." I adjust the top hat I found in old Uncle Edward's trunk. "Cheswick, red ribbon."

Cheswick purrs and promptly nudges the green ribbon laid out on the rug with his nose.

"Ah," I mutter contemplatively. *"Colorblindness."*

Aunt Eleanor shakes her head. "And how long did it take you to teach Chessy this trick?"

"Two days. Oh, apropos of absolutely nothing, we may have to make him more treats."

"Stella—"

I already know what she's going to say. *We need to have a*

talk about your next steps. Though Aunt Eleanor was easy on me while I regained my strength, it's now been nearly a month since my fever broke. With Livvie away, she's got no one to distract herself from wondering what to do with me.

"So I've sent a letter to Mr. Elmhurst," I say. "I think 'Letters to Fiona Flippant' has run its course. I was never as good at it as Mum was, anyway. I want to ask him to take me on as an apprentice. My plan is to be so annoyingly persistent that he will have no choice but to put me on to his staff."

"Or fire you."

I balance the top hat on my knee. "Oh. Well that's true." I nibble on a biscuit to buy myself some time. "I really do not want to be a nanny or a servant, Aunt Eleanor."

"I know." She exhales. "I could write to Jane—"

"Absolutely not." I wrote the Fitzroys a letter of condolences, delivered along with some of Aunt Eleanor's sipping chocolate mixes. I've heard nothing back, which is fine. The correspondence had a finality to it, on my decision.

"An entire house, Stella. Not to mention the allowance."

"I won't have that held over my head for the rest of my life. When I said I no longer wanted a thing to do with the Fitzroys, I meant it. Well—" I leap to my feet. "I'm off for a walk."

"Your third of the day—"

"It's good for the soul!" I call out, halfway to the door.

But when I open it, there's a commotion on our steps.

It all happens very fast—a man has his fist raised to knock on the door, sees me, frowns, I scowl back, he asks for the man of the house, I say, *He's dead,* so he asks for my mistress, I threaten

✦ 315 ✦

to push him down the steps, and all the while, another man carries a weeping Katherine Chen into the house.

Him I recognize from the house over the hill. "Mr. Stetson!"

He nods to me, his pale face red as a radish. "Miss Sedgwick, where's Mrs. Witherson?"

Aunt Eleanor comes into the hallway from the sitting room. "What's happened? *Who is this?*"

"Kitty Chen," I whisper. The girl is moaning in pain and clutching her ankle.

Mr. Stetson sets her down on our sofa. "There was an accident. Miss Chen's carriage wheel broke, sending them down a hill." He gestures toward the driver. "We'll have to see if we can replace it."

Aunt Eleanor wipes her hands on her apron. "Of course, and the young lady can stay here for the time being. I'll call upon the doctor to see her."

I look back at Kitty, who's already fainted.

Aunt Eleanor and I share a curious look, our brows raised identically.

By the time the town physician arrives and Kitty wakes, I've eaten three ginger biscuits and had two cups of tea. Well, the second cup was hers, but she was resting, anyway, and it was getting cold.

"Miss Chen?" I ask tentatively.

Kitty looks up at me. Her face is bloodless as she looks around. "Stella? Where am I?"

I kneel next to Mr. Granger, who's wrapping her ankle in cloth. "You're in Addyshire. This is my aunt's house."

❖ 316 ❖

"Oh! Did I faint?" She touches her head. "Where's my driver, Mr. Donnelly?"

"He's fine, he's fixing the carriage. And you'll be fine as well; Mr. Granger here has been tending to my own scrapes and bruises since I was a child."

"A foolhardy child," he murmurs.

I shrug. "And he hasn't grown a sense of humor since."

Kitty manages a weak smile. "I'm terribly sorry to have put you out."

"Oh, nonsense. Would you like some stew? It's my aunt's famous recipe. It won a prize at the last Addyshire fair, though some weren't too fond of the spice, fair warning."

"Too much spice," Granger mumbles.

She smiles sweetly. "I was wondering about that delicious smell. That sounds lovely, thank you."

I let Mr. Granger finish up while I prepare a bowl. The whole kitchen smells like allspice, pepper, garlic, and roasted meat. I tell you, I will never leave Addyshire again if it means going without my aunt's recipes. I fix myself a bowl as well.

When I return, Mr. Granger is wrapping up his belongings.

". . . and lots of rest, you'll have to keep off of it for at least a few days." He looks to me, nods. "Give my best to Mrs. Witherson, Stella. And watch it with the sweets, you'll rot your teeth."

"Yes, yes," I whisper, showing him the way out.

Two spoons in, Kitty seems to approve of the stew. "It's delicious, thank you."

"I'm happy you like it."

We fall into a slightly awkward silence. It's hard to look at her like this. Even without the accident, she'd still have the dark circles under her eyes, and the overall lack of cheeriness that made her so infuriatingly endearing weeks ago.

Oh, shite, here it goes—

"I have to confess," I blurt out so quickly that I can hardly believe it. "It was me. I exposed your father. I am Fiona Flippant. I ruined your engagement. It's all my fault."

I'd expected more of a reaction, but she only nods. "I know."

"I should not have done such a thing for the sake of starting conversation, and I—" I pause, gasping on my breath. "I'm sorry. *You know?*"

"I mean, I *guessed*." She shrugs. "I knew that you were at the opera. And I knew . . . knew you weren't very fond of me."

I nibble on the inside of my cheek.

"See, it made sense. Your reaction to what I said about the column that day we had tea. Even more so, your presence in London coinciding with the new letters."

Well, when she says it that way, it seems so obvious despite my added characters. "I apologize. It was cruel of me, and you have never been my enemy, Kitty. But, if I am being honest, I didn't once think about the collateral—" I pause once more. "No, that's wrong. Perhaps a small part of me wanted to embarrass you as well. I was jealous, you see, at how well you seemed suited to society life in a way that I never could be."

She purses her lips and scrunches her mouth from side to side like a child who has a secret. "I don't deserve your apology, seeing as I . . . Well, I sought retaliation. I was there in Paris."

I inhale sharply.

"I wanted to surprise Fitzroy. He'd confided to me about his father, but he'd been so distant from me otherwise. I thought— well, Paris! What a place for a proposal."

"You saw us."

"Yes. And after Jane's wedding, after Fitzroy told me he wouldn't be proposing, after I'd lost everything, I wanted to embarrass you the same way you embarrassed me."

I feel like I should be angry, but I only feel a little sad. "Then why mention Olivia?" I ask incredulously.

She looks away in shame. "You always seemed so immune to everything. You know, at my first London party, I once had a man ask me if I could see properly." She scoffs. "At first, I couldn't understand what he meant. And then it hit me. I cried. Right there, in front of him."

"Imagine knowing all of the things a person could be in the world, and deciding to be prejudiced. Sometimes I pity them. Being hateful just seems so miserable." I fidget guiltily. "Truthfully, I always thought you were having a much easier time than I was. People never seemed to sneer at you the way they did me."

She laughs, but there's no humor in it. "Oh, no, believe me, I've heard many horrible things. And I felt worse knowing that I let them get to me. You, on the other hand. I've never seen you stumble. I thought hurting your cousin might hurt you more. I regretted it instantly, I swear. I wrote to the Désirs, I took ownership for starting the gossip. I hope it was enough."

"All is well, Kitty. You needn't worry." I consider my next words for a moment. The way she's described me as unfeeling and invincible sets my teeth on edge, though I'm having trouble determining why. "But you're wrong about me. I may seem headstrong, but every comment *does* hurt. I've felt my otherness entirely. I might appear unaffected, but I'm not. I feel it all."

She nods. "I understand, and I apologize."

"And let me apologize to you. It seems we've both misjudged each other."

She smiles, dimples forming in her cheeks.

I take the fullest breath I've enjoyed in weeks. I roll my shoulders, relishing that a weight has been lifted.

She cleans off her spoon. "You know, due to my father's very public infidelity, my whole family has been torn apart."

I brace myself, but Kitty only smiles a little.

She shakes her head. "And for the first time, I needn't worry about what anyone thinks. I feel like if I can survive all of London gossiping about me, then the worst is over. And with Fitzroy no longer being a realistic suitor for me . . ." She mulls her next words over. "Know this. . . . It was a marriage of convenience for both of us. I mean, I could've done far worse. He's kind, he's handsome—I've heard horror stories of matches made to cruel men. And even if we didn't love each other, at least, at least I'd be near Gwen?" She pauses. Something about her tone has changed, and I can't quite tell why.

I feel silly. I did not once stop to think that perhaps Kitty did not love Nathaniel and that she was being pushed into a marriage that she did not truly want in the same way I'd feared for myself.

"We should've been friends this whole time," I say.

❖   320   ❖

She giggles. "Who says we can't be friends now?"

I smile back. "Then what a lucky coincidence that you were passing through town and happened upon our door."

She blushes slightly. "It's not entirely a coincidence, actually. I was going up to Enderly to see Gwen, and, well—"

There's a vicious knock at the door.

"Oh, that must be your carriage—"

"*Kitty! Stella!*"

I snap back to her. "Why, is that Gwen?"

And now Kitty's slight blush becomes something fierce.

I go to the front door. "Gwendolyn! What are you doing here?"

She throws her arms around me and gives me a quick squeeze before running into the sitting room.

Kitty looks relieved and embarrassed all at once, the blush growing. "*Gwen.*"

Gwen's out of breath, her blond hair all a mess. I watch as she flings herself to her knees in front of Kitty. "I was at Enderly— waiting for you—oh, by the way, how are you, Stella?"

"Oh, I'm fine—"

But Gwen's hardly listening; her attention is so focused on Kitty. "And a servant informed me that your carriage had been turned over by bandits!"

"Bandits?" Kitty laughs. "God, I hate gossip—"

"You're all right, then?"

"Of course! Gwen, if my carriage was overrun by bandits, what were you going to do? Take them on all by yourself?"

"I hadn't thought that far ahead! By the time I was on my

❖ 321 ❖

way, I saw the men fixing up your carriage here!"

"Oh, it's my fault. We were on the way, but I got nerves, and I yelled at Mr. Donnelly to stop the carriage, and it surprised him, and the horse jolted—"

"Nerves? Why?"

Kitty smiles sheepishly. "You know why. You *always* give me nerves."

"Oh, Kitty!" Gwen is wide-eyed with amusement and tenderness. "Thank God you're all right!"

All this, and I'm just standing there, completely ignored by the two of them. Good God, this is a fascinating thing to watch. They continue on like this, speaking rapidly, their sentences breathlessly fitting into each other's like puzzle pieces. My eyes dart between them. It's as if I'm not even here! Foreheads bent toward each other, hands clasped in each other's, Gwen pushing back Kitty's hair so she can get a good look at her face—

Oh.

Oh!

I resist slapping my palm to my forehead.

Thinking back on my time spent with both Katherine and Gwen, their affection for each other now seems so apparent. Of course, it all makes sense: Gwen's reluctance to take any courtship seriously, and Kitty's insistence on marrying Nathaniel to remain close to her. I thought Gwen might resent Kitty for having all of his attention, but Gwen must've been jealous of *Nathaniel*! I hold in a laugh. It seems that Olivia and Samuel are not the only ones with the ability to melt my heart.

+ 322 +

"I'm just going to get some more tea," I say casually, hiding my grin. "Go on, catch up, you two."

And of course, lost in each other's eyes, neither pays me any mind at all.

32

Aunt Eleanor and I watch through the window as the beautiful carriage makes its way up the hill and toward our home.

I wring my hands. Olivia's return should not make me so nervous. She's my cousin, for heaven's sake. My best friend. Being engaged wouldn't change her, I know it. Even if we haven't spoken in a month and our last words to each other were harsh and cruel, I know she's still my dear Livvie.

Okay, I do think it's a little odd that Aunt Eleanor and I are all dressed up. Cheswick mews beside me. For God's sake, poor thing's wearing a *miniature cravat*.

"This is ridiculous," I say.

Aunt Eleanor shushes me.

I point at the carriage. "It's not like they can hear me!"

When the carriage does arrive, Aunt Eleanor and I greet them on the steps.

The attendants come out. They go around the doors to open them. I see the furs first and then the long silken dress.

Then her face. Baby-faced Olivia Witherson seems to glow from within, and she looks like the most refined woman in all of England.

There's mud, grass, and stone, but neither of us cares. With one look, we run giddily toward each other and into a hug.

As Aunt Eleanor takes Mr. Désir on a tour of our home, I get Olivia all to myself, which is lovely. She tells me about Paris— the art, the culture, how the people take some getting used to, but she doesn't feel quite so lost.

"And I'm learning French quite fast, my tutor says." She lowers her voice. "Though it was a bit awkward when I tried to explain that I had a pet cat, and ended up saying *quite* a different word. Turns out, French for cat is *chat*, and *chatte* is, uh, a rather crude term for erm, something else." She gestures vaguely toward her privates.

I throw my head back in laughter. "No! Why wasn't I there? How could I have missed such a perfect moment?"

She giggles. "Stella, I've never been so embarrassed in my life."

"Well, at least you're doing something. I feel like I'm just twiddling the days away. I've taken to talking to myself, but in my defense, Cheswick isn't a very good listener."

She sighs, and I tense up. That is Livvie's *verge-of-tears* sigh.

She rubs her eyes. "I'm sorry. I just hate to think of you here and me so far away."

"You needn't worry for me."

She looks up at me. "I know. You can take care of yourself. You're clever, cunning, beautiful, and you have a fortune given to you by a kind man."

I smile thinly. There will be time to talk about this later. For now, I want to comfort her, and I don't want her to worry about me. "But you see, I have many good fortunes already." I squeeze her hand tightly. "I have my hair, I have my humor—"

She chuckles.

"What!"

"Nothing!"

I laugh with her. "Well, I think I'm a fine writer, even if no one will believe it unless my work is signed by a pen name. I have my health, for now, though it's entirely possible that subsisting on seven cups of tea each morning will haunt me in the future, but I suppose we'll see to it when it comes. I have Cheswick—"

"Cheswick?"

"What, you don't plan to leave me *utterly* alone here, do you?"

She's crying now, but it's a relieved sort of cry, rather than a sad one.

I wrap my arms around her. "And I have you, my dearest Olivia, even if you'll be a whole country away from me—practically on the other side of the world, I think. I have Aunt Eleanor, who loves me for my quirks, and Lady Tess, who loves me in spite of them."

She snorts, and she sniffles.

"And if that is not enough to make any young woman happy,

then she must be the most spoiled creature on this earth."

"Stella, I will miss you more than I think I can bear."

"Nonsense, you'll thrive as the lady of Mr. Désir's house. We both know it'll suit you so finely that everyone will think you were born to do it." I make my voice snooty and stuffy. "Ah yes, Lady Désir, the most perfect woman on earth—*wait*, you're French now." I put on an obnoxious accent. "*Oui oui, bring me ze fromage et les garçons!*"

She closes her eyes and laughs. "The cheese and the boys?"

I sigh. "We can't all have personal tutors."

She rubs her lips together. "Erm. So, speaking of boys. You and Fitzroy?"

"Oh, heavens, that's all done with." I play with my hands, needing something to distract myself. "It's your time, Livvie. Let's not speak of anything but your nuptials. Besides, now that *you're* rich, what do I need an inheritance for? Will there be rooms for me in your new estate?"

She puts her hands atop mine and squeezes. "And here I thought that Stella Sedgwick was no runner."

I try to play off my sudden anxiety with a scoff. "And what do you mean by that?"

She shrugs. "Dunno. Maybe that I thought if anyone would fight for what they wanted, it would be you."

"But I don't—" I bite on the inside of my cheek. Despite everything, this is the one lie I cannot seem to say aloud.

Olivia pulls me into the tenderest hug. "If you really want to move on from him, fine. But you'd better be certain, Stella. I'd hate to see my favorite person buckle to her own pride."

I let myself sink into the hug, a little stunned. I've been trying my best to forget Nathaniel altogether, and now find myself wondering what could have been if I'd let myself choose him.

Familiar footsteps approach from the hall. I gather myself quickly, pushing away such dangerous thoughts and blinking back tears. Sure enough, Aunt Eleanor leads Samuel into the sitting room—oh, the woman is *beaming*. If Lady Tess were here, the entire house would be filled with triumphant, diabolical laughter.

I rise and curtsy. "Pleasure as always, Mr. Désir."

"It's lovely to see you again, Miss Sedgwick." He holds his hands out to me.

I have a mind to say, *Hurt her, and I'll mount your head on a spike*, but Aunt Eleanor is glaring at me like she's reading my mind, so I settle for the hand-holding instead.

The first few days after Livvie leaves are fine, really. I miss her dearly, and I keep wanting to tell her about the funny things I've found in a book, or show her my improved cross-stitching, or ask her to accompany my walks, but I can't. And every moment where I think of turning to her only to find myself alone teaches me something painful—I've never not been by her side in the past few years, and now I don't know what to do with myself.

I take my walks alone. I keep my stitches to myself—Aunt Eleanor is a much harsher critic. I read and read and read, studying the craft of the words and thinking of how to improve my own talents.

Sometimes I feel like I can't breathe.

It's not loneliness exactly. It's more the thought that I've been left behind. With Livvie in Paris and soon to be married, and Gwen off on holiday, I feel like everyone is moving on to great things without me.

And then there's the matter of Fitzroy.

I hate you, Nathaniel Fitzroy, I think glumly. If only it were true. I'd give anything to hate this boy who so firmly holds my heart in jeweled fingers. What I would do to be free of him. Sometimes I hold the little bundle of letters that Jane left me with. I can't bring myself to burn them, but I can't seem to work up the courage to read them, either.

"Stella, still lounging about?"

I wave absently at Aunt Eleanor, a pillow pressed firmly to my face. "Perhaps. It's only ten. Pretend I'm still asleep."

I can practically *hear* the pause for her eye roll. "Sit up, there's a parcel for you."

"Cursed words! The last time you said that, you shipped me off to Kendall Manor."

"It's from Mr. Elmhurst."

I fling the pillow, and it nearly clips Cheswick, poor thing. "Oh, well, why didn't you say so!"

She hands over the square package and throws her hands up in exasperation.

With little care for neatness, I rip off the packaging. It's a book, with a note attached. I gasp. "He'srequestedareviewabout—"

"*Stella*. Breathe, girl."

I inhale. "Mr. Elmhurst has requested a column on the latest

❖ 329 ❖

novel by one Juliette Spear." I swallow hard. "It's a romance—romance and courtship and the season." I clutch the letter to my chest. He's suggested a number of pen names, and while I'm not thrilled about that, I must bear it. Fiona Flippant was never the right fit for me, and I'm happy to move on to this.

Aunt Eleanor raises a brow. "And you'd be okay with that? Writing about dresses and dancing?"

I can hardly keep the smile off my face. "It's a *book review*, Aunt Eleanor. Then when I've gathered a following, I can petition to write other things, opinion pieces, can you believe it? This is just the start! The start of everything!" I stand and pose dramatically. "Stella Sedgwick, book reviewer for *State of London*. What a dream!"

"Silly girl." Her face is softer now, amused but affectionate. Lightly, she brushes a stray curl away from my face, her fingertips lingering on my cheek. "I want to tell you to temper your expectations, but you've done nothing but exceed them, haven't you? I'd be a fool to doubt you."

Mr. Elmhurst has given me until the end of the month, but I devour the book in a few hours, I can't help it. I only take breaks when Aunt Eleanor demands my attention for meal times. She thinks reading at the table is rude, and I get to tell her that *I'm working*, which . . . doesn't change her opinion at all, unfortunately.

By three in the afternoon, I begin organizing my thoughts, which are a jumble of themes, character growth—and what was with all of those odd metaphors involving wind and the color red?

For a moment, I feel completely out of my depth. Maybe Lady Tess put him up to it, out of her own pity for me. There's something else burning up inside me that I can't shake. I know I should be happy with this opportunity, but I realize now that my dreams are not what I thought they were. I don't just want to be offered a seat at this table that belongs to Elmhurst and his staff. I want to set the table alight, watch it devoured by my flames, and replace it with something entirely new. Maybe it starts here, at *State of London.* But a paper where I must hide my true name will not be where I end. I have a dream now, as foolish as it might be. My own paper. My own staff, filled with Black writers like me. A novel, maybe. The road will be hard, I know, but I'm up for the challenge.

Until then, this review needs writing, and I need a walk. Fresh air solves everything, and I have to take in all the walks I can before winter starts and the snow begins falling. I pull on a thin coat and my uncle's old wide-brimmed hat and push through the front door.

"Where are you off to?" Aunt Eleanor calls from the kitchen.

Drat. "Just a walk!"

She pokes her head out. "Fancy going up to Enderly?" It's a question, but the tone of her voice very much implies a demand. "You should have gone to pay your respects by now."

My tummy flips. Immediately, I feel anxious. "We sent our condolences."

"It's not the same thing as showing your face, and you know that. I've cut some flowers from the garden, and I'd like you to hand-deliver them. I'll have Mr. Townsend take you, yes? He's managed to spruce up the old hansom."

I know she's right. I remember how annoyed I was when the Fitzroys sent their own flowers and condolences by courier after Mum died. It'd seemed so impersonal, considering I'd known them for years. Had that been Jane's doing as well?

Reluctantly, I take the flowers.

We arrive at Enderly in half an hour. Thankfully, Mr. Townsend is a talker, and thoroughly distracts me with stories about his rambunctious grandchildren. It helps, having something to think about besides my own nervousness.

The stone pathway up to the massive house is busy. Men are moving pieces of furniture, statues, artwork, and heavy trunks into wagons, and unloading other items into the house. Nathaniel has wasted no time in redecorating, it seems. It's disorienting for a moment. I have to weave out of the way of two labor hands attempting to maneuver a dining table. Clutching the flowers, I work through the maze of carts and stop only to let the men carrying cloth-covered paintings pass in front of me.

I look back at the cart. It seems like an absurd amount of artwork, but one in particular catches my attention.

I still, narrowing my eyes at the remaining framed piece. The protective cloth is bunched up at the corner, revealing thick black paint swirled into a cloud at the end of two weaved plaits.

I can't resist. Before I can stop myself, I yank up the cloth.

It's *me*.

I like that my hair takes up most of the frame, and that my deep brown skin seems to glisten in the sunlight. He's spun golds and reds into the background, mimicking dawn. I look contemplative, my brow turned down, even with the slight smile on my lips. There is care here, from the perfect detail in each of my thick lashes, to the intricate curl in each strand of hair.

"Do you like it?"

I have to lift my head all the way so the wide brim of my hat does not hide him.

And there he is. Nathaniel Fitzroy waiting at the top of the steps, eyes raised at me in wonderment. There's a small folio in his hands. He looks like he's just woken up, but is still so exhausted. The top of his black dress shirt is unbuttoned, and his curls are uncombed and messy. Just the way I like him. A little undone.

He smiles. "That one's my favorite."

I blink away the tears that have inconveniently pooled in my eyes. "It's lovely. It's—" I shake my head. "Well, it's me. Does saying it's beautiful make me arrogant?"

"You like it, truly?"

I nod, unable to wipe away the smile on my lips. "It's *beautiful.*"

I walk up to the bottom step, away from the fray of the workers.

He remains on the top step, hands on his hips. "I'd offer it to you, but I don't think I can part with it."

A tickle blooms in my chest. I look up at him. He smiles down at me.

"Flowers," I sputter, holding up the bouquet between us. "For you. Oh, Nate. I'm so sorry about your grandfather, and I should've come by sooner."

"You were ill, I know." He takes the flowers, his fingers lingering on mine before he pulls away. "And I have something for you, actually. It's the title to Kendall." He lifts the folio.

I take an involuntary step back. "I can't—"

He raises his hand. "Well, it's a little late for that, seeing as Mr. Fitzroy's eldest grandchild and grandson have already deemed it done. Take it. It's yours. It's what my grandfather wanted, and it's only a small token in apology for what he let happen to your mother."

I run up the steps two at a time to get to him. I take the folio, open it, and see that the spot for my husband has been filled in with the signature of a rather vague *M. Sedgwick*, a man who doesn't exist.

Nathaniel laughs a little. "The viscount, Lord Amberlough, arranged it. Funny how rules can be bent if you have enough money to spend."

I look at him, blood pounding in my ears and thrumming in my veins.

I don't know what comes over me, but I snap the folio shut and throw my arms around Nathaniel. He pulls me into his arms, exhaling in surprise. I've never been held like this, so tightly that his heartbeat seems to beat in my own chest. He runs his fingers up and down my back. I tuck my face into his neck, and he doesn't seem to mind the wet tears against his skin. It's silent, except for the sounds of our own relieved breaths.

A shock of fear runs through me, and I break away to hold him at arm's length. *"Are you engaged?"* He opens his mouth to speak but I don't give him a chance. "I know your sister has some match in mind, and if you are, well, I don't want to know! In fact, I think I should leave now because I can't hear the words."

"What? Stella, I—"

I hardly hear him. I spin and begin pacing, keeping my head down to spare myself the look on his face. "And I can't see you again, not ever. I just—I can't bear knowing that my best friend has married someone who is probably kind, yes, and beautiful, and fine and perfect, I'm sure, but could never ever love him as much as I do."

I exhale, dropping my head. Silly, foolish tears.

He places a gentle touch on my wrist.

"You what?" he asks softly. "Did I hear that correctly? Or was it just my hopeful imagination?"

I'm so stunned with embarrassment that all I can manage is a half nod. He circles his arm around me. With his free hand, he takes mine, lacing our fingers together.

His words are soft. "Look at me, Stella."

"No, no, I don't want to."

He laughs and tucks a hand under my chin.

I look up and find him gazing down at me with hopeless brown eyes. He studies my face just like he did that night in his grandfather's library at Kendall, like he can't get enough of me. I shake my head—at him, at myself. At this predicament I've allowed myself to fall into love with Nathaniel Fitzroy, how ridiculous, how unfair.

But when Nate dips his head toward me, our foreheads touching, I feel at ease. There's a moment where I don't think either of us is breathing. I know nothing but the look of his eyes and the feeling of his thumb stroking my hand.

I touch his cheek. "If you don't marry some nice genteel lady, then you're a fool."

He pulls me closer. Our hands are tightly clasped between us. "*Yes*. I am a fool. So be it."

I rise onto my toes as he lowers his mouth to meet mine. It's a brief, gentle kiss, a test, as if neither of us is sure this is really happening. Just that brush of his lips against mine sends lightning through me, and my mouth burns with the need to be reunited with his.

My hand on the back of his neck, I guide him down to me once more. This kiss is pure bliss, his perfect, full lips soft against mine. I rest my hands against his chest, relishing that sliver of skin, the feel of his heartbeat against my palm. I do not care if any of the workers or staff see us. I don't care if a million scandal sheets bear my name for this. Let them all know that Stella Sedgwick has finally met her match.

Nate pulls away and holds me desperately, his face nuzzled into the crook of my neck. It's a perfect embrace of relief, of comfort, of knowing there is no one else we'd prefer to share this with.

He sweeps his lips up to my ear. "Stella," he whispers. "It's always been you, my love."

Of all of my fortunes, I think this may be the greatest of all.

EPILOGUE

December 1868

S pring and summer are often called the most romantic months, but I quite like the winter. Forget summer loves and blooming roses; they are nothing compared to the pearly, snow-covered hills of Enderly cupped by darkness, the sound of the crackling orange fire, the feel of a warm mug against my palm, and of course, the young man sitting across from me.

Our bodies are mere meters apart, our quiet breaths in synchrony.

I don't want to break this sweet little reverie, but I must say, "Does it really take this bloody long to paint a portrait?"

He looks up at me from over the canvas and rolls his eyes. "Keep fidgeting like that, and you won't have an ear."

I laugh, and he smiles wide.

Snaggletooth!

"Have you decided where you're going to put this one when it's done?" he asks.

"I have," I reply, grinning to myself. At home, in my library, right next to the portrait of me and my mother from nearly a decade ago. Nathaniel had found it in the basement of Kendall Manor, along with scores of things the late Mrs. Fitzroy had deemed unworthy of care. For my nineteenth birthday, Nate restored it. I think Aunt Eleanor and I scared him with how hard we'd wept at the sight of it.

He flicks his gaze up at me once more. "All right, let me put you out of your misery for today, my little love."

I jump from the stool and pretend to stretch my legs. But Nate knows all of my tricks, and he lifts the canvas away from me before I can peek. "Nice try," he says.

"I do look forward to seeing the final portrait, sir."

He slips his hands around my waist. He's done so many times, but it always sends a jolt of pleasure down my spine. He must notice, because he grins in that satisfied, mischievous way that I love. "Just a few more sittings—be patient."

"You know it's quite impossible for me to be patient."

I push him away lightheartedly. He follows me into the hallway, playing with the ribbon on my dress.

"I must leave you now," I say, reaching for my scarf. "It is not proper for a young, unwed lady to spend so many hours in the company of a single man."

"Oh yes," he says, his fingers now gliding like silk across the small of my back. "Because you're all about propriety."

"But of course!" I rest my hand delicately on my chest. "And my aunt will worry, it's such an icy night."

He gazes down upon me with such wonder, I must remind myself to breathe. "Then kiss me before you go, Miss Sedgwick, so that the memory of your touch might keep me warm tonight."

I lift onto my toes and kiss his forehead, his eyes, and finally, I brush my lips against his. His body trembles as he exhales, sending a warm tingle down my spine.

I don't know how this all ends. Perhaps we will grow sick of each other in a fortnight. Perhaps I'll one day say yes. Maybe I'll die of consumption—not the most satisfying ending, but I've been reading a fair few of novels lately, and my, they are bleak.

But while I know little about love, I know I'm enjoying this: his fingers running the length of my shoulder blades, his eyes so focused on me, like he can't seem to look away. Or the way he calls on me at Kendall Manor with a small drawing for me and gifts for Aunt Eleanor. It's the way he not only listens, but *hears* me, and gives me the permission to take up as much space as I wish to.

I kiss him, savoring the taste of his lips, the heat of his touch. He cradles me close to his body. "I'm going to marry you one day, Stella Sedgwick."

My face warms, but I feign shock. "Why! Is that a threat, Mr. Fitzroy?"

"Oh no." He brushes my forehead with his lips. "It's only this young man's dream."

Heavens.

We kiss until our lips are sore. It is hard to say goodbye,

but I must get back to my aunt. She's been so tender lately with Olivia touring France, so I must keep her company with my witty jokes and poor musical skills.

Nate kisses my fingers and reluctantly lets me go.

When I arrive at Kendall, the house is quiet. Aunt Eleanor has fallen asleep by the fireplace in the great sitting room with Cheswick napping at her feet. She's taken to the new house well, and I am ever thankful that she's here with me.

I curl into the armchair across from her. It's the perfect spot to do a bit of writing. I have many letters to send—to Olivia, to Gwen, and to Kitty—but first, a letter I've been putting off for too long now.

Dearest friends,

Before you read this note, I ask that you find a comfortable seat and a mug of your favorite tea. I come to you on this wintry day with bittersweet news. The end is here for "Letters to Fiona Flippant," my pride and greatest accomplishment. I have enjoyed being your confidante and your friend, but as I've always said, there must be time for new dreams, and new schemes.

Yours, in confidence,

G. & S.

ACKNOWLEDGMENTS

Third book down! It's such an honor to write for kids, and I'm grateful to the teens and tweens (and older!) who have picked up this book.

Eternal thanks to Laura Rennert for your expertise and support on our first book together. I'm so lucky to have you and the Andrea Brown Literary Agency in my corner. Here's to many, many more!

Big shout-out to Claire Stetzer and Bess Braswell for being the first to push this book toward publication. This book might not exist without y'all—thank you, thank you! To my editors, Tara Weikum and Sarah Homer—this book is better for all the work you poured into it. Thank you for seeing all that Stella's story could be. Thank you to Ana Deboo for the vital fact-checking. And to everyone at Harper who touched this project, massive thanks for putting together the book of my dreams! In production, Danielle McClelland, Melissa Cicchitelli, Becky Langdon, and Gwen Morton; in marketing and publicity, Shannon Cox, Jenn Corcoran, and Mimi Rankin; and the entire sales team.

The cover still takes my breath away whenever I see it. I'm so happy I had Baraka Carberry's illustration and Kathleen Oudit, Andrea Vandergrift, and David Curtis on design. My girl looks so good front and center.

A very special thanks to Dr. Caroline Bressey at University College London, whose work in demystifying and conceptualizing the lives of Black Victorians was tantamount to creating Stella's world. While there's many a creative liberty taken here, I found your work to be a treasure trove of information that informed so much of my writing. To Beverly Jenkins, Vanessa Riley, and so many other authors writing our love stories, your Black-centered historical romances paved the way for this one, and I'm endlessly inspired.

This book would not have been possible without the friends and family members who supported me along the way. I love you all so much. To Maya Prasad, Linda Cheng, and Candace Buford especially, thank you for showing me that this book could be more than just a soothing little project for my eyes only. Forever thankful to have such a fierce critique group to call friends.